PENGUIN BOOKS

The Half Burnt House

Alex North was born in Leeds, where he now lives with his wife and son. He studied philosophy at Leeds University, and prior to becoming a writer he worked there in the sociology department. *The Whisper Man* was published in more than thirty languages, was a *Sunday Times* and *New York Times* bestseller and a Richard and Judy Book Club pick. It is in development as a major Hollywood motion picture.

The Half Burnt House

ALEX NORTH

PENGUIN BOOKS

PENGUIN BOOKS

UK | USA | Canada | Ireland | Australia
India | New Zealand | South Africa

Penguin Books is part of the Penguin Random House group of companies
whose addresses can be found at global.penguinrandomhouse.com

First published by Penguin Michael Joseph 2023
Published in Penguin Books 2023

001

Copyright © Alex North, 2023

The moral right of the author has been asserted

Typeset by Jouve (UK), Milton Keynes
Printed and bound in Great Britain by Clays Ltd, Elcograf S.p.A.

The authorized representative in the EEA is Penguin Random House Ireland,
Morrison Chambers, 32 Nassau Street, Dublin D02 YH68

A CIP catalogue record for this book is available from the British Library

ISBN: 978-1-405-94527-1

www.greenpenguin.co.uk

MIX
Paper | Supporting
responsible forestry
FSC® C018179

Penguin Random House is committed to a
sustainable future for our business, our readers
and our planet. This book is made from Forest
Stewardship Council® certified paper.

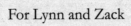
For Lynn and Zack

'If you could see the future,' Sam asked her, 'would you want to?'

It was the end of the school day and they were sitting outside the sixth-form building. There was a roundabout there with a stone edge and a circle of flower beds in the centre, and Sam and Katie met there every afternoon at the end of lessons. They were seventeen years old. As teenagers do, they sat and gossiped. They complained about her parents.

They asked each other questions.

If you could see the future, would you want to?

Katie thought about that. It was exactly the kind of question that had made her fall in love with Sam in the first place, but in that moment it made her uneasy. Sam was handsome and charismatic – full of talent and ambition – and for some unfathomable reason he seemed to be in love with her as well. That made her happy, of course, but she was also frightened of losing him. Next year they would both be going away to different universities, and that upcoming separation felt like a threat looming on the horizon.

What was going to happen to them then?

'Katie?' Sam prompted.

'I don't know.'

'Why not?'

'Because what if you saw something you didn't like?'

'Then you'd be able to change it.'

'Maybe.'

It was a warm afternoon with only the slightest of breezes. She watched as a group of kids drifted past them, hitching their bags up on their shoulders, talking and laughing. They were heading down the sunlit drive that led to the nearby village, while others were wandering away towards the bus stop. It was a reminder that she and Sam would have to part ways shortly. Katie lived close to the school, whereas his house was a bus journey away.

For a long time Katie had felt like a spare wheel in her family; it was her younger brother, Chris, who her parents doted on. But over the last year Sam had made her parents a *lot* more interested in her life than they had been previously. Her mother especially was suspicious of him, and overly keen to monitor their relationship and keep it from going too far. If Katie was not home on time after school, there would be questions. At weekends she and Sam were not allowed to be alone together. If Katie went round to his house, her mother was always careful to ensure his parents were home too.

The resentment that caused had been growing steadily, simmering away inside her, a little hotter every day. What she *wanted* to do was to spend as much time as possible with Sam before they were separated, and it seemed desperately unfair that her mother believed she was entitled to intervene.

'*Could* you change it, though?' Katie wondered.

'What do you mean?'

'Well, if you just saw the future, you wouldn't know how you got there. So anything you did to avoid it might actually be what led you to it all along.'

Sam considered that.

'You're so clever,' he said.

'That's why you love me, right?'

'No. It's just *one* of the reasons.'

She leaned her head on his shoulder and he kissed her hair.

They sat like that in comfortable silence for a few seconds, and she closed her eyes, enjoying the sunlight on her face.

But then Sam started to say something and stopped.

She opened her eyes. 'What?'

He hesitated, which made the familiar anxiety flare up inside her. They hadn't spoken about what was going to happen next year, but she was sure university must have been on his mind as well – that he might be worrying about what was going to happen too. Perhaps that had been what had prompted his question. Maybe he'd decided it was better to end things now.

Katie leaned away and looked at him. 'Sam?'

'I was just thinking.'

'Yeah, about what?'

'That my parents won't be home for an hour or so.'

Her chest tightened for a second, and then her anxiety evaporated. He'd said it so casually, as though the words meant nothing at all – just an observation, really – but the weight of his suggestion hung in the air, and despite the warmth of the afternoon she shivered a little.

She wanted to go back with him so badly.

'I can't,' she said.

'Yeah, I know.'

'I mean . . . I want to. I just can't.'

He nodded. Katie wondered what was going through

his mind. Was he losing patience with her? Had he already? There had been no pressure from Sam on that level at all, but she couldn't help feeling she'd just failed a test of some kind. And she supposed that she had. Because even though her parents didn't seem to care very much about her, she was still being good, wasn't she?

Still doing what she'd been told.

'One day, though,' she said.

'One day.'

She looked to her right – and there was Chris, walking slowly along the road towards them. As always, he was alone; she didn't think he had any friends. His hands were tucked in his pockets and his head was bowed. He was fifteen but looked younger and smaller than his age, and Katie had to wait for him every day and walk home with him. Her mother insisted. Katie supposed it made sense. They were at the same high school, after all, and were both going to the same place at the same time.

But while she loved her brother very much, she was not his keeper, and the sight of him now caused the resentment inside her to blaze even brighter. God, he even *carried* himself like he didn't belong. Why couldn't he look after himself instead of her being expected to do it? Why didn't her life matter to her parents as much as his?

Sam saw Chris approaching them.

He sighed and stood up, hitching his bag on to his shoulder.

'I'll see you tomorrow,' he said quietly. 'I love you.'

'I love you too.'

Then he stood in front of her, waiting for her to stand

up and kiss him goodbye as she always did. But she was still looking to her right, watching Chris walking towards them, and the feeling of resentment that had been building inside her finally spilled over.

She looked back at Sam. 'No,' she said. 'Wait.'

If you could see the future, would you want to?

You can't, of course. A life is lived forward. The present is a vantage point from which every moment in the past is inevitable and every moment in the future invisible. Most of those moments won't be important, but a handful will turn out to be pivotal – shattering, even – and you never know which until it's too late.

As Katie boarded the bus with Sam that day, she didn't know that a local man named Michael Hyde was leaving his house right then.

That he was walking towards his car with a knife in his hand.

She spent an hour at Sam's house that afternoon. She had made a decision to do what *she* wanted to do for once, and it was thrilling. She would deal with the consequences later – and really, how bad could they be? Sam walked her to the bus stop afterwards, their hands clasped tightly together and their upper arms pressed against each other. He kissed her goodbye. When the bus set off, Katie smiled at him through the window until he was out of sight, and then she looked straight ahead, smiling to herself instead, her body full of warmth and light. It felt as though she hadn't just discovered a secret but somehow become one.

After getting off the bus, she walked home slowly. She was more than ready to have whatever argument awaited her there, but she also wanted to hold on to that feeling inside her for as long as possible. And besides, it was a beautiful afternoon. The sun was still bright and warm, and there was a lovely cast to the light that brought out fresh colours in the world around her. Everywhere she looked, it was like she was seeing things for the first time. As though everything had changed.

And of course it had. She just didn't know it yet.

Katie reached their road.

As she turned the corner, the scene before her made no sense. They lived in a quiet area, but the street ahead was crowded with police cars and vans. Everywhere she looked, she saw red and blue lights flashing. The sight of it all stopped her in her tracks. Her gaze moved to the yellow cordon that had been set up across the street, with what seemed like crowds of police officers moving around behind it. Part of her was aware there should have been a great deal of noise, but for a few seconds it was like being underwater, and all she could hear was her heartbeat thudding dully in her ears.

Something terrible has happened.

She would always remember the sickening, sinking feeling inside herself. And she would remember what came along with it: the desperate urge to go back in time and change things.

Please, she would remember thinking.

Oh God, please.

Because right then, she would have given up Sam for that chance.

She would have given up herself.

She would have given up anything.

Katie took a few faltering steps forward, unsure at first

whether her body would work properly – and then she began to run. One of the police officers saw her coming and intercepted her at the tape. She didn't know it at the time, but he had been expecting her. Her parents had called Sam's house while she'd been on the bus and learned she was on her way.

'Hey,' the officer said gently. 'Hey.'

Katie ignored him. He was tall and solid, and she had to step to one side in order to stare past him at the scene beyond the cordon.

She didn't understand what she was seeing – not right then. But she took it in anyway, and even seventeen years later she could still see it all so clearly whenever she closed her eyes.

The old red car, abandoned at an angle across the pavement, where it had swerved in to block Chris's path.

The blood spatters from where he had been stabbed repeatedly.

And the larger pool of blood, in the gutter, where Michael Hyde had begun his desperate attempt to cut off her brother's face.

PART ONE

I

You can't do this. It's not allowed.

Alan Hobbes looks up from the book on his desk. He listens carefully, but the only thing he can hear is the silence ringing in the room. There is nobody else here. He sent everyone home earlier and is alone in the house. Or at least, he is for the moment.

And yet the voice of his brother, Edward, echoes in the air from across the years.

Hobbes stares at his bookshelves for a few seconds and then shakes his head. He is old now; that is all it is. Everything is swimming together as the end approaches. And really, that is fine. They say that people's lives flash before their eyes as they die, and what else can that mean except that the nature of time changes as death approaches? Or rather – he corrects himself – that our *perception* of it does, so that we finally begin to see time for what it was all along. A journey seems to take place step by step while you're on it, but if you could look down from above you would see the whole route laid out below you. You would understand that the beginning, middle and end all exist at once, and that they always had and always would.

It is not something to be afraid of.

Hobbes looks back down at the notebook on the desk. The time he has left is limited, and he needs to concentrate. Because death is coming for him. He can feel it approaching steadily and inexorably. It will be arriving at the house in just a few short hours, whereupon it will open the door downstairs and creep up one of the twinned staircases that lead to his rooms.

And then it will all be over.

Except that isn't true. His *own* journey will end tonight, but others will continue. Has he been careful enough? Is everything in place? It is difficult to be sure, especially as there are other drifts than the perception of time that come with old age. But he has done his best.

He thinks of those people he has never met and never will, but who he feels he knows so well.

Right now, Katie Shaw is at home, making dinner. She is worrying about her daughter, her marriage and one of the children she teaches. She is blissfully unaware of the turn her journey will take tomorrow and where it will lead her.

Detective Laurence Page is listening to classical music at home. He doesn't know Hobbes's name yet.

And Christopher Shaw, of course.

Christopher will be here soon, which reminds Hobbes again that time is short. He can see death edging ever closer in his mind's eye – a knife in its hand – and the thought of what is going to happen spurs him on.

It is 4 October 2017.

Hobbes picks up the old pen.

You can't do this, he remembers. *It's not allowed.*

Even so, he begins to write.

2

'Holy shit,' Pettifer said. 'Would you look at this?'

Laurence was doing exactly that.

He had his shirtsleeves rolled up and his arm resting on the sill of the open passenger window. He had been staring idly out for some time, watching as they left the old factories and office blocks of the city centre behind them, and then the suburbs full of crammed houses. Now they were passing through the more affluent neighbourhoods to the north. It was aspirational here: a world of sprawling bungalows, detached mansions and enormous gardens.

But there were even richer locales ahead.

'How the other half live,' Pettifer said.

'And yet die like the rest of us.'

'Yes, well. Let's try not to upset anyone at the scene, shall we?'

'Don't worry.' Laurence closed his eyes, enjoying the sensation of the fresh air rushing over his face. 'I will behave.'

'Do you need to have the window open?'

'I like the wind.'

'Could you close it?'

'I could,' he said happily. 'It is within my power. But I'm not going to.'

Pettifer sighed. She had fallen into that trap before.

But she did have a point, Laurence thought. Not

about the window, or him behaving (although, of course, there was that), but about the divisions of wealth within the city. At the same time, it was *also* interesting that it seemed a fresh observation to her. Laurence had come to this city – this country – as an infant, shortly after his mother's death, and one of the many things he had inherited from his father was an immigrant's sense of curiosity. Many of the other officers seemed to take the city for granted, whereas Laurence had never quite shaken away the sensation of being an outsider. Of not quite belonging. Of seeing the city as something that needed to be understood. The way he thought about it was this: his colleagues were excellent at reading the time on the clock face, but it often seemed to surprise them to discover there were cogs behind it that made the hands turn.

A short time later, he opened his eyes.

They were driving through countryside now. Fields sprawled away into the distance on either side. Some were dotted with cattle or crops, but most seemed empty. Perhaps they were simply being left fallow? Laurence wasn't sure; his knowledge of the agricultural industry was cursory. But it was difficult to shake the sensation that the land here belonged to people who owned so much of it that they could afford to leave acres barren and untended, forgotten afterthoughts in their vast inventories.

Laurence yawned.

'How much further?' he asked.

'I'm afraid I can't hear you because the window is open.'

'I don't believe you.'

She didn't reply – this time avoiding another familiar trap. Laurence smiled to himself. He liked Pettifer a lot. They had been working together as partners for more than three years. They complemented each other well, in that they annoyed each other in precisely the right ways unless it was important that they did not.

A minute or so later, she slowed down and flicked the indicator. They turned right on to what seemed to Laurence little more than a narrow dirt road leading off between the trees that were packed in tightly on either side. The muddy ground beneath the car had hardened into an undulating wave, and the tyres rolled from one side to the other as Pettifer navigated the twists and turns.

'Mr Hobbes liked his privacy,' Laurence said.

'I guess so. But if you had as much money as that, wouldn't you?'

'I honestly don't know how much money he had.'

'No, well' – Pettifer ducked her head slightly, peering out of the windscreen at the winding track ahead – 'clearly enough to get away from other people. Which I have to say has always been a dream of mine.'

'And of all the people who know you.'

The world suddenly brightened as the dark trees fell away, curling off to either side to form a black perimeter round a large sunlit clearing. The dirt track beneath the car became an immaculately maintained driveway of pale gravel that led in a straight line across an expanse of neatly trimmed grass.

The house was about a hundred metres ahead – although, Laurence thought, leaning forward himself now, *house* barely did the structure justice. There was a three-storey building at the centre, and taller wings stretching out on either side, every visible edifice topped with towers and turrets. His gaze moved over the face of the property. There were almost too many windows to count. Some were aligned in neat rows, while others appeared to be just randomly placed dark squares. Taken as a whole, the building looked like a curve of jawbone, inverted and pressed into the land.

Two police vans were parked out front.

A few officers were dotted around.

The *house* – he needed to think of it as something – loomed ever larger as they approached. Looking up, Laurence noticed that part of the roof in the middle was more jagged than the rest. Whatever room had once been up there was now partially exposed to the air, and he could see a few blackened struts of wood sticking up. An old fire. The bricks below were scorched and the window directly beneath had shattered and not been repaired.

The tyres crackled as Pettifer brought the car to a halt behind one of the vans at the entrance. One of the uniformed officers approached the vehicle.

Laurence held out his ID. 'Detective Laurence Page,' he said. 'Detective Caroline Pettifer.'

'Yes, sir. Ma'am.'

They got out of the car, and Laurence looked at the entrance before them: two enormous wooden doors beneath a stone arch. They were far wider and taller than any human would require.

'Good Lord,' he said. 'You could ride a horse through there.'

Pettifer walked round the car and stood beside him,

hands on her hips, looking up. 'Told you so,' she said. 'The other half.'

A sergeant led them inside to the scene.

Through the doors there was a large reception area, the floor made of cracked black and white tiles. Laurence looked up as they walked; the ceiling was two storeys above. Ahead of them, separated by a vast mirror, two wooden staircases curled upwards. There were no windows, and dust hung in the air, and yet there was the hint of a breeze coming from somewhere.

He and Pettifer followed the officer up one of the staircases, which joined the other on a small landing. Another pair led up from there, curving round each other like a figure of eight, so that they turned back on themselves again as they ascended. The arrangement seemed pointless to Laurence – whichever route they chose, they ended up in the same place – but eventually they emerged into a large area he estimated must have been above the entrance hall. Despite the solid floor beneath his feet, he was aware of a vast distance stretching away below him, and it felt like if he fell, he would be falling for ever.

'This way, sir.'

'And ma'am,' Pettifer said.

'Yes, ma'am. Sorry.'

A thin corridor led away to the left with an open door at the far end. As they approached it, Laurence could see officers moving in the room beyond. He was expecting another grand, ornate space, but his expectations were confounded. He and Pettifer followed the officer into a small area that, in some ways, reminded him of the modest confines of his own flat. Looking around, he saw little in the way of furnishings: a single bed against one wall, on which the victim was still lying; a trolley of medical equipment beside it; an old television on a stand, angled towards the bed. He looked to his left. There was a small open-plan kitchen area there, and a closed door next to it that he assumed led to a bathroom.

And at the far end of the room, an archway.

He stared at that for a moment. It clearly led away into some deeper chamber of the house, but the blackness there was impenetrable. Laurence could hear the faintest rush of air emerging from it, and the sound reminded him of something breathing.

He stepped over to the bed and looked down at the victim.

Breathing was clearly not a sound Alan Hobbes would be making again. The old man's lower body was still beneath the covers, but he was exposed from the waist up. His head was tilted at an unnatural angle, all but severed by a vicious knife wound.

The cause of death, at least, was clear. But Laurence also scanned the man's exposed scrawny torso, taking in the additional stab wounds there. The bed sheets below the body had once been white but were now saturated with blood. Whoever had murdered Alan Hobbes had taken their time in doing so, and the old man had clearly been too weak and feeble even to begin to fight them off.

It was too early to form an opinion, but Laurence found himself working through possible scenarios. Hobbes was clearly rich – or *had* been, he supposed, given you famously couldn't take it with you. Money conferred privilege, but rarely came without problems of its own. You made enemies along with it, and there would always be people who wanted to take it from you once you had it. The torture could suggest either – it was impossible to say right now. But Laurence was already confident that the motive would ultimately reside, as they so frequently did, in the dead man's bank account.

Pettifer was standing beside him. He was sure she would have formed the same opinion. He was about to voice it anyway, as it was important to be first, but then there was a cough from behind them.

They both turned round.

The man standing there was not a police officer. Instead, he was dressed in an expensive-looking three-piece suit, and his brown hair was gelled into neat curls. He was thirty at most, and obviously trying to appear older than he was. *Like a little boy trying on his father's suit*, Laurence thought. Which he might have considered uncharitable if the man hadn't also been curling his lip slightly as he looked between Laurence and Pettifer, as though trying to work out who was the superior.

Laurence saved him the bother. He beckoned to the nearest uniform.

'Excuse me,' he said. 'Who is this young man, and why is he in my crime scene?'

The uniform, predictably, looked slightly helpless.

The man coughed again. 'My name is Richard Gaunt,' he said. 'I'm a lawyer at the firm that deals with Mr Hobbes's estate. We look after his investments and finances.'

Good God – Gaunt was actually extending a hand, as though this was a business meeting rather than a room with a murder victim lying on the bed.

'Which doesn't explain why you're here.' Laurence nodded towards the body behind him. 'I mean, the paint is barely even dry yet.'

He felt Pettifer tense slightly beside him.

Gaunt lowered his hand. 'It was me who found Mr Hobbes this morning,' he said quietly. But then he rallied. 'And actually, I have permission from your superior. I spoke to DCI Barnes earlier. It was considered useful for me to be here, as I have knowledge of the property's inventory.'

Laurence looked at Pettifer, but she just raised an eyebrow at him.

'And *is* anything missing?'

'I don't know yet.' Gaunt glanced towards the dark archway at the far end of the room.

Laurence followed his gaze. A camera flashed. It was pointing at the corpse on the bed, but the light briefly illuminated a corridor beyond. Old stone walls. Cobwebs clinging to the ceiling.

And that faint rush of air.

There were no windows here, Laurence noticed. It was a room without a view. But one with a breeze.

He turned back to Gaunt. 'You said you found the body this morning. Why were you here?'

'I had an appointment,' Gaunt said. 'Mr Hobbes had requested a meeting to discuss his finances. I was given a key and told to let myself in – although the door was open when I arrived.'

Laurence frowned. That bothered him. Not the open door, as such, but the arrangements. Why would a key be required? Hobbes had been an old man, and the trolley beside the bed pointed to him relying on some degree of medical assistance. Surely there must have been carers? That aside, the property was large and must have required a team of staff to handle general upkeep and maintenance.

'So there was nobody else here?'

'That's correct.'

'Mr Hobbes had no family?'

'No.'

'And no staff at all?'

Gaunt frowned. 'Not this morning. That's the strange thing. I've worked on behalf of Mr Hobbes for a few years now, and there's always been quite a team on site whenever I've visited. I handle the accounts, so I have most of their contact details. I've already spoken to a couple of them today.'

Laurence felt a flare of annoyance. First of all, this man was in his crime scene, and now he appeared to be conducting their investigation for them.

But waste not want not.

'And?'

'The two I spoke to both said they were dismissed yesterday afternoon,' Gaunt said. 'And from what they told me it was the same for every other member of staff. They were all told by Mr Hobbes that their employment was no longer required. He thanked each of them individually – warmly, I'm told – and said they would be contacted shortly about severance pay and references.'

Laurence fell silent for a moment, considering that.

Obviously Gaunt's words by themselves could not be trusted, and so he and Pettifer were going to need to spend a great deal of time verifying his claims. But he also suspected Gaunt was telling them the truth. And if so, what did that mean?

He turned his back on the lawyer and stared at Alan Hobbes's body. Another camera flash went off, the bright light emphasizing the man's pale, emaciated frame and the vicious injuries that had been inflicted upon him.

'It's like he knew,' Gaunt said quietly.

Laurence didn't turn round. Instead, he crouched down slowly. From this angle he could see Hobbes's face. It was contorted in an expression of sorrow and suffering so acute that, even in death, it was easy to imagine he was still feeling pain.

'It's like he knew,' Gaunt said again. 'Like he knew this was coming and was ready for it.'

3

It was an afternoon for premonitions. The first came after work, as Katie drove out of the school grounds and saw her brother for the first time in two years.

He was sitting on a bench just outside the main entrance: a dishevelled figure with his head bowed and long hair trailing down, dressed in old jeans and a stained jacket that he was pulling tightly around himself. Katie's heart started beating faster. The encounter had come out of nowhere, and there was no time to be sure what she was feeling. Part of her *longed* to see Chris again, but she was also frightened of why he had come back after all this time, and what he might want.

She slowed the car down as she reached him.

Chris noticed her approaching and looked up. But then she met his eyes through the window and immediately turned her head away and sped up again. Not Chris at all. Just another young homeless man. Even after two years she would have recognized her brother straight away. However much he might have changed in that time, there would have been no mistaking the scar that ran down the side of his jaw.

Calm down, Katie.

If you're going to do this, then focus.

She turned the steering wheel carefully, breathing slowly to steady herself. She had the address of the house she was heading to, but she didn't know that part of the city well and had to rely on the GPS on the dashboard. In a strange way, that took some of the pressure off. It meant she didn't need to think about the fact she probably shouldn't be doing this. Instead, she could dutifully follow the blue line on the screen, as though the start and end points of her journey had been defined for her, and that driving the route between them was inevitable and beyond her control.

Even so, the nerves returned as she neared her destination.

You shouldn't be here.

She parked up outside a semi-detached house on a nondescript street. Most of the properties here had seen better days, but the area itself was neither rich nor poor, and there was certainly nothing to single out this house in particular. It was a home you would drive past without noticing. And she supposed that, on one level, that was the reason she had come here.

She got out of the car and shivered a little. After an endlessly oppressive summer, the air the past few weeks had become colder and sharper. Every morning the trees were a little barer, the pavements carpeted with more and more fallen leaves. Right now, the sun was bright and the breeze mild, but there was a wistfulness to both, as though, even if the year wasn't dying quite yet, it had accepted it was going to.

She walked to the door and rang the bell.

A woman answered a minute or so later. Her greying hair was tied back in a loose ponytail, and she was wearing a pale blue outfit. Katie wasn't sure if she had just come back from work or was about to head out. But then she registered the weariness on the woman's face and reminded herself it could be both.

'Mrs Field?' she said.

'Yes.'

'Nice to meet you.' Katie smiled. 'My name's Katie Shaw. I'm your son's form teacher.'

The smile wasn't returned. Instead, Mrs Field folded her arms and leaned against the door frame, looking even more tired now than she had a moment ago: a woman working two jobs who was about to be given a third.

'What's he done now?'

'It's not what he's done,' she said. 'It's that Gareth has missed several days of school already this term, and he was absent again this morning.'

Mrs Field blinked and then looked away to one side. Katie could almost see the calculations that were running through the woman's head. She hadn't been aware of what Katie had just told her, but she was also wondering how to make this new problem she'd been presented with go away as quickly and painlessly as possible. A moment later, she looked back at Katie.

'Yeah, that's right. Gareth was off sick today.'

'Nobody called the office.'

Mrs Field shrugged. 'It was busy this morning.'

Katie was sure it had been, and that with everything else Mrs Field had to deal with she was doing the best she could. But it was also clear the woman had no idea where her son had been today.

'I think it's important,' Katie said. 'I'm concerned about Gareth. He was already showing signs of falling behind the other students last year. If these absences continue, I'm worried he's going to struggle. I really don't want that to happen.'

Mrs Field snorted slightly. 'Yeah, that would make the school look bad, right?'

'No, that's not it at all. I'm thinking of your son.'

'Oh, so you're saying I'm not?'

Katie started to reply but forced herself to stop. Deep down, she recognized that Mrs Field was lashing out at her as a form of defence, and it was important not to respond in kind. Instead, she tried to picture what Mrs Field was seeing right now: this smartly dressed younger woman who had arrived on her doorstep, smiling, pretending to act friendly even as she stuck the knife in.

'That's honestly not what I think at all,' Katie said. 'I am absolutely sure you care very deeply about your son. But, like I said, I'm concerned too. I don't want him to slip through the cracks.'

'It's always the same with you people, isn't it? All targets. All box-ticking. It's not like Gareth has ever done well at school anyway.'

Which was true, Katie thought. From his academic record there was nothing exceptional about Gareth Field at all. In his own way he was just as average as this house, this street, this whole area. But that was the point. It wasn't the special kids you needed to hold a hand out to. It wasn't the terrible kids either. It was whichever ones you saw falling.

'I know it's hard,' Katie said. 'I know what teenagers are like.'

'Do you?'

'Yes.'

Mrs Field looked her up and down, and then snorted

again. Katie supposed it was understandable; she was in her mid-thirties and didn't look old enough to have a child that age. But then she pictured Gareth Field in her mind's eye – not a troublemaker; just a lonely boy, slight and timid, isolated from the other children in his class – and the image segued into memories of Chris back when he had been a teenager. The way she would see her brother walking along the school corridors by himself, always slightly hunched over, as though he were holding something close to his chest that other people might try to break.

And which someone eventually had.

'Yes,' Katie said again. 'I really do.'

I know how people can be lost.

I know how people can get hurt if you let them.

But Mrs Field didn't reply.

'Let me know if there's anything I can do to help,' Katie said. 'Please.'

Then she turned and walked away. She had tried to do what she could. Maybe her words would make a difference – that was all she could hope for. But when she reached the car and glanced behind her, she saw the front door was already closed.

When Katie got back home, she was greeted by the sight of Siena, her three-and-a-half-year-old daughter, sitting on the settee, her little feet poking off the edge. As always, Siena was draped in her flag. The television was on, and she was so engrossed in whatever cartoon it was showing that she didn't even glance up. Katie looked around the living room, then leaned on one foot and peered through into the kitchen.

Sam was nowhere to be seen.

She could hear the faint sound of music beating somewhere below her feet.

Keep calm, she told herself. *She's fine.*

She shrugged her bag off her shoulder, fighting off the panic in the back of her mind, and then kept her tone even.

'Hey there, Snail,' she said. 'Remember me?'

'Mummy!'

Siena got up and toddled over to her, the flag pulled over her shoulders like a cape, and then offered a gentle cuddle that Katie kneeled down gratefully to accept.

'Daddy downstairs?'

'Yes.'

'And have you been good for him since home time?'

'No.'

Katie ruffled her soft hair. 'Good.'

She stood up and headed through to the kitchen, and then to the door that led down to the basement.

She and Sam had fallen in love with their cottage the first time they'd laid eyes on it. It had been at the end of a long month of house-hunting, and the estate agent had brought them to the property with the manner of someone showing a prospective owner the last and most hopeless dog in the pound. The cottage was small and cramped, the walls speckled with mould, the paint flecked, the wallpaper peeling. It smelled damp, and felt it too.

But as they looked around, Katie found she gradually stopped noticing the many things that were wrong with it and began focusing instead on the things that felt right. The exposed wooden beams in the front-room ceiling.

The layout of the rooms. The way in which she could – almost without trying – already furnish the spaces in front of her. Bookcases here; a settee there; the bed like that with the wardrobes opposite. It was the strangest feeling, as though a future version of her knew this place by heart, but the her right then hadn't yet reached that point in time.

She and Sam spent the next two years renovating it, doing the work themselves when they could and stretching their budget on a monthly basis when they needed help. Ever so slowly, it had become not just a house but a home. And it turned out that everything had fitted exactly where she'd imagined it would. Where *both* of them had.

For Sam that meant the basement.

The music grew louder as she opened the door and headed down the stone steps. The basement was the size of the living room above, but even that was barely enough space to contain the equipment her husband had amassed over the years. There were guitars and bass guitars stored upright in a cluster of stands by one wall. A drum kit in one corner. Racks of the headphones he used for his silent discos. A keyboard that seemed longer than the average human being. The floor was a swirl of foot pedals and cables, the latter concentrated round a table covered with computer equipment, where Sam was standing right now.

He had his back to her and was staring intently at one of the screens. From what she could see of the detail there, it might have been monitoring the vital signs of a whole hospital ward.

'Hey,' she said.

'Hey.'

Sam pressed a button and the music stopped.

'Listen,' Katie said, 'I don't know if you remember, but we have a child?' She held her palm out at waist height. 'Little person, about this tall? Arrived a few years ago now, I guess, but the occasion was reasonably memorable.'

She tried to keep her tone light-hearted, but inside she was seething. Siena was fine, and she knew she was worrying needlessly, but that did nothing to still the alarm sounding in the back of her mind. Sam had been down *here* and Siena had been up *there*, and that meant *she had not been safe*. Because that was the way the world worked. You couldn't make assumptions and take chances. You didn't know when bad things were going to happen until they already had, and by then it was too late.

Sam turned round and smiled. Despite herself, the cold feeling inside her melted slightly. Whenever he smiled like that, she felt the years dropping away. His hair hadn't changed over the years, and his smile made him look so much like the carefree teenage boy she'd fallen in love with that it was often hard to remain angry.

'But she's fine, right?' Sam said.

Katie folded her arms. 'Well, she was watching television.'

'Television is very educational these days.' He checked his watch. 'And I needed to sort this. You're back later than usual.'

'I went to one of my kids' houses on the way home.'

'How come?'

'You remember me telling you about Gareth Field?

He wasn't in school again today, so I decided to talk to his mother.'

Sam frowned. 'I don't know how these things work, but are you actually allowed to do that?'

'Allowed to look up the address on the school computer system and call round at the house unannounced? No, not really.'

'Could you get in trouble for it?'

'*Possibly*,' she said. 'Time will tell.'

'Time does do that, yes.'

Sam was silent for a moment. Then he sighed.

'You can't help everyone,' he said quietly. 'You're not *responsible* for everyone. You do know that, don't you?'

Katie didn't reply, and for a few seconds the atmosphere in the basement felt awkward. Then she heard Siena calling from upstairs.

'Mummy? Daddy?'

The sound broke the tension in the air. She looked up at the ceiling for a moment, then back down at Sam as his eyes widened in pretend shock.

'Shit,' he said. 'I remember now.'

Once back upstairs – and with the television firmly off – Katie sat next to Siena on the settee, reading with her. This was one of her favourite parts of the day, snuggled up tightly beside her daughter. The book in front of them was already far too young for Siena; it had big pages, with simple illustrations and the corresponding words written below them. But Siena had always loved it, which meant Katie loved it too.

'Sun.'

Siena pointed at the right drawing.

'That's right,' Katie said.

'And moon.'

Siena giggled at that: a gorgeous sound that made Katie smile. On this particular page Siena always left that image until last. She and Sam had told Siena it was the first word she ever said, and since then the moon had been magic to her. Every night she insisted on saying goodnight to it.

Katie turned the page.

Siena pointed. 'Van.'

'That's the one.'

'Helicopter.'

'You're a genius, kid.'

As her daughter continued pointing and naming the illustrations, Katie allowed her mind to wander, thinking back to what Sam had said to her downstairs. *You can't help everyone.* The two of them had fallen in love as teenagers and been together ever since, so he knew her well – far too well sometimes. But he was right, and she needed to remind herself of it more often. At the same time, knowing it was true never did anything to dispel the urge to help, or to soften the sense of guilt she felt when she failed.

And as her mind wandered, the second premonition arrived.

'Red car,' Siena said.

Katie blinked, snapping back into focus, and looked down at the page. There was a picture of a car there, but it was blue.

'What do you mean?' Katie said slowly.

'Red car, Mummy.'

Her heart fluttered in her chest and a trickle of cold ran down her spine.

Red car.

'What –'

But then she heard a buzzing sound. Her phone ringing – over on the table. She stood up and walked across, shivering slightly, caught off balance.

She registered the number on the screen and answered the call.

'Mum?'

'Katie?'

Her mother sounded disorientated. Upset. Which frightened Katie because weakness had always been the very last thing her mother would show the world.

Something terrible has happened.

'It's me, Mum. What's wrong?'

For a second there was no reply. Just a hiss of static on the line.

'It's Chris,' her mother said softly. 'It's your brother.'

4

A couple of minutes later, Katie was back on the settee pulling her boots on, her fingers trembling slightly. Sam walked in from the kitchen and leaned against the door frame.

'Who was that?'

'Just Mum.'

'What did she want?'

'I'm not sure. Something to do with Chris. I'm heading over now.'

A moment of silence.

'Is he dead?' Sam said.

Katie stopped and looked up. Her husband had his arms folded in a way that reminded her a little too much of Mrs Field earlier. She looked down and knotted her laces too tightly.

The last time she had seen Chris was more than two years ago. It had been on what should have been their father's birthday, except that Dad had died three years earlier, and what was left of their family had gathered at her mother's flat in his memory. She and Sam had arrived early with Siena to help her mother prepare a meal. Chris turned up later. He was allegedly no longer using, but there had been too many betrayals over the years, and Sam had been sceptical beforehand. His patience had always been thinner. Katie had looked at Chris carefully when he arrived. That was something she had become

34

used to doing – trying to work out what stage he was at in the endless cycle of addiction – but that day she found him hard to read.

Regardless, her mother was overjoyed to see him. Katie remembered how she'd bustled around the kitchen, happily batting away the offers of help, while Chris played with Siena in the front room. But when Katie took the first of the dishes through to the table, she found her daughter abandoned on the settee. Because her brother had already snuck out by then, taking with him the money he had found in her handbag.

And despite her mother's protestations, Katie had called the police.

And none of them had heard from him since. She and Sam had never spoken about it, but she imagined that, as time passed, they had both made the same assumption: at some point there would be a body found in some shabby flat, or an old tent, or face down in the canal. It had always seemed the inevitable destination of her brother's life, and even if Sam had not quite *wished* for that outcome, she knew he had at least been relieved to have Chris gone from their lives.

She reminded herself now that was only because Sam cared about her. That it stemmed from what he'd tried to get her to accept over the years: that people choose their own paths, and however much you love them there comes a point when they have to take responsibility for the journey they've embarked upon.

And that it's not your fault when they do.

Is he dead?

'I don't think so.' Katie stood up. 'But she didn't want to talk over the phone.'

'What does that mean?'

Katie walked over and kissed him. 'It means I won't be long,' she said.

He didn't reply.

It was growing dark as she drove on to her mother's street. She passed the point where Hyde had attacked Chris all those years ago without looking at it, and then parked just past a driveway flanked by two large stone pillars.

She locked the car, then made her way down the driveway in the gloom. From the outside the building looked impressive – and perhaps it had been once. It remained a stern, imposing Victorian mansion, with towering soot-black stone walls and tall, austere windows. But at some point in the building's history the interior had been clumsily converted into four flats, each a single drab corridor with a handful of rooms leading off to either side.

At the bottom of the drive Katie stopped and looked to her left. There were four garages there; one for each flat. Theirs was padlocked shut, the metal doors as brittle and fragile as old parchment. She remembered on countless summer days seeing her father sitting at a trestle table inside it, threading wick through a plastic container then tacking it in place while wax heated in a cheap pan on the stove beside him. The ramshackle shelves around him were always filled with rainbow rows of candles. As a child, the bright colours had made her happy, but it had been a bittersweet feeling because she also knew they needed to sell those candles, not store them. The thing that made her saddest of all was when her father locked the garage of an evening, and then walked slowly back to the house, as though he had a pain in his hip that got worse every day.

She made her way down a set of steps and let herself into her mother's flat.

'It's me,' she called.

After a moment, her mother's voice drifted from the far end of the corridor.

'I'll be through in a minute.'

'OK.'

The curtains were open in the front room, but the fading light from outside barely illuminated it. Katie stepped on the switch that turned on the standing lamp in the corner, bathing the familiar furnishings with dim light. Nothing had really changed in here over the years. The threadbare settee; her mother's worn old armchair, with its coarse, itchy fabric; the alcoves lined with makeshift shelves, still filled with dusty books that had mostly been her father's and hadn't been slid out of place in years. There was the same ancient wooden table by the window, as solid and heavy as if it had grown up through the bare floorboards below.

Katie walked across. A half-completed jigsaw was laid out on the table. She tilted her head, squinting down at it, and then felt a jolt as she recognized the image. The jigsaw must have been custom-made from a family photo. It showed her mother and father standing with their backs to a window full of rows of brightly coloured candles, and Chris and Katie side by side in front of them. She remembered that day. There had been a brief period when her father's business had been successful enough to warrant renting a shop, and this picture had been taken when the four of them went to see it for the first time.

She stared down at her younger self standing beside her brother. The two of them smiling.

'That was a nice day, wasn't it?'

Katie turned to see her mother standing in the doorway.

'Yes,' Katie said. 'It was. You'll strain your eyes in this light, though.'

'My eyes are just fine, Katie.'

'Yes, Mum. I know.'

Even so, she forced herself to look away as her mother made her way slowly over to the armchair, leaning on the stick she used to walk with. The sight of her always broke Katie's heart a little these days, but it was important never to show it. Her mother refused to acknowledge that her abilities were dimming and failing, even though it must have been as obvious to her as it was to Katie. She had always been so strong. While Katie's father had sometimes struggled to make a living, her mother had worked at a care home, taking on long, back-breaking shifts. Her whole life, she had been someone other people relied on. The reversal of that was intolerable to her.

Which only reminded Katie of how shaken she'd sounded on the phone.

She waited until her mother had eased herself carefully down into the chair, and then went and perched on the arm of the settee, her hands clasped between her knees.

'What's going on, Mum?' she said quietly. 'What's happened with Chris?'

'He's gone missing.'

'I know that. He went missing two years ago.'

'No, he came back, Katie.'

Her mother blinked and looked at her helplessly.

'He came back to me,' she said. 'And now he's in danger.'

It had started about three months ago, Katie's mother told her, with a knock at the door. It had taken her some time to open it, but when she had, Chris had been standing on the doorstep. He had been an addict for much of his adult life, and borderline homeless for most of that, but she told Katie that he had been dressed in neat clothes and looked healthy and well.

'I'm not making this up,' she said.

'I didn't think you were.'

'I mean about him being well.'

Katie said nothing to that. While she was prepared to believe her brother had reappeared, she was far more sceptical about him no longer using. But her mother had never given up on Chris, even though Katie had watched her heart break a hundred times over the years. She was a proud woman, and always seemed inured to when the inevitable occurred – when Chris relapsed, and then drifted out of contact until the next time he needed something. Katie was worried for her sake that this was going to be another example of history repeating itself. However proud you might be, there are only so many times a heart can break and mend.

'It was properly *him*,' her mother said. 'He seemed so happy and together. Not like he used to be. Like he was *meant* to be.'

'Where had he been all this time?' Katie said.

'He didn't want to talk about it. I respected that.'

'OK, then. What did he want?'

'Just to see me. Is that so hard to believe?'

'No,' Katie lied. 'What happened next?'

'He kept calling round.'

Twice a week, her mother told her, and always at the same times, which Chris had claimed fitted in with his work schedule. Which was new. As far as Katie was aware, her brother had never held down a legitimate job for any length of time, but the details of his employment were another mystery her mother had respected. Regardless, Chris hadn't asked her for money, and didn't seem to want anything beyond reconnecting with her. The puzzle on the table had been a present from him, she said. There had been one day he'd wanted to look through some old photographs, and he'd had it made afterwards from photos she'd let him take away.

'Why didn't you tell me he was back?'

Her mother hesitated, and Katie leaned forward.

'Mum?'

'Because he didn't *want* you to know.'

She was gracious enough to allow Katie a moment of silence then, and not to mention that the last time Katie had seen Chris had been when she'd called the police on him. But Katie thought about that anyway, and the sadness of it all ran through her. Had Chris hidden from her out of shame because of what he'd done? Was he angry with her for reporting him to the police? Or had he simply assumed it was *her* who wouldn't want to see *him*, and had decided to spare himself the pain of facing that?

Regardless, it hurt badly that the two of them had come to this. There had been so much love between them once.

Katie took a deep breath. 'OK,' she said. 'What makes you think he's in trouble?'

'He's gone missing again. He didn't turn up yesterday.'

Katie's heart sank at that, but her mother put up her hand.

'I know what you're thinking. I know what a stupid and foolish old woman you think I am.'

'Oh, Mum.' She closed her eyes for a moment. 'I really don't.'

'Yes, you do – you *do*, Katie. And perhaps you're right. But it's different this time. He's not answering the number he gave me; I think his phone is switched off. And the last couple of weeks he's been acting strangely.'

'Strangely how?'

'Like he was looking over his shoulder the whole time. Like he was scared of something. Or *someone*.'

That seemed likely to Katie. Even if she took her mother's word for it that Chris was no longer using in the present, he certainly had the kind of past from which people might emerge to haunt him.

'Yes.' She sighed. 'It's certainly possible he was scared of someone.'

'Like him,' her mother said. 'That monster.'

Katie looked at her.

Even after all this time, her mother couldn't bring herself to say the name *Michael Hyde* out loud. Nobody had been able to explain why Hyde had attacked Chris that day, beyond the fact he had a history of mental health issues and had been experiencing spiralling delusions in the days leading up to it. Hyde seemed to have been cruising the streets at random that afternoon. In a different universe the victim might have been someone else. In this one it had been Chris.

That monster.

Part of Katie wanted to tell her mother that Hyde was just a man. That it was all in the past now and that he was no longer any kind of threat to Chris.

But her daughter's words from earlier began echoing in her head.

Red car, Mummy.

Red car.

5

Laurence left work precisely on time that day.

Which was not to say that he stopped working. Even as he drove home, his mind was on the case and not on the route. He understood the necessity of the workplace, but it did not suit him. Noise and bustle; too many people; too much *distraction*. While he liked and respected his colleagues – and Pettifer especially – the truth was that he did his best work on his own. While he had never sat down and crunched the numbers, he thought it entirely possible he had put in more hours alone in his flat than he had at his desk in the department.

And what a flat! Nobody could accuse it of being large, even for a single man, but equally, nobody could deny its efficiency. As Laurence opened the door, the soft light in the front room turned on in recognition of his arrival, revealing the clean floor, the matching furniture, the state-of-the-art stereo system. The alcoves were lined with neat rows of books, separated by a settee that faced the large plasma screen mounted on the opposite wall. An open alcove led through to a kitchen that hummed with soft blue light. Like the rest of the flat, everything through there was top of the range, so that the room would not have looked out of place in a spaceship.

Laurence was not a rich man, and he was frugal; he spent money only on the things that mattered to him, and those things were few. At the top of that list was the place he lived, which he had spent both years and considerable amounts of money making *just so*. Everyone has different priorities, of course, but to Laurence's mind your home was where you started and finished the day. If it didn't make you happy – if it didn't fit you as best you could make it – then you were at as much of a disadvantage in life as you would be going to bed or work hungry.

The flat also knew him well. As Laurence walked into the kitchen and put the bundle of papers he'd brought with him on the table, the arrival of the Bluetooth connection in his phone had already started the coffee machine. He set up his laptop and connected it to the department's intranet. By the time he'd set some gentle music playing in the front room, the coffee was ready. He poured himself a cup, then sat down at the table and sighed happily to himself.

And then he set to work.

When he was a child, his father had often sat him down for serious talks. Laurence remembered many of them, but one in particular had always resonated with him.

'Laurence,' his father said, 'you are born with advantages and disadvantages in this life. We do not all share the same starting line. Now, one of your disadvantages is the colour of your skin. People will judge you for *what* you are rather than *who*, and that means you will sometimes have to work twice as hard and twice as smart as them in order to be considered half as good.'

Laurence had nodded dutifully.

Then his father had winked at him. 'And one *advantage* you have is that this will not be hard for you.'

He read methodically through the paperwork beside him now. He remained convinced that Alan Hobbes's murder had been motivated by financial concerns – but if that somehow turned out not to be the case, he would only have wasted thirty minutes. And he favoured a holistic approach to these matters; it was always better to have as much information as possible.

To understand the ailment, first understand the organism.

And so, within half an hour, he had a decent if rudimentary understanding of Hobbes's career and business interests.

There had been some surprises within the material. From the house he had visited that afternoon, he had assumed Alan Hobbes had been born into a rich family – that he was *old money* – and had then spent his life idling. Not so. Hobbes appeared to have been raised in relative poverty, and had made his fortune in his twenties through a series of extremely shrewd investments. Over the years, he had bought shares in a vast web of lucrative companies and held an extensive portfolio of properties.

And yet he had not really been a *businessman* at all.

It turned out that Alan Hobbes had actually been *Professor* Alan Hobbes. He had been a senior lecturer in the Philosophy department of the city's university, where he had received his doctorate close to fifty years ago, and then worked until his retirement a decade earlier. Which was curious. The man's financial investments had provided him with exponentially more money than his teaching; there had been no need for him to work to support himself. Which made it clear to Laurence where the man's heart had been, and implied the money he'd made elsewhere had been a means to that end.

And it was not obvious that Hobbes had cared about money beyond that. Before Laurence now were details of the man's numerous charitable donations and quiet philanthropic gestures – so many, in fact, that, at the time of his murder, Alan Hobbes had been worth far less than his grand house would have suggested to an outsider. In the years since his retirement, the man had given away more money than most people could dream of earning in a lifetime.

Laurence poured himself a fresh cup of coffee and pondered.

Who would have wanted to hurt Alan Hobbes? He gave every appearance of having been a good and decent man. Laurence looked again at the man's business dealings. There was nothing obviously suspicious there, but you never knew what deals might have been done behind the scenes, and what resentments might have ended up simmering as a result. And when it came to investments, there was Hobbes's rate of success to consider. The man seemed to have had an uncanny knack for being in the right place at the right time.

Until, of course, he hadn't.

It's like he knew.

Like he knew this was coming and was ready for it.

The lawyer's words from earlier. They made Laurence consider the circumstances leading up to Hobbes's murder, and the actions the old man had taken.

Dismissing all his staff.

Arranging for Gaunt to turn up the next morning.

Almost as if he was waiting for his killer to arrive,

46

his murder simply another appointment that had to be met.

Laurence slid the laptop across and performed a search for Hobbes at the university. The page loaded slowly, so while he waited he opened the online case file. It included a list of all the employees registered as working for Alan Hobbes. Updates were gradually being added as each one was spoken to, and Laurence scanned a few of the reports that had arrived since he had left the office. There were several still unaccounted for, but so far everyone interviewed had confirmed what Gaunt had told them.

Laurence leaned back in his chair and rubbed his mouth thoughtfully.

The obvious question was *why* Alan Hobbes had surrendered his life without a fight. He seemed to have accepted his death was coming – as though, after a life of good fortune and luxury, a debt had become due and he had been resigned to paying it.

Like he had made a deal with the Devil, Laurence thought.

Not literally, of course. Laurence was not a religious man. Even if he had been, he suspected such a deal would be functionally impossible – that the Devil would most likely end up exasperated, throwing his little red hands in the air at the flood of applications. But *figuratively* there was something there. Especially when Laurence remembered the look of pain and sadness etched on the dead man's face.

Laurence's mobile rang.

It was still in his jacket pocket. He fumbled for it, saw it was Pettifer, then accepted the call and held the phone to his ear.

'Hello there,' he said. 'You have reached your boss. Please leave a message after the –'

'You're not my fucking boss, Laurence.'

'Technically no, but we both know the truth deep down.'

'Working hard?'

'Of course,' he said. 'Yourself?'

'Not only working hard but working *smart*,' she said. 'Check your inbox.'

'Hold the line. Your call will be answered as soon as –'

'Just do it, Laurence.'

With the phone still pressed to his ear, he reached for the laptop and scrolled through until he found the email. When he opened it, he read the message twice and then looked down at the attachment.

Hobbes had had a camera installed in his room.

Laurence opened the footage Pettifer had sent him.

The CCTV camera in Hobbes's flat had been located high above the door. He supposed that was some consolation for him not having spotted it at the time – and, of course, for all her talk of smartness Pettifer hadn't noticed it then either.

Nevertheless.

He was still kicking himself a little.

When the video opened, he noted the time stamp on the bottom. Assuming the information was accurate, the clip had been recorded on the day of the murder, beginning a little before eight o'clock at night and running for approximately five minutes. Pettifer had explained it was the last available footage that could be retrieved from the camera. Which gave Laurence pause. It seemed a step beyond the capabilities of modern technology to imagine the surveillance system had simply winked out of existence at the same time as its owner.

All will be revealed, he told himself.

He pressed play.

He was presented with a grainy black-and-white image, the recording disappointingly low-resolution. The angle was decent enough, at least, taking in most of the main room. Hobbes was already in situ, lying in the bed where he had been found today. But he was alive here. The quality was just good enough for Laurence to make out the covers moving gently over the old man's chest. He appeared to be sleeping, with his head tilted back a little and his mouth slightly open.

Laurence watched as a line of static rolled slowly up the screen. When it reached Hobbes, it seemed to make his body convulse as it passed over him, his expression momentarily twisting into something else before the static moved on, leaving just his peaceful, sleeping face again.

There was no sound.

No other apparent movement in the room.

As another roll of static crept up the screen, Laurence's attention moved from the old man on the bed to the archway in the wall behind him. On screen, the blackness there seemed even more absolute than it had while standing in the room. He remembered the faint rush of cold air that had been coming from it earlier.

A figure emerged suddenly from the darkness of the archway.

Laurence paused the video and peered carefully. The figure was little more than a pale smear, like an animal

49

caught on a trail cam, and he imagined most of the frames would yield similar results. There might be better evidence in motion, though, and so he set the footage playing again.

The figure stepped cautiously out of the darkness of the archway. With the low quality Laurence could tell that it was a man, but not much more than that. He saw what looked like jeans. Some kind of jacket. Dark hair. And the man appeared to be holding something. Laurence turned his head to one side, but couldn't make out what it was – only that the man was clasping it between his hands and pressing it to his stomach. Whatever it was, it wasn't big. It didn't look heavy. And yet there was something about the way the man was holding it – almost nervously – that suggested it weighed on him in a different way.

The object glinted slightly.

Is anything missing?

Laurence remembered the way the lawyer had glanced at the archway.

I don't know yet.

He watched as the man stepped beside the bed and stood there for a few seconds, staring down at Alan Hobbes. Laurence cursed the lack of audio. Was the man talking to Hobbes? He was turned away from the camera, so it was impossible to tell. If so, there was no response from the old man. Hobbes appeared to remain asleep, lying there in the bed with the covers over his chest gently rising and falling.

A line of static rolled over the pair, making them both jitter.

The man turned away from the bed and walked

towards the door, his head bowed, his face entirely out of sight.

And then he disappeared from view.

Damn it.

Laurence leaned back. It was perhaps too much to hope that the murder had been caught on camera, but the footage might at least have had the decency to offer a viable view of a suspect. As things stood, he didn't think they would get anything from it on that score. But. Accentuate the positives. This had been recorded well after members of staff were all supposed to have been dismissed, and even if it was low quality, it might still be good enough to identify one if they had come back.

Laurence stared at the screen.

There were only a few seconds left of the recording, and he watched as another roll of static began its steady ascent up the screen. Laurence leaned forward and peered more closely as it reached Alan Hobbes.

And then the entire screen was filled with a face.

Laurence pulled back – his heart leaping from the shock. The whole frame was white for a couple of seconds, before an eye moved into view, filling the screen, looking this way and that, and then the man leaned away from the camera, his entire face clearly visible now, and stared directly into the lens for the briefest of moments.

And then the screen went black.

His phone rang.

Laurence glanced down, his heart beating hard. Pettifer was calling him back.

'So,' she said when he answered. 'What do you think?'

'I think give me a minute.'

'No,' she said. 'Please just tell me *how good* this is.'

He ignored her and set the footage playing again, pausing it towards the end. The frame gave about as clear an image as it was possible to get. The man in the footage was about thirty years old, with pale skin and earnest-looking eyes. Long hair. A spread of freckles across his nose and cheeks.

And a scar that ran down his face from the side of his eye to his chin.

Tell me how good this is.

'I'll do you one better,' he said. 'I'll tell you *who* this is.'

6

That was a nice day, wasn't it?

Katie remembered her family going to see her father's first shop. After toiling for years in the garage, he had been able to rent a small unit in Barton Mill on the outskirts of the city, close to the countryside. Katie was thirteen then; Chris, eleven. The old mill was situated on the bend of a curving hill, with a river churning away below. It appeared impossibly precarious to her: a huge stone edifice half supported by thick black wooden struts that stretched almost endlessly down to the muddy banks beneath. When they got out of the car, she walked across to the fence and leaned over the railing, peering at the water. It was so far below her that for a second she felt dizzy.

'Wow,' she said. 'Come and look at this, Chris.'

She heard the *chit* of his trainers behind her as he walked across to join her.

'Chris, don't,' her mother called sharply. 'It's dangerous.'

Katie looked over her shoulder and saw Chris frozen halfway between her and her parents at the car, pulled equally in two directions at once. There was a slightly helpless look on his face, as though he wanted to be brave but knew deep down that he shouldn't. That he should do as he was told.

Katie watched him deflate a little.

He turned and walked back to their parents.

By then she was used to them being overprotective of Chris. On one level she understood it, because she often had the same impulse. Her brother was small, but there was a vulnerability to him that wasn't simply down to his size. It was something more innate. A sense that he was desperate to find his place in the world but was perpetually at odds with it, like a puzzle piece that didn't quite fit.

Even so, it didn't escape her attention that her mother hadn't called to *her* just then. That it had been Chris she was concerned about, not Katie.

Never her.

She followed her family inside.

The Mill was a new conversion. Everything smelled of sawn wood and floor polish. A corridor led between units with glass walls, many dark and empty but several already occupied. Their parents wandered further, but Chris stopped by a unit. This shop was closed and dark, and her brother formed binoculars with his hands and peered in through the window. Katie stopped beside him. Close to the glass she could see a display of elaborately decorated boxes painted with beautiful, swirling imagery. Dungeons & Dragons; Space Explorer; Dark Knight. There were racks of dice: regular ones, of course, but also ones with ten and twenty and a hundred sides. A little further in, battalions of tiny, intricately painted figurines were arranged on a sculpted table.

She looked up at the sign above the door.

GODS PLAY DICE.

'What is this?' Chris said.

'Role-playing games,' she said.

'What's that?'

'It's when people pretend to be elves or soldiers, or

whatever, and then they roll dice, and stuff happens depending on the number. A fantasy game. Make-believe.'

He was silent for a moment. 'It all looks so *cool*, doesn't it?'

Katie considered that. She had never played anything like it herself but had a vague conception of the kind of person who did, and *cool* wasn't the first word that sprang to mind. But it would have been unfair to say so. Chris seemed hypnotized by the sight in front of him now, and if it turned out *he* was going to be that type of person, then she didn't want to be mean about it.

'Yeah,' she said. 'It looks really cool.'

He looked at her hopefully. 'Maybe we could play it together some time?'

'Yeah,' she said. 'Your birthday's coming up.'

He smiled at her, and any resentment she'd felt outside disappeared for now. Their mother and father had been arguing a great deal recently – about work; about money; about who did what and who didn't do enough – and even though they always tried to keep it from them, the atmosphere at home had been tense. Chris was more sensitive than Katie and had spent more time clinging to her than she was comfortable with. There had been a fair few moments over the last year or so when he'd bugged the hell out of her. But that smile of his always undid the damage. It made him look about half his age, and had the kind of purity that made him seem like a small flame you wanted to cup your hands around and protect.

Of course I'll play a game with you, she thought.

Because I love you.

'Come on, loser,' she said.

55

The unit her father had rented was a couple of shops along. A plain sign above the door read WICK'S END, which was a joke she'd had to explain to Chris after having it explained to her first. Her father was unlocking the door as they caught up. When the lights came on, she almost gasped in shock. An enormous rainbow filled the window before her. The plywood shelves within were lined with candles of different shapes and sizes, all arranged by colour in a bright, beautiful display that covered almost every square inch of the glass. At first glance it was impossible to take in the sheer intricacy of it – how each candle came together to build the whole display – and for a moment she was transfixed by it.

'*Voilà*,' her father said quietly.

Katie looked away from the window and towards her mother.

She was standing by the doorway, one hand cupped under her other elbow, her gaze moving over the sight before her. It was hard to work out what she was thinking.

The unit was small, but her father had worked hard to maximize the available space. There were the racks and shelves around the walls, and against the window, and the effect of the colours was even more impressive in the shop. Outside, Katie had felt like she was observing a rainbow; in here, it was more like she was standing inside one. To her right was a counter with an old cash register and thin sheets of packing paper. Behind that, a sink unit and counter, the latter covered with pots and pans she recognized from the now empty garage back home. They looked battered and out of place, but it was equipment that had served her father well over the years.

She looked at him. He had a strange expression on his

56

face, as though he wanted to be proud but wasn't quite sure if he was allowed to be.

'What do you think?' he asked them.

'It's amazing,' Katie said.

'Really?' He beamed at her for a moment – but then corrected himself. 'I know it needs a lot of work. But it's a start.'

Chris was looking around with the same sense of wonder he'd had outside the role-playing game shop. It would occur to Katie years later that he often approached the world that way – that it was as much a part of him as the vulnerability. It was another thing Michael Hyde would take from him.

'Do people really buy *this many* candles?' Chris said.

'Not all at once,' her mother told him.

She had been silent until then, still hugging herself and looking around, as though she wasn't sure what to make of what she was seeing. But then she stepped over to her husband, put her arms round him, and hugged him tightly. After a moment's hesitation, he embraced her back. Even though Katie didn't fully understand everything that had gone on between them, she felt it in the air anyway: some kind of tension dissipating.

'It's perfect,' her mother said.

'No, it needs a lot of work.'

She rubbed his back. 'Not all at once,' she repeated quietly.

As well as a phone number for Chris, Katie's mother had an address for him too. He had even left her a spare key. But her mother no longer drove, and she wanted Katie to see if he was all right. The idea of doing so filled her with dread. Despite her mother's assurances that he was no longer using, her mind immediately conjured up an image of Chris lying dead in his flat, and she couldn't imagine how it would feel to find him like that. And even if he was fine, what would it be like to see him again after all this time?

'If you're that worried about him,' Katie said, 'we should call the police.'

Her mother shook her head. 'He would never want the police involved.'

Once again, her mother was gracious enough not to mention what had happened the last time Katie had seen Chris. But it hung in the air anyway.

And so, back in the car, Katie texted Sam to let him know she was going to be a little longer than she'd expected, and then drove south into the whorl of dual carriageways that circled the city centre. The street lights filled the car with alternating waves of amber and shadow, and they washed over her in time with the anxiety that was throbbing inside her. Along with the familiar feeling that what she wanted was always less important than her brother.

Of always being second best.

The GPS took her past the city's floodlit prison, which sat on the crest of a hill like a castle, and then along streets lined with flat, hard-edged houses. A single main road ran through the suburb in which Chris had made his home. She drove past shuttered convenience stores, charity shops and minimarkets, interspersed with the bright windows of intermittent takeaways. She caught sight of a few shapes huddled in the doorways, and a couple sitting hunched together in the shadows of a bus shelter, but the street was otherwise almost eerily deserted.

She indicated and pulled in.

At first glance the address Chris had given her mother looked like a bust. Number fifty-three was an estate agent's, while the windows of number fifty-five beside it were filled with rolls of carpet and squares of dull-coloured fabric. Both were closed. She was beginning to think her brother must have lied once again, but then she noticed an unmarked door between the two businesses.

She leaned forward and peered up through the wind-screen. There was a second storey above the fabric shop, almost invisible against the night sky. Its windows were dark.

OK then.

Katie checked her mobile phone.

No reply from Sam.

She wasn't sure what to read into that silence. Maybe he was pissed off at having to put Siena to bed himself. More likely, though, he was concerned about her. He would be worried about what her brother coming back into their lives meant. Certainly if he knew where she was right now, he would very much want her to turn round and drive away.

She looked up at the dark flat again and wondered if perhaps she should do exactly that. Her mother might have felt it was her job to be here, but if there *was* something terrible waiting inside the flat, she had no obligation to see it. And if Chris was in some kind of trouble, it wasn't her duty to risk her own safety by getting involved. Especially when he had made it clear he wanted nothing to do with her.

For a moment she felt torn between what Sam and her mother wanted from her, in the same way she remembered her brother being caught between her and their parents outside the Mill.

Forget about them for a minute, she told herself. *What do you want to do?*

She thought back to that day at the Mill again – how her brother's smile had made the resentment waft away, like the sun cutting through a cold morning's mist. And then she remembered, a few years later, crying at the sight of him in the hospital when they had been finally allowed to visit. While her brother had survived the attack, Michael Hyde had left him with so many scars. The one that ran prominently down his face; the ones on his body that were less visible; the ones in his mind that only he could see. And while nothing is ever so clear cut and simple, it had always seemed to her that their paths colliding that day had knocked Chris off course and set him on the path he had followed since.

The guilt from that had never left her.

She remembered how she had felt as she ran towards the police cordon, and it seemed to her now that what she *wanted* to do was the wrong question. What mattered far more was what she would be able to live with herself for not doing.

So she took a deep breath.

Then slipped the phone into her jacket pocket and got out of the car.

7

Katie shivered. Night had fallen properly now, and it was cold, but this whole area seemed rough and she felt vulnerable out of the car. There was noise coming from further up the street: the sound of people outside a pub, an angry edge to the echoing laughter. She glanced across the street behind her. A forbidding metal block of public toilets rested on a grass verge there, and a skinny man, bald and shirtless, was pacing back and forth on the pavement, talking to himself and gesticulating with his thin arms.

She turned to Chris's door and rang the bell.

There was no response, but the flat above her was so dark and silent that she hadn't expected one. She tried the key in the lock, part of her hoping it wouldn't turn.

But it did.

She stepped inside and closed the door behind her.

There was a thin set of stairs directly ahead, leading up to a dark landing above. She stood still and listened for a few seconds, but everything was quiet aside from the thud of her heartbeat. Nobody was here. You can tell when a place is empty; the silence just has a different quality.

Of course, that didn't mean Chris wasn't here.

She found a light switch, and then made her way up the stairs to the landing above, breathing slowly and carefully the whole time. The air smelled slightly stale, but – mercifully – no worse than that. It didn't take long to explore the flat. There were only four small rooms: a living room, a kitchen, a bathroom and a bedroom. She steeled herself as she stepped into each one, but there was no sign of her brother.

Katie stopped on the landing. She felt slightly out of breath – she hadn't realized how much she had been bracing herself to find something terrible. And so on one level she was relieved. But there was also space for a little anger to creep in. For the worry and concern Chris had caused their mother through his behaviour. Just as he had so often in the past.

But the flat was far nicer inside than she would have guessed from outside. The carpets were all new; the walls had been freshly painted; and while the furniture was sparse and functional, each piece had clearly been carefully chosen. As an adult, she had become used to Chris finding the cheapest lodgings on offer, using them up until there was nothing left, and then moving on. But this place felt different. It had more of a settled feel to it, as though he'd found a house and made an effort to transform it into a home.

She couldn't remember him ever doing that before.

She walked back into the front room and looked around. There was a television on a stand, a settee and an armchair, and two small shelves stacked with a random selection of second-hand paperback books. *The Death House; The Stand; The Doll Who Ate His Mother*. She found a few bits of personal debris scattered on top of the shelves – a faded library card; a spread of small change; a couple of half-burnt tealight candles – and at one end a hundred-sided dice.

Katie picked that up and ran it between her fingers. It was one they'd played with together – part of the set she'd saved up and bought for his birthday. But it was so old now that it had the polished feel of a pebble, and so many of the numbers had rubbed away that it would be impossible to use. Even so, it brought a pang of nostalgia and sadness. She wondered why Chris had kept it. As a reminder, perhaps, of simpler, happier times. Or maybe of the more serious games he had spent his life playing and losing since. She put it down again.

There was a cheap mobile next to the television. It was out of charge, and so she assumed this was the phone her mother had tried to call. Which begged the question why it was here when Chris wasn't, and why it had been left to run out of power. There had been a time when a mobile phone, however inexpensive, would have been good currency for him. But she didn't recognize the model, and there was no sign of a charger.

The bedroom was small. There was just enough space for a double bed with a wardrobe on one side of the headboard, and a small table on the other. The bed was unmade, and there were clothes scattered across it. She opened the wardrobe. While a few clothes remained, it was filled mostly with empty wire hangers.

Almost as though Chris had left in a hurry.

Like he was looking over his shoulder, she remembered.

Like he was scared of something.

She moved round to the table. There was a drawer built in below. When she opened it, she was greeted by the smell of wood and dust drifting up.

There were a few sheets of paper inside. She picked one out and saw it was an old, faded letter printed on

63

university-headed notepaper. It hadn't been delivered to the flat, and both the address and the name of the person – James Alderson – meant nothing to her. But directly underneath she spotted a glossy sheet of photographs, and she put the letter aside and picked those out instead.

There had been four originally, taken in a booth, but one had been clipped away. The remaining three showed the same image of the same two people. She recognized Chris, leaning into the picture on the right-hand side, and yet at the same time she didn't. For one thing, he looked *healthy*. He was tanned and freckled, he'd grown his hair out into a style that really suited him, and his smile was as genuine as she could remember seeing since he was a little boy. And, most importantly of all, he didn't seem remotely self-conscious about the scar that ran down the side of his face.

He was pressing his cheek against that of a man Katie didn't recognize. She guessed he was about thirty years old – although, like her brother, there was something about his face that made him seem boyish and younger. He had long brown hair, round glasses and a smile that matched her brother's in terms of happiness.

She turned the photos over and recognized her brother's handwriting there.

Mr Christopher Shaw, Esq. and Mr James Alderson Jr, Esq.

So he had a boyfriend – another sign that he had been building a life. She put the photos back in the drawer, and, as she did, she noticed the sheet of paper directly underneath. It looked like it had been printed off the internet and showed a black-and-white photograph of a stern-looking man with a broad moustache. He was dressed in a smart black suit with a flower in the lapel. Beside the picture, above a dense wall of small text, the headline read: THE DESPICABLE HISTORY OF JACK LOCK.

The front door opened downstairs.

Katie froze, and then listened carefully. For a moment she could hear nothing beyond a slight rush of outside air from below. Whoever was down there was hesitating. There was something about the silence that made her think it wasn't her brother.

That it was someone like her who shouldn't be here.

'Chris?'

A man's voice calling up.

'James?'

She heard the front door close, followed by a tentative series of creaks as the man made his way slowly and cautiously up the stairs. Katie glanced desperately around the room – but there was nowhere to hide. She closed the drawer quietly, and then pulled out the key and clenched it between her knuckles.

As she heard the creaks reaching the top of the stairs, she stepped out on to the landing with her fist raised.

'*Shit!*'

The man flung his arm up to protect his face, and then stumbled and lost his footing, falling backwards on to the floor against the wall.

'Don't!' he cried out. 'Please! No need!'

Her heart was hammering. She recognized him – it was the shirtless man she'd seen talking to himself across the road. Except now that she was seeing him up close, cowering on the floor in front of her, she realized he wasn't actually a man at all. He was barely older than the sixth-form boys at school. He was bone-thin, his skin

65

almost blue, and there was a mottled, cup-shaped scar curling beneath the bristles on his closely shaved skull. When he looked up, he seemed more scared of her than she was of him.

'No need,' he repeated.

Katie hesitated. Then she put the key away and took out her phone, keeping her distance. He didn't seem much of a physical threat, but she wasn't taking any chances. She tried to summon a little of the authority that she didn't feel.

'You've got about two seconds before I call the police,' she said. 'What are you doing in here?'

'I saw the lights.' He started to get up.

'Don't,' she warned him. 'Just stay where you are.'

He settled back. 'I thought Chris and James were home,' he said.

'So you know them?'

'They're friends of mine. They used to give me money sometimes. I live opposite.'

He gestured with his head in the direction of the street. It took her a moment to realize he was referring to the old toilet block across the road. Then he looked back at her again, a little more suspicious now.

'Who are *you* anyway?' he said. 'Are you one of the people watching them?'

His choice of words sent a chill through her.

Like he was scared of something.

'What's your name?' she said.

'Ben.'

'OK, Ben. I'm Katie. I'm Chris's sister.'

'He never said anything about a sister. And you don't look much like him.'

'Maybe he didn't tell you everything about his life. I'm here because his family is worried about him. What did you mean *one of the people watching them*?'

He hesitated.

'Talk to me, Ben,' she said. 'I'm trying to help Chris too.'

And after another few seconds of silence, he did.

He told her that Chris had moved into this flat about a year and a half ago, and Chris had been kind to him from the beginning: saying hello and giving him money as and when he could. James Alderson, Chris's boyfriend, had arrived on the scene about a year ago. Alderson was doing a PhD in art at the university, and Ben said he had been nice too.

And for a while everything had been fine.

'But then I saw Chris . . . maybe last week?' Ben said. 'He looked more nervous than usual. You know how he always seemed so calm and in control of himself, right?'

'Yes,' Katie lied.

'Well, he wasn't like that any more. He was really on edge.'

Chris hadn't wanted to tell Ben what was wrong at first, but finally he'd relented. He thought someone was following him, and because Ben had his eyes and ears on the street, Chris asked him to keep a lookout and let him know if he saw anything suspicious. Anyone loitering in the area who didn't belong or seemed like they were watching the flat. Any cars that looked out of place.

'What kind of car?' Katie said quickly.

'A posh one, Chris said. Like something a rich person would drive.'

That settled her slightly.

'And did you see anything?'

'I don't know.' Ben looked uneasy. 'Maybe – but not a car. A man. It was the middle of the night when there was nobody else around. I didn't really see the guy. He was standing in a shop doorway a little way along the street. Hardly moving. I thought he was a shadow at first.'

'What did he look like?'

'I couldn't see him properly. He was tall, though. Big. And there was a bad feeling coming off him. It's usually peaceful at that time, and I like being out and about because nobody else is. But that night my skin was tingling. I had this feeling like there was something dangerous nearby. And when I spotted this man, I realized it was *him* I was scared of. That he was someone who enjoyed doing really bad things to people.'

'What happened afterwards?'

'I told Chris – this was a few days ago. And then I saw him and James together. They had these big rucksacks on, like they were heading off on an adventure. I've not seen them since.'

'Did you see the man in the doorway again?'

'No. But I've *felt* things. It doesn't seem safe around here any more.' He looked upset now. 'Are Chris and James in trouble?'

Katie thought about it. Then shook her head.

'I honestly don't know. But, listen, there's some change beside the TV. It's not a lot, but I'm sure Chris would be happy for you to have it.'

Ben looked at her warily for a second, then stood up and disappeared into the front room. A few seconds later, he emerged back on to the landing, nodded at her once, then made his way back down the stairs.

She waited for a couple of minutes, trying to calm herself down. And thinking.

She had been reluctant to come inside, but if nothing else, she had imagined doing so would at least provide an answer as to what had happened to her brother. Instead, all she had found were questions. Was he in trouble? While she couldn't necessarily trust everything Ben had just told her, she was sure there had been grains of truth in there. The flat really did feel abandoned. And that chimed with what her mother had said – that her brother had been scared of someone.

But who?

Someone who enjoyed doing really bad things to people.

Katie went outside and locked the front door behind her. There was no sign of Ben; she was alone on the street right now. But it *felt* like she was being watched. There was an itch at the back of her neck.

Leaves skittered across the street as a cold breeze picked up.

You should go home now.

Yes, she thought. She really should. Perhaps she wouldn't have been able to forgive herself if she hadn't checked in on Chris, but there were limits. Her brother wasn't her responsibility any more. Whatever trouble he might have got himself into, it wasn't her job to get him out of it – especially when she had her own family to think about.

There's only so much of yourself you can give.

She got in the car and started off.

But she kept checking the rear-view mirror as she drove. The traffic was relatively sparse, but there were a few vehicles behind her, and even though the idea she might be being followed was ridiculous, she still found herself keeping an eye on them, and feeling a sense of relief as each one turned steadily off.

By the time she passed the prison there was only one left.

It was a fair way back, but it seemed to be maintaining a steady distance, keeping pace with the speed she was driving. Its headlights were on full beam, so that it was impossible to make out the size of vehicle, never mind the type or colour, and whoever was behind the wheel was lost in darkness.

Her heart began beating a little faster again.

The car followed her as she drove back towards the main roads that circled the city centre. However much she varied her speed, it kept the same steady distance behind her.

After a while, the main road divided into two lanes, the left peeling off in the direction of her village. She signalled and took the turn, watching the mirror as she did, then turning her head to look out of the window. The car stayed on the main road – but suddenly accelerated so hard that it was out of sight almost before she could see it properly. The street lights bleached the vehicle of colour.

But she caught the briefest flash of a fish-white face staring out at her.

She turned back and stared ahead, gripping the steering wheel tightly. Her heart was thudding. And even though she tried to tell herself it had just been her imagination – that the vehicle had simply been behind her, and not following her at all – Siena's words came back to her again as she drove, and she felt her nerves begin to sing.

Red car, Mummy.

And what did that mean?

Something terrible and incomprehensible.

Something that had always been coming for you, but which you wouldn't even see until it swerved in out of nowhere and changed your world for ever.

PART TWO

8

It is 6 March 1956.

Alan is ten years old and he is looking down at the body of his mother. She is lying in the kitchen, her skull cracked like a broken cup and her blood already drying between the tiles. An hour earlier, he listened to his father repeatedly smacking her head against the floor there – a sickening sound that was barely muffled by the closed door and which is still replaying in his head now.

So much so that he can barely hear his brother.

Alan turns slightly, faint and adrift. 'What . . . what did you say?'

'That I *told* you not to come in here.'

Edward is standing in the kitchen doorway. He is nearly two years older than Alan, and when their father left the house he told the two of them that Edward was in charge while he was out. In addition to the usual rules, neither of them was to enter the kitchen. But Alan has disobeyed their father, and there is a furious look on Edward's face. Edward has always done what he's told; to him their father's word is law. Even now, with their mother lying dead in a pool of blood, he remains at the threshold of the room.

Alan looks down at his mother.

The out-of-body feeling is intensifying, as though something inside him is wheeling upwards and looking down at the whole spinning scene from above. It is not the sight of the blood or the aftermath of violence that still hangs trembling in the air. On both counts he has seen worse. It is not even grief yet. It is the knowledge that everything has changed. That some taut link binding the family's existence has snapped and there is nothing left to hold it together. There is a sense of *unravelling*.

He looks back at Edward. 'But . . . he's killed Mum.'

Edward stares at him, his face set hard. '*Deus scripsit*,' he says.

God has written it.

Alan blinks at that. How can his brother be so calm? But then Edward has always had more of their father in him than Alan. It is Edward who was taken out the last time their father brought home a girl; Edward who crouched down over her in the night and joined in the work of making her into an angel.

'Get out of there now.'

Trembling slightly, Alan does as he is told; his brother is a head taller than him and there will be a beating in it for him if he doesn't. Then Edward closes the door, shutting their mother's body away.

'What are we going to do?' Alan says.

'What we were *told* to do. Now stop crying.'

Alan touches his face, surprised to find the tears there, and then follows Edward through to one of the front rooms. They sit in silence for a time. What they have been told to do is wait for their father to return home, but Alan has no idea how long that might be or what will happen afterwards. Surely even Edward must feel it too – that this is different from the other times. That everything is different now.

Or can be.

And while the situation feels like a dream, the sensation inside him is more akin to having just woken from one. A kind of clarity has come over him. Five years from now the man who will adopt him is taking him for an eye test. As the optician slides the lens into place and the world swims into focus, the sensation is the same.

He blinks again.

'Where are you going?' Edward says.

Alan doesn't know; he hadn't even been aware he had stood up. And yet here he is – standing – as though pulled from his seat by someone he can't see.

'I . . . I need the toilet.'

Edward appraises him coldly, and for a moment Alan wonders if his brother will tell him to sit back down.

'Don't be long.'

Alan steps into the hall, his gaze quickly moving away from the closed door of the kitchen and over to the downstairs bathroom, its own door slightly ajar. His footsteps echo as he walks towards it, a scratching sound against the tiles. But as he reaches the bottom of the staircase, he pauses, and a strange thing happens.

The sound continues.

Scritch.

Very slowly, Alan turns his head to look up the stairs. The landing above, where they double back on themselves, is dark and empty. The air is still. But while there shouldn't be anybody else in the house, he senses a presence up there anyway, somewhere high above him.

Scritch.

Like a fingernail curling against wood.

He glances back. Across the hall, the door to the front room is open, but the angle is such that Edward is out

77

of sight. Alan turns back to the stairs. And, after a moment's hesitation, he starts tentatively up them. Each creaks gently under his weight. When he reaches the first landing, his heart is beating hard and the silence has begun buzzing.

Scritch.

The sound draws him up all the way to the top floor of the house, and then down the dark corridor that leads to his father's chambers. The heavy oak door there is closed, but when he reaches out for the iron handle, it turns with a quiet *cricking* noise.

The door opens.

He swallows nervously.

Edward has been in here before, but Alan never has. This room is out of bounds; it is one of their father's strictest rules. Alan blinks as he looks around now. It is a gilded room – far richer than the rest of the house. The carpet is soft and plush, the furniture ornate and expensive. Glinting brass fittings surround an elaborate fireplace in the chimney breast. The walls are bare aside from a single painting, hung so as to overlook the whole room. Alan finds himself staring at it for a few seconds in horror. It shows a tortured saint, arms nailed out, half the skin of his face peeled off and hanging down like a necktie, the ridges of exposed muscle dotted with beads of blood.

Scritch . . .

He looks ahead.

There is a closed door at the far side of the room. And even though the scratching sound is no louder here than it was in the hall far below, he can tell it is coming from somewhere on the other side.

Beckoning him.

He walks slowly across the room, every footstep further into this forbidden place like a blasphemy that sets the silence ringing a little louder.

He reaches the door and presses his ear against the old wood –

SCRITCH.

– and then jerks back, his heart fluttering in his chest like a bird.

There is something on the other side of the door. He takes a few seconds to calm himself and then reaches out and turns the metal ring.

Pulls the door open towards him.

A narrow stone corridor. There is very little light, but he can just make out what seems to be a large room a short distance ahead. And, as he stares into the darkness there, he has the impression that something is looking back at him. A shadow within a shadow.

He whispers, 'Is someone there?'

But then he senses a different presence, this time behind him.

'What are you doing?'

He turns quickly to see Edward has followed him upstairs.

His brother is standing on the far side of the room, his eyes filled with rage and his face contorted with hatred and disbelief. Alan can tell Edward would kill him for this disobedience right now if he could.

But Edward always does what he is told – always follows their father's instructions to the letter – and he has remained beyond the threshold to the chamber. His fists are opening and closing powerlessly by his sides.

'*Get back out here now.*'

Alan stares at him like a rabbit caught in headlights. Even if it means a beating – or worse – the instinct to obey the order is strong. It is all he has ever done in the past. Except that everything has changed now, hasn't it? An end is approaching. A chance for things to be different. And he realizes *that* feeling is much stronger than the urge to follow the order he has been given.

Because he doesn't have to do what he has been told any more.

He turns back to the open door. He takes a step into the dark corridor.

'You can't do this,' Edward screams behind him. 'It's not allowed!'

But he does.

It is 4 October 2017.

Alan Hobbes puts the pen down and then leans back in his chair, taking a few seconds to massage a wrist bone as large and swollen as a knuckle.

A slight breeze wafts through the room.

Even from a distance of sixty years, he can still clearly remember what awaited him that day in his father's inner chamber. The darkness in the room. The silence that seemed to coil in the air. *Is someone there?* He had been certain he had felt a presence, and yet the room had been empty when he stepped inside; any possible source for the sound he had heard absent. But somehow there had been a faint light in the room, and it had drawn him across to a wooden desk against one wall. And it was there that he had found his father's notebook, resting neatly in the centre, its pages laid open towards the middle.

Hobbes looks down at it now.

He no longer thinks of Jack Lock as his father. His father was a good man named George Hobbes. Approximately eighteen years before this moment, George Hobbes is dying, and Alan is holding tightly on to his hand, telling him how much he loves and admires him. But Jack Lock is his biological father, and the notebook before Alan now is filled with the man's life work.

The dense black scrawl of Lock's spidery handwriting fills every page from top to bottom and side to side. It has always been all but illegible, composed of language that is familiar but somehow unrecognizable. You need to look at it from just the right angle to decipher what has been written – and even then you can't quite be sure, as though the words might take on different meanings for different readers. The pages are not numbered, and the tales it tells occur out of chronological order, as though Lock simply picked a page at random to write in, gradually filling in the whole as he went. There is no index. But Hobbes's experience is this: if he flicks through the book without trying, the story he is searching for finds him rather than the other way around.

He does so now. And as he concentrates as best he can on the passage before him, he pictures his brother, older now, walking down a corridor towards a truth so awful that no man should ever have to face it.

Which is Alan's fault.

He picks up the pen again.

Edward.

Hobbes is aware of how much pain his brother has caused to others over the years: the lives he has taken and the damage he has done. But while Hobbes despises him for that, he can't escape a feeling of sadness too. He sometimes finds himself wondering about the scatterings of cause and effect that have taken the two of them from the exact same past to such very different presents. But, of course, while they are both products of their upbringings, much of Edward's life has been wholly constrained by it, and the same cannot be said of Hobbes.

But even so, they both know the terrible pain of losing a child.

Hobbes glances behind him towards the far corner of the room.

Then he turns back to the book before him. And as he continues to write, the quiet *scritching* of his pen whispers in the room.

9

The nightmare was always the same.

Edward Leland spent a few minutes lying still, listening to the soft instrumental music that had been programmed to wake him. The dream itself never did. And, as always, it lingered now: a memory from thirty years earlier that played out as a series of jerky and indistinct images in his mind, as though he were watching newsreel footage from the distant past. Some mornings he even fancied he could hear the rattle of film in an old projection wheel.

The quiet tapping of his footsteps on the tiled floor of a long corridor. A single bright window far ahead. The police officer walking on one side of him, the nurse on the other. The nurse could sense his grief and loss and wanted to put a consoling hand on his shoulder, but she resisted, perhaps sensing something else about him as well.

The open door far ahead.

Are you sure you're ready for this, Mr Leland?

Yes. I need to be sure.

And then the sight that awaited him inside that room.

He had stood there for some time, gradually becoming aware of a terrible sound building in the air. It had made no sense at first, but then he had realized the noise was coming from him. It was something between a scream and a sob, and it grew louder and more desolate as he stood there, staring down at *the thing* – he could no longer think of it as a child – that was lying before him.

Finally understanding what had been done to his son Nathaniel.

That was a long time ago now, of course.

Leland slid out from beneath the silk sheets, then walked a little stiffly across the heated floorboards. Lights set into the ceiling bathed the room in calm blue light. At the bedroom door he slipped on the robe that was hanging there, knotted it tightly at the waist, then stepped through into the chamber beyond, the music following him and gradually wafting away the last traces of the nightmare.

A freshly delivered tray of toast and coffee was waiting for him on the table, along with the usual pile of carefully folded morning newspapers. A clean suit and his laundered gym clothes were hanging on the oak wardrobes that filled one wall. He sat on the leather settee, ate his breakfast, and then drank orange juice and coffee as he worked his way through the papers.

The business news first, of course.

His gaze moved steadily over columns of figures, lists of stocks and shares, reports of market fluctuations and boardroom restructuring. That whole world moved so quickly that most of the information was better gleaned online, but to Leland that always felt like watching a video that never paused. He preferred to start his day by studying individual frames. Frozen moments.

After the business pages, the general news.

Political stories interested him vaguely. While patterns of power could occasionally be discerned between the lines, nothing truly important would be reported here; newspapers were, after all, designed for the cattle's consumption. The photographs could sometimes be worthwhile. Every now and then he recognized a face in the background, usually caught by accident behind whatever politician or adviser was the intended focus of the shot. They always reminded him of the pictures you saw of innocent, smiling subjects, the photographer failing to notice the predator lurking in the bushes behind.

Finally he moved on to the crime stories.

Even after so many years, Leland was not dead to the effect of these. There was always a trace of excitement as he flicked through the pages. For some reason the reports of war and associated atrocities held little appeal. It was the smaller, everyday items to which he gravitated, and over which he lingered. Today's news brought a familiar list. A teenage boy stabbed in a park; a man found deceased in woodland; a woman beaten to death by her boyfriend. The papers rustled quietly as he worked his way through them. Tragedy was its own unending video, and there was satisfaction to be had in concentrating on individual frames here as well.

The terrible things that happened because they were meant to.

Because God had written them.

He found only a single mention of Alan Hobbes. It was a short column in the local newspaper, and it gave very little detail. A former university lecturer and businessman – not even named yet – had been found dead in his home. Police had opened an investigation but were not making further comment on the situation at this time. The scarcity of information did not particularly surprise Leland. Even in death, men like Alan Hobbes – and indeed himself – were adroit at staying out of the public eye.

Leland drained the last of his coffee. Remembering.

You can't do this.

Their father had told them both many things over the years, including something that Leland had understood implicitly: that he was special and his brother was not. Because he was the one who did as he was told. He was the one who was destined for the grandest things in life.

And he still remembered the anger he had felt as he watched Alan walking away from him down the corridor.

Stealing what he had.

And because of that, what was *right* and *meant to be* had become crooked.

Leland looked down and realized his hand was trembling.

He put the cup carefully on the tray.

A long time ago now.

Except Leland knew better than most how little meaning *time* had in the grand scheme of things.

After breakfast Leland put on his workout clothes, left the house, and made his way past the greenhouse and down the vast garden behind. He was walking a route that pre-dated him: a flagstone path that had been here since he had been brought to the property as a twelve-year-old boy.

It was a cold morning. The sky ahead was grey and

implacable, and there was bite and sharpness to the air. Although the gardener had trimmed the lawn earlier that week, the grass was already patchy and dishevelled, its colours muted. The trees that edged the property grew more skeletal with every passing day, and all that remained in most of the flower beds were brittle shivering stems, just a few wilted petals still clinging on stubbornly here and there.

Halfway down the garden, Leland stopped and stared back at the house behind him, which had once belonged to the man who had raised him as a teenager. A good man. A rich one, as well – his father had been correct about the greatness that would be delivered to Edward. Giles Leland had done his best to raise Edward, just as Edward had done his best to hide his true nature from him. He had bided his time. And now it had been close to two decades since Giles Leland had been forced to cede control of the family's businesses to his adopted son, and then been confined to a nursing home to live out the handful of years remaining to him.

Leland had only visited him once. The man had been barely recognizable at that point: a distressed figure, sobbing uncontrollably, unable to understand *what he had done wrong*. How had this cuckoo arrived in his nest without him realizing? Edward had stared down at him without compassion. The only pity he had been able to summon was for the fact that, even then, the man still believed the choices he had made might have been different.

Somewhere in the grey distance now the sky rumbled.

Leland turned and walked down the path.

He reached the bottom of the garden and turned

right, ducking beneath an arch of sharp brambles and then following a path constrained on either side by tight coils of foliage. A minute later, he emerged into the hidden garden beyond. The gardener was not allowed here, and the grass ahead was thick and tangled, but a rough path was worn through it, leading to a squat building at the centre.

When Leland reached the door, he looked to his right.

There was an area at the edge of the garden where the grass was absent and the soil was exposed. He had turned and flattened it numerous times over the years, always under cover of darkness. A short distance below the surface lay the remains of the angels he had made over the years.

As God has written.

He turned back to the door and opened it.

The garage was wired up to the main building, and he reached into the darkness and flicked the switch. The strip light suspended from the roof began humming, growing slowly in strength, and the shadowy interior before him gradually transformed into a blood-red sea criss-crossed by black lines. The building was full of old iron: benches, frames, racks of old weights. The crimson light created a fractured web from their interweaving angles.

Leland left the door open and made his way through to the weight bench at the back of the room. This was one of the earliest presents from his adoptive father. The body of the bench, made from hard wood, had been polished smooth by years of sweat and pressure, and the iron struts were speckled with rust. The bar resting across it was flaky, the weights on either end locked and immovable, the metal fused into place.

Leland laid down and pressed out twenty repetitions.

While he remained stronger than he looked, he was in his seventies now and the weights he lifted had diminished with age. The bench had deteriorated too. He could hear it protesting with each repetition, and then the rattle and shudder when he placed the bar back on the struts. Every day the structure felt more and more precarious, as though it might collapse beneath him at any moment. But it was wrong to fear that. *Worse* than wrong – a blasphemy. Because whatever would happen would happen. The story was already written and it would unfold in the way it had been intended, just as the flower contains the seed that contains another flower.

Deus scripsit.

Leland sat up. His view of the corrugated ceiling above swung backwards out of sight, replaced by the bright rectangle of the open door at the front of the garage. A large man was standing there, waiting patiently and politely. Mr Banyard, one of his more trusted associates.

Leland beckoned him in. 'It's done?'

Banyard nodded and handed him the mobile phone he had taken from Alan Hobbes's flat. The phone was scant compensation for what he had really been sent to retrieve, but it might offer a route to it. It had been locked, of course, but when you have the necessary resources that becomes a simple matter of time, and breaking the security in this instance had taken less than thirty-six hours.

'Thank you,' Leland said.

The man nodded once, then turned and picked his way back through the garage. Leland's expression remained blank as he watched him leave, but a fire was burning inside him at the thought of what was to come. For now, though, he put the phone to one side and lay back down on the bench.

It trembled as he began pressing the weight again.

But it stayed firm. The past held and the present played out.

As God has written.

IO

Whenever Laurence thought about what had happened to Christopher Shaw, it was Michael Hyde's car he kept returning to.

He remembered the scene of the attack well. The road taped off, the kerbs lined with police vans, their lights flashing rhythmically in the afternoon sunshine, the bloodstains on the pavement. The ambulance that had rushed Christopher Shaw to hospital was gone by then, but Hyde was still present – out of sight inside one of the vans – along with the passing delivery driver who had intervened in the assault and helped save Christopher Shaw's life.

And then the girl running towards him at the cordon.

But before that there had been a moment when Laurence had found himself all but hypnotized by Michael Hyde's car. It had swerved off the road in front of Shaw, and it rested there still, angled at a slant across the pavement, with the driver's door hanging open and its interior illuminated. What struck him about it was how *piecemeal* the car looked. It was as though it had started off as one vehicle a long time ago, and then almost every part of it had been replaced in the years since. Sections of bodywork did not match the chassis; one segment of the roof didn't fit the rest. Everywhere he looked, the colours were different shades of red. The vehicle appeared a patchwork of parts: a mixture of the present and a dozen different pasts and, as Laurence had stared at it, it seemed to shift between time periods, as though it somehow existed in all of them and none of them at once.

Seventeen years later, he found himself looking at it again.

It was one of several photographs arranged on the table before him. The office he shared with Pettifer was small. There was enough space for a desk and a computer each – facing away from each other in opposite corners of the room – and this semicircular table, placed against one wall, at which they were sometimes forced to sit cramped together, elbow to elbow, annoying them both enormously.

Fortunately Pettifer was yet to arrive.

Laurence looked down at the photographs.

The car, yes.

And Michael Hyde obviously. This particular picture was the mugshot after he'd been taken into custody following the assault on Christopher Shaw. There were several others on file, but they all ultimately showed the same individual. Hyde was a small man with weak and insipid features. His pale, unhealthy skin appeared to have been wrapped around a skull that lacked any form of underlying bone structure, and his hair was sparse and tufty, like patches of lank grass.

Not a winner in life's genetic lottery, Laurence thought. Hyde had only been in his mid-thirties when this photograph was taken but could easily have passed for two decades older. And yet, while unpleasant, he was not an obvious physical threat. A grown man could have smacked him down without issue – and, indeed, a man had done just that.

But Christopher Shaw, of course, had not been a grown man.

Laurence turned his attention to photographs of the boy. Shaw had been barely fifteen years old when Hyde attacked him, and there was a strange contrast between their appearances. While Hyde looked older than he was, Christopher Shaw appeared far younger. It made the images themselves harder to view. The wounds to Shaw's side, where Hyde had plunged the knife into him. The defensive injuries to the boy's thin forearms. And the angry slice down the side of his face. In the photograph of that particular injury, Shaw's jawline was horribly swollen, the stitched cut there forming a stark black tramline on the risen hill of his skin.

Laurence leaned on the table. Just as with Hyde, there were other photographs of Christopher Shaw on file. The wounded boy in these pictures had grown into a troubled young man who had accumulated mugshots of his own over the years. But Laurence had been unaware of that when he watched the CCTV footage last night. It was this particular image that he had recognized.

Shaw as a victim. Not only of Michael Hyde but of chance.

The door opened suddenly, with too much force, and Laurence jumped. And was then annoyed with himself as he looked up to see Pettifer grinning at him.

'Gotcha.'

Laurence picked up his phone and held it to his ear without dialling.

'DCI Barnes?' he said. 'I'd like to report an attempt on an officer's life.'

'When I'm really trying, it won't be an attempt.'

Pettifer closed the door, put her bag on her chair, and shrugged off her coat. Then she came and stood next to him, looking down at the photographs.

'This our boy?' she said.

'It is. Or rather, it *was* our boy. Back in the day.'

'You worked this case?'

'Yes. Although it wasn't really a case as such.'

'What happened?'

Laurence considered just handing her the file and letting her read through it for herself, but then relented and filled her in with the basic details. The way Hyde had attacked Shaw and attempted to cut off his face before a passer-by intervened and subdued him.

'Motive?' Pettifer said.

'The passer-by? Probably common decency.'

'*Hyde*, I mean.'

Laurence shrugged. 'He was delusional. Paranoid. By that point he already had a fair few burglaries on his record. Breaking and entering. Setting fires. He told us he had been hearing voices and driving around for days. When he saw Christopher Shaw, he felt like he had to attack him, but he didn't understand why. Basically Shaw was just in the wrong place at the wrong time.'

'What happened to Hyde?'

'Twelve years for assault with intent,' Laurence said. 'He didn't have an easy time of things in prison. He was attacked several times and beaten so badly that he almost died. Men like him don't have a good time inside.'

'I have no problem with that.'

'Do you not? I'm undecided. Anyway, he was released from prison a few years ago. He's registered disabled. As of this moment in time he has not reoffended.'

Laurence walked over to a whiteboard mounted on the opposite wall. He picked up a cloth and then wiped away a swathe of notes.

'What are you doing?' Pettifer said.

'Clearing some space.'

'Did you even check what was there?'

'Yes, it was very important.'

He took the top off a marker and began writing, the nib squeaking against the whiteboard.

A) Christopher Shaw attacked by Michael Hyde
(3 May 2000)

Pettifer was holding the photograph of Shaw's injuries. 'How is this relevant?' she said.

'It isn't. I was just killing time until you arrived.'

She glared at him and put the photograph down.

'But it isn't totally *irrelevant*. I don't think it necessarily has any bearing on the murder of Alan Hobbes. But it does provide context. If you want to understand the ailment, first understand the organism.'

'What the fuck is that supposed to mean?'

'You're aware we haven't been able to locate Christopher Shaw overnight?'

'Yes, of course.'

Laurence gestured towards a folder on the table. It was filled with a sheaf of paper nearly a centimetre thick.

'That is the file we have on Christopher Shaw,' he said. 'Those are all incidents that occurred in the years following the attack by Hyde. Have a look through. You will note a downwards trajectory in the course of this young man's life.'

Pettifer sighed, and then Laurence waited as she flicked through the file, working quickly through the various arrest reports, the photographs, the court records and recommendations. Since his late teens, Christopher Shaw had lived a vagabond existence. Drugs were a constant feature, but there had also been a number of arrests for shoplifting, soliciting and public disorder.

'The last sighting of him was two years ago,' Laurence said. 'He stole from his sister on what should have been their father's birthday, and she reported him for the theft. Her statement is in the file here. It seems like she finally lost patience with him.'

'Yeah, I don't blame her.'

It wouldn't actually have occurred to Laurence to blame anyone. But he remembered Katie Shaw from the time of her brother's assault – how he had met her at the cordon that day, and how upset she had been. How she had blamed herself for what had happened. It had been obvious to him that she loved her brother, and he imagined it must have taken a great deal for her to cut him off the way she eventually had.

He turned back to the board.

A) Christopher Shaw attacked by Michael Hyde
(3 May 2000)

B) Katie Shaw reports CS to the police
(3 September 2015)
– CS disappears

'After that,' he said, 'Christopher Shaw seems to have dropped off the face of the earth.'

'Until now.'

'Yes. There is no record of Christopher Shaw working for Alan Hobbes. He's not listed as an employee. But he certainly seemed familiar with the layout of the house. And, as we have seen, he also appeared to remove something from the property. I couldn't tell what he was holding. Could you?'

Pettifer shook her head. 'It was too grainy to see properly.'

'But it's reasonable to assume that it was deliberately chosen – and that it was why Shaw was there.'

He added more notes to the board.

C) Alan Hobbes murdered (4 October 2017)
– staff dismissed
– business dealings / investments
– charitable donations
– Philosophy lecturer

D) CS present at scene (4 October 2017)
– no record of employment by Hobbes
– apparent theft from property
– disabled security camera

'Do you think Christopher Shaw killed Hobbes?' Pettifer asked.

Still looking at the board, Laurence considered the question. While they were awaiting a precise time of death, it was clear that Christopher Shaw had been in the room with Alan Hobbes shortly before his murder. He had stolen something. He had disabled the security camera. Such things did not weigh in his favour. If it turned out he was *not* involved in the killing, they were remarkable coincidences.

But coincidences happened.

'I don't know,' Laurence said. 'What's clear is that we need to find out where he is now, and establish why he was at the scene two evenings ago. As to the former, obviously there is no current address for him on the system. He remains as entirely vanished as he has been for the last two years.'

'So we start with the family.'

'Yes,' Laurence said. 'Or, rather, *you* start with them.'

Pettifer frowned. 'Which is fine,' she said. 'But what are you going to do?'

Is anything missing?

Laurence thought of the lawyer looking towards the archway.

He took out his phone.

'Look into the possible *whys*,' he said.

11

Katie slept badly. Every time she was about to drop off, she thought about Chris, and the constant sense of unease had her skimming the surface of sleep for most of the night. Where was he and what had caused him to run away like he had? However much she told herself he wasn't her responsibility, the question kept her tossing and turning. When the alarm went off the next morning, the trill of music from her phone seemed especially loud, its happy tone almost painfully at odds with how she felt.

She rolled over quickly to turn it off, her head thick and groggy.

'Mummy!'

Siena calling through. Katie sat up and rubbed her face. Beside her, Sam was lying motionless under the covers, facing the weak light streaming in through the curtains. But she could tell he was awake, as the gentle snoring that had accompanied her through most of the night had finally come to a stop.

One of them had slept well at least.

'Can you get Siena?' she asked him.

He yawned but showed no immediate sign of moving.

'I guess that's a no then.'

She went to Siena's room to find her sitting up in bed, smiling and happy, excited for the day ahead, as she always was. The sight of her wafted away a few of the cobwebs.

'Morning, Snail,' she said. 'Sleep well?'

'Moon.'

Siena pointed across the room towards the window. She had always found the night sky comforting, and Sam had left the curtains open for her at bedtime, the way she liked. Katie could see a stretch of blue-grey sky out there now. Shreds of pale cloud.

'In the night, yeah?' she said.

Siena nodded happily. 'Moon came to see me.'

'That's nice. Now let's go and loudly wake up your father.'

As Katie showered, she did her best not to resent Sam too much. Because as far as he knew, everything was fine. Katie had given him a radically truncated version of events when she returned last night. So he knew it was something to do with her brother – that Chris had come back and disappeared again – but nothing more than that. Nothing about the flat or the car she'd seen. When it came to her brother, she and Sam maintained a policy of don't ask, don't tell. Even so, she had sensed his disapproval and had tried not to let it rankle. Sam cared about her and so he worried.

It would have bothered her more if he didn't.

She turned off the shower. Then she got dressed and headed downstairs. Sam was in the front room, fully engaged now in getting Siena prepared for the day at nursery. In the kitchen Katie found a cup of coffee ready on the side, and two slices of bread waiting in the toaster. Sam came to the kitchen while she was buttering the toast.

'Thanks for this,' she said.

'No worries. I like to be of some use.' He leaned against the counter. 'You OK this morning?'

She put the knife down and licked her finger. 'Yeah, I'm fine. Why wouldn't I be?'

'Ah, you know. We didn't talk much last night. Or maybe I just didn't ask.'

I wouldn't have expected you to, she thought. Despite everything, that made her feel sad. Don't ask, don't tell was fine, as far as it went, but right then it would have been good to be able to unload a little of what she was feeling.

'I'm fine,' she said.

'Why do you think Chris came back?'

'I don't know. Maybe it really was just because he wanted to see Mum. But God knows what's happened to him now.'

Sam hesitated. 'Are you going to try to find him?'

'No. I wouldn't even know where to start.'

'You'd find a way,' Sam said. 'I know you. You're very clever.'

'That's why you love me, right?'

'No. It's just one of the reasons.'

Katie smiled at him. 'You don't need to worry,' she said.

He leaned away from the counter and rubbed her upper arm. 'I just don't want you getting hurt,' he said. 'That's all.'

She felt a twist of pain at that. It had been upsetting when her mother told her Chris hadn't wanted to see her. It broke her heart to think their relationship had deteriorated so badly that he might not know she loved him and wanted him to be safe, and that she always would.

I just don't want you getting hurt.

Too late.

But then she heard Siena laughing in the front room, and she put her hand over her husband's, pressing his palm against her arm. The warmth of it was reassuring.

'Don't worry,' she said. 'I won't.'

The Tadpoles nursery was based in a side room of the local community centre. When Katie parked up and took Siena inside, she was greeted by the usual chaotic scene. The children were running amok, and the air was filled with noise and the mingled smells of toast and juice and floor polish. There was an impression of barely controlled carnage about the place, but Siena herself seemed entirely unconcerned. She toddled off without a backward glance, the Snail flag draped over her tiny shoulders like a cape, and then planted herself down on the worn carpet and began talking at another child.

One of the caregivers appeared beside her, holding a stack of plastic plates.

'I've been forgotten already,' Katie said.

The caregiver gave her a wry smile. 'It's better than the alternative, believe me.'

Katie raised her eyebrows. 'This is very true.'

She was relieved by how easy her daughter found it to settle. Regardless of what she was faced with, Siena always had such confidence. It was reassuring on one level; the fact she felt so protected reflected well on Sam and her, and it was good she was secure enough to love life so carelessly. At the same time it unnerved Katie. In an ideal world a child *should* be able to be like that, of course, but she knew this world was not always a safe and happy one. That all it took was one mistake. One crossed path you never saw coming.

She started to leave, but then the caregiver called to her.

'Oh, Mrs Shaw? I almost forgot.'

'Yes?'

The worker took a step closer to her, lowering her voice slightly. 'Just as a follow-up to what happened yesterday,' she said, 'we've heard back from the police. There's nothing much they can do right now, but they're going to have an officer drive past every so often for the next few days.'

Katie stared at her. 'I'm sorry,' she said. 'I'm not following.'

'I told your husband when he picked up Siena yesterday.'

'He didn't mention anything.'

The caregiver looked a little surprised. 'Oh – about the car?'

'What do you mean?' Katie said. 'What car?'

The worker gestured to a side door, which opened on to a small garden gated off from the street.

'Some of the children were playing outside after lunch,' she said. 'A couple of them told staff there was a man parked up in a car, and they thought he was watching them. When we went over to check, there was nobody there.'

'Was Siena one of them?'

'I'm not sure. A few of them were out there. But –'

'What colour was the car?'

The caregiver started to reply, but the sudden urgency in Katie's voice had startled her. She looked at her a little strangely.

Katie thought quickly. 'Just so I can keep my eye out, I mean.'

'Oh, I see.' The woman relaxed a little. 'No, the kids couldn't give them a description at all. Not of the car or the driver. That was the main reason the police said there wasn't anything they could do beyond send an officer out every now and then.'

'Right.'

'It's probably nothing,' she said. 'You know what imaginations they all have at this age. And the safety of your children is our number-one priority. You have nothing to worry about.'

Katie looked across at Siena, still sitting on the floor and talking happily to the little girl beside her. Guileless and innocent.

Safe.

You have nothing to worry about.

'Yes,' Katie said.

And although she was trembling inside, she managed to keep her voice even. 'I'm sure that's why my husband didn't mention it.'

'Why didn't you tell me about the car?'

'What?' Sam said. 'What car?'

'At the nursery yesterday.'

She was sitting in the driver's seat outside, her phone pressed to her ear, trying to contain the anxiety inside her. Our experiences and fears collect in the backs of our minds like dry kindling, and Katie's were constantly smouldering. What the nursery worker had told her had sent a lick of flame across them. They were burning brightly now.

'Oh,' Sam said – too damn casually for her liking. 'I don't know. You were out. And then . . . I guess I forgot. What did they say?'

'That the police can't do anything. They didn't get a good description.'

'Yeah, that's what they told me too.'

'That it's *probably nothing*.'

'Exactly. And anyway, the security there is really good.'

'Yes. I know that.'

She glanced at the building beside her. She had every faith in the measures they had in place. The solid front door with its keypad; the high railings outside; the security cameras at every entrance and exit. She'd noted them all down approvingly when they'd first looked around because if they hadn't been here, then Siena wouldn't have been either.

'So no big deal, right?' Sam said.

'I think it's a big deal. You should have told me.'

'Sorry. It didn't seem that important. Like I said, I just forgot.'

Katie sat there for a moment. Her nerves were still humming, but there was anger mixed in with the anxiety now. She didn't believe him. While her husband likely did think it was *probably nothing*, that wasn't the reason he had neglected to mention it. He hadn't just forgotten either. No, he had kept quiet because he had decided it was better she didn't know. Because he thought she worried too much. That she was prone to overreacting.

How dare you? she thought.

It wasn't his call to make to keep things from her like that – especially when it involved their daughter. It wasn't his place to police her reactions as though he knew what was best for her.

'Katie?'

'Still here,' she said blankly. 'But I do have to go. Love you loads.'

'OK. Love you too.'

She ended the call and then sat there, staring out of the window at the nursery, trying to dampen down that fire in the back of her mind. She was pissed off with Sam because he *should* have told her, but what she was feeling right now wasn't really his fault. He didn't know what had happened at her brother's flat or about the car she'd seen on the way back. Of course, she had no idea herself whether it actually had been following her, or if it was just that her nerves had been on edge. And, regardless, there was no reason to believe it was connected to anyone who might have been watching the children here yesterday.

But what if it is?

What if there was danger circling her family and she just couldn't see it yet?

The thought set the anxiety inside her burning more brightly. What if this was one of the moments when if you allowed yourself to imagine everything was fine, you ended up regretting it for ever? She thought back to what she'd been told last night – that James Alderson, her brother's boyfriend, was a mature student doing a PhD in Fine Art at the university. There had been an address on the letter he'd been sent. She could just about remember it.

A fool's errand, perhaps. But it was something.

Katie took out her phone and called in sick to the school.

And then, spurred on by that anxiety, she started the car and went in search of James Alderson.

Laurence stood still for a moment, questioning himself.

Before he had arrived at the Philosophy department on the edge of the university campus, he had been expecting something else entirely. Philosophy conjured up images of quiet contemplation. Laurence recalled kneeling by the hearth in their small house while his father sat reading in an armchair. Dust in the air; warmth on his face; a safe silence undisturbed beyond the gentle crackle of the fire and the quiet turning of pages. And yet the building before him now – a newly built block of polished black marble, sandstone and glass – looked like a place more suited to laboratory experiments than those carried out within minds.

The doors slid apart as he stepped forward.

He was expected, and one of the secretaries in the main office pointed him in the right direction. He wandered down a corridor that wouldn't have been out of place in a modern office block – clean carpets; pine-scented air freshener; anonymous modern art prints hanging between the wooden doors – and finally reached the office of Professor Robin Nelson. It had been left slightly ajar in anticipation of his arrival, but he rapped gently with his knuckles anyway.

'Come in.'

He pushed the door wider. The room contained an oak desk, with papers and used mugs strewn around the computer there. The shelves lining the walls were crammed tightly with books and even more sheaves of paperwork, some of it occluded by randomly placed trinkets and photographs. A tattered rug had been spread out near the door. *This* was more like it, Laurence thought happily. The office felt lived in, as though the occupant, upon being granted a sterile new office, had made a concerted effort to transport every last crumb of dust across from their old one.

Nelson stood up and walked round the desk, extending a hand. Laurence shook it. The professor had a slightly foppish swathe of brown hair and was wearing a red-velvet jacket over a checked shirt. He was only in his thirties, Laurence guessed, which seemed young to be a professor, never mind head of department.

Nelson seemed aware of that himself, and even slightly embarrassed by it.

'It's more an administrative position than anything else,' he explained as he cleared a seat for Laurence. 'Or a prison sentence. All it really means is lots of extra work and headaches. The role changes hands every five years, and the smarter ones find a way of avoiding it.'

Laurence glanced at the wall of books. He figured Nelson was pretty smart.

'How long do you have left to serve?' he said.

'Three years, ten months, two weeks and two days.'

Laurence laughed as he sat down. 'I'll try not to take up too much of it,' he said. 'Especially given why I'm here. I'm sorry for your loss.'

'Thank you.' Nelson looked slightly pained as he returned to his own seat. 'I can't really take that, though. I didn't know Professor Hobbes well at all. He actually retired before I started here – although he did return for guest lectures on occasion, so we met in passing. But I can tell you that he was *very* well liked for the most part. Everyone here is shocked.'

Laurence frowned.

' "Well liked *for the most part*"?'

'Oh – just a turn of phrase really. As a person, is what I meant. He was a good guy – and a brilliant teacher too, by all accounts, which is what matters most. *Devoted* to teaching. Generally speaking, his students loved him. But one particular subject he taught – the one he specialized in – can be difficult for some people to process. It can upset people.'

'Determinism?'

'Yes.'

Laurence had spent a little time reading up about it last night and understood the basics of the arguments well enough. But there was often no harm in appearing to know less than you did.

'Can you run me through it?'

Nelson looked delighted. 'Yes, of course! Well, I can try – it's not my area. But the basic idea is a very simple one. Here.'

He searched for something in the mess on his desk. He found a pen, held it up for a moment, and then dropped it on the desk. Laurence watched as it clattered against the wood.

'Now,' Nelson said, 'why did the pen fall?'

'Gravity.'

'Exactly. The laws of physics – everything in the universe obeys them. Every effect has a cause.' Nelson touched the side of his head. 'But the *human brain* is part of the universe. It's made up of the same basic matter, and so it follows the exact same physical laws. Which means that every action you take, every decision you make, is caused by the state of your brain immediately before it. And that state is caused by the one before that. And so on, meaning that all your decisions are predetermined. There's a famous thought experiment called Laplace's demon?'

Laurence had heard of it. But he waited.

'OK,' Nelson said. 'So, imagine a creature – a demon – that understands all the physical laws in the universe. It also knows the exact state of every atom at a single moment in time, all the way down to the smallest part. It follows that the demon would be able to work out *everything* that had ever happened or ever would. All of it would be inevitable, from the first moment of the universe to the very last.'

Laurence considered that. It made him think of the case file he'd been looking through earlier. Michael Hyde's red patchwork car angled across the pavement. Christopher Shaw – a boy who had simply been in the wrong place at the wrong time.

An attack that could have happened to anyone.

'What about random chance?' he said.

'There's no such thing.' Nelson shook his head. 'It only feels that way because we don't have the knowledge the demon has. In physics, some events at a really small level do appear to be random – but that doesn't help you and me. All it means is that our actions are caused or random. Which doesn't leave much room for *us* to be doing anything.'

'You mean free will?'

'That's right. Do you drink, Detective?'

Laurence raised an eyebrow. 'Is it that obvious?'

'Not at all.' Nelson laughed. 'It's just an example, because I certainly do. But on an evening, when you're deciding whether to open that bottle of wine or not, it might *feel* like you're free to make up your mind either way. But you aren't. What will happen will happen. What happens was *always* going to happen. You had no more choice than the pen did just then.'

'That's depressing.'

'In many ways.'

'And this was what Professor Hobbes taught?'

'Part of it,' Nelson said. 'What I just described is the materialistic approach to determinism – based on science. But there are others. One logical approach, for example, argues that all statements have to be true or false, even ones about the future. But another is based on the idea of God. That was Professor Hobbes's specialism.'

'Oh?'

'Many religions consider God to be omniscient – all-knowing. And if God knows the future, then the future can't be changed.'

'That's depressing for God too.'

Nelson laughed again. 'Yes. It would reduce the universe to the equivalent of a bauble on His table, wouldn't it? Nice to look at from time to time, perhaps, but not exactly full of surprises. Or the kind of moral choices that God is, let's say, traditionally supposed to be interested in.'

'Yes. Maybe I should stop arresting people.'

'Oh no, don't do that. But actually, yes, the whole

subject does open up all kinds of questions along those lines.'

'You said it upset people?'

'Sometimes. Especially if they're prone to that kind of thinking. For some people the idea that you don't have a real choice can feel like it robs the world of meaning and purpose. For other people . . . well, I suppose you could use it as an excuse to do anything you wanted.'

'In which case you were always going to anyway?'

'Yes! Because it was inevitable you would encounter the theory.'

Nelson smiled, proud of his teaching.

'Did Professor Hobbes ever get any trouble on that level?' Laurence said. 'Hate mail. One of these conflicted students harassing him. Negative attention. Anything like that?'

Nelson thought about it.

'Not to my knowledge. But, like I said, he hasn't taught here in years. And all that was before I started working here.'

'Could you look into it for me? See if anything has survived?'

'I can try. I mean, I don't think it would be a very long list.'

'By chance, my favourite kind of list.' Then Laurence nodded in thanks and stood up and walked towards the door. As he did, Nelson came out from behind his desk.

'Do you really think this has anything to do with what happened to Professor Hobbes?'

Laurence hesitated. Most likely it didn't. At the same time, he thought about Laplace's demon. He couldn't shake what he'd been told yesterday and had been lingering in his mind ever since – that from his behaviour, it appeared Alan Hobbes had known his death was coming before it arrived.

But if that were true, why had he done nothing to avoid it?

'I don't know,' he said. 'But thank you for taking the time to talk to me.'

As he opened the door, a thought occurred to him.

Although I suppose you didn't have a choice, did you?

13

Katie slowed the car as she reached the bewildering network of road names around the university campus.

There were Victorias and Alberts here, Edinburghs and Georges – and for each of those there were Streets and Avenues, Groves and Terraces. The red-brick buildings were tall and thin, packed in tightly together. Most were student houses, but some had been bought up by different faculties, the former living rooms converted into receptions, and the twisting staircases leading up to old bedrooms that had been transformed into makeshift offices and workspaces.

A few minutes later, she found the correct road and parked up outside a house that, at first glance, was indistinguishable from its neighbours. She slipped her phone into her pocket, then got out of the car, opened the gate, and made her way up the overgrown garden to the front door.

There was a panel of buttons on the wall there, one for each of the six flats within. The scrawl next to number six was almost illegible, but when she squinted more closely she could just about make out Alderson's name. Instead of pressing the buzzer, she tried the door handle – and was almost surprised when it turned. The front door opened inwards with a creak. She stepped inside and closed the door quietly behind her.

A drab, dark corridor. The floorboards were bare and

the walls had been mostly stripped of paper. There were two closed doors ahead, one on either side, and a staircase leading up a little further on.

She headed across and up.

The first floor smelled of wood and paint. Again, there were two doors. The one on the right-hand side was slightly ajar, and she could hear the sound of a radio coming from within, along with someone whistling to themselves. She crept past quickly. There was another staircase at the end of the corridor. She made her way up to the second floor. The corridor up here ended at a door open on to a small, grimy-looking toilet that didn't appear to have been cleaned in a long time. The two other doors were both shut, but when she walked down to number six and tried the handle, she found this one was unlocked as well.

She stepped into the room and flicked the light switch.

Nobody here. It was about the size of a large bedroom, although it was obviously no longer intended to be used as one. James Alderson was an art student, and this was the studio space the university had provided him with. The bare floorboards were speckled with dry, crusted paint, and the only real furniture in the room was a table on which a board was balanced, with a spread of reference material beside it. There were tins of paint against the base of one wall, along with congealed trays and matted brushes and rollers. Stacks of canvases were leaning against one another.

But it was the far wall that caught her attention.

A single enormous canvas there stretched almost from floor to ceiling. It was composed of perhaps a hundred smaller paintings, and it was the colours and shades of each of those, taken together, that created the larger image that filled the canvas. There were a few empty rectangles – paintings that remained to be added, she assumed – but even in its unfinished state, she recognized what it was: the picture of Chris and James Alderson she'd found in her brother's flat. The one where the two of them were crammed in a photo booth with their faces pressed tightly together, both of them grinning and very much in love.

She walked across slowly.

As she did so, the overall image of Chris and Alderson dissolved, and it became easier to see the smaller pieces that made up the whole. She looked at the ones Alderson had used to create the illusion of his own face. From what she could tell, most of them appeared to be pictures of himself at various stages of his life, but there were several that depicted different people and places, and she had no way of knowing who they were or what they might mean.

But when she looked to the right, the smaller paintings that made up Chris's face were immediately familiar. As with Alderson, there were pictures of him at different ages. A few that had clearly been taken recently were mixed in with images of him as a young man, a teenager, a little boy. Her gaze moved here and there, each image tugging at her memory. There were pictures of their parents. In one, they both looked so young, so *striking*, that for a moment it was hard to believe it was really them.

And there were pictures of her.

Katie stared at those, feeling something between wonder and loss. There was one of Chris and her standing side by side as teenagers, a cake in the background.

A birthday, she assumed – although whether hers or his, she couldn't recall. Another showed the two of them as little children, squatting together on a beach, wearing matching sunhats and building a sandcastle. They were filling a bucket with their plastic spades, and Chris was grinning at the camera, his familiar floppy hair and guileless smile already present even as an infant.

There was the photograph Chris had printed on the jigsaw for their mother. The four of them standing outside her father's shop, the picture taken when they had all been happy, just a few years before Michael Hyde had swerved his red car across her brother's path and changed everything.

And Hyde was here too.

She recognized his face with a jolt. The painting Alderson had done was based on the photograph that had been used in the newspaper, which had been taken by the police after Hyde was arrested. It was the local paper, of course. Chris had survived the attack, and even with the injuries he'd suffered, his story hadn't been deemed newsworthy enough to spread beyond the area.

She forced herself to look at Hyde. He had an ugly face – a mean one – but the expression on it here seemed lost and bewildered, as though he wasn't quite sure what he'd done or why.

Katie leaned a little closer, peering at him.

Is it you my brother is scared of?

Was it you outside my daughter's nursery?

Hyde stared back at her from the painting, his expression still confused, as though even if she'd been able to ask him those questions in person he wouldn't have understood them clearly enough to answer.

She leaned away again, her gaze moving to one of the pictures of Chris as a baby. In this one he was staring off to one side. But then she tilted her head and frowned. Something about it wasn't right. The nose and the eyes. The shape of the whole face. There were other photographs of her brother as a baby in the composition, and in each of those she could already see traces of the man he would grow up to be.

But this one didn't look anything like him at all.

She stepped back from the painting. As she did so, the individual images of the past disappeared, vanishing into the larger picture of the present they had been arranged to create. Then she turned round and walked over to the table, and began to search through the material Alderson had been working from. Most of it was photographs, but halfway down the pile she found something else. It was a small torn piece of newspaper. There was no date visible, but the paper was brittle and yellow, and it was clearly many years old.

The baby on the canvas.

The print composing the child's face was long faded now, and the words beneath barely visible. But she could still just about read them, and as she did so she felt a shiver run down her back, like a cold finger tracing the length of her spine.

Nathaniel Leland, 7 months, remains missing.

A door opened downstairs and the distant sound of the radio became a little louder.

'Hello?'

A man's voice calling up from the landing below.

Then the creak of a foot on the stairs.

'You guys back?'

She held her breath and kept still. *Just a student*, she told herself. Nothing to worry about. And yet she didn't want to be discovered here. So she waited. There were a few more seconds of silence, and then she heard who-ever was down there retreating, followed by the sound of a door being closed.

She looked at the newspaper clipping again. Who was this child? But that was a mystery she couldn't solve right now, and so she folded the clipping carefully and put it in her pocket.

You guys back?

The man downstairs must have been referring to Chris and Alderson. And while they weren't here now, if they had been once, then perhaps they would be again. She found a chunky pencil, the tip sharpened roughly with a knife, then leaned over the blank canvas on the table and began to write.

Chris. It's Katie. I want to know you're OK. Please call me.

She added her mobile number. Then she stared at the message for a few seconds, hesitating.

Unsure.

But in the end she did it, adding another line in under-neath. One that had felt blocked in her head for a moment, but which then seemed to unspool out of her.

I love you.

Katie leaned the canvas against the wall, where any-body walking into the room would see it. And then, after one last look at that painting behind her – at all those pasts that had come together to create the present – she headed out of the room, closed the door behind her, and crept quietly downstairs again.

Thinking:

Who were you so frightened of, Chris? And where the hell are you?

14

A park.

It was in the middle of the city, and nobody's idea of a destination: just one of the centre's few remaining squares of something approximating greenery. There were no flower beds here, and the trees were arranged in ugly unplanned bunches, the grass between them dotted with fallen leaves. The paths criss-crossing the area could be walked in half a minute or less, and most people kept to the pavements outside instead.

Not a special place to anyone.

Except them.

Chris and James were sitting on an old bench, their rucksacks on the ground in front of them. They had spent most of the day so far aimlessly walking the streets of the city. It was something to do. Now they were sitting quietly, drinking takeaway coffee in silence – or a *sort of silence*, Chris thought. Because it was that awkward kind of quiet when it felt like a lot was being said without it being spoken.

He looked up. The sky above was a shade of grey that couldn't even bring itself to promise rain. It was just a blank, featureless expanse, entirely uninterested in the world below it. For many years that was how he had thought of the city in general. Other people saw it as home, but sleeping rough on its streets had given him a different perspective. Everywhere you looked – if you looked – you saw shuttered windows, boarded-up door-ways, unfriendly faces. Even the shops seemed to stare at you suspiciously. And the message you received if you could bring yourself to listen was loud and insistent. You don't belong here. You're not welcome.

And for a long time he had believed that was true.

He didn't any more, but that made him think about Alan Hobbes, and he wasn't ready to do that just yet. The question came anyway. The one that was hanging unspoken between him and James right now.

What the fuck are we going to do?

A different memory.

This was a year and a half ago – maybe a month or so after he'd got clean, and at a point when he had still been unaccustomed to the freedoms available to him. During his time in the clinic the rules had been strict and his routine rigorously regimented. When he emerged on the last day, blinking at the harsh light, it had been as though he were experiencing the world for the first time, like a newborn child. A month after that, it had still felt alien to him that he could leave his flat at will – his own flat! – and go wherever he wanted. By that point he was working for Alan Hobbes, but the requirements of the job were far from arduous or time-consuming. There had been nothing much demanded of him at all, beyond basic household tasks, being available on call to attend to the occasional request, and – this most of all – sitting and listening to the old man when he was taken by the desire to talk.

On a day off he had wandered into the city centre one lunchtime and found himself here, sitting on this bench, eating a sandwich from a plastic package, with a take-away cup of hot coffee beside him.

Soaking in the silence.

Minding his own business.

Chris had seen the man from the back to begin with, his attention caught first by his long hair and the large waterproof coat he was wearing, and then by his behaviour. The man was taking photographs of the cluster of trees across from them both. He kept squatting and holding his camera to his face, standing and checking the screen, then shifting position and crouching down again.

The whole time he was moving gradually backwards in Chris's direction, like a chess piece slowly manoeuvring itself into position. Chris might have mistaken it for a deliberate approach if the man hadn't been so clearly unaware of his presence.

In the month or so he had been out, he'd barely spoken to anyone. There had been Hobbes, and a couple of the other workers at the house when their paths crossed, but nothing really initiated by him. And there was no reason to speak to this stranger now, of course, beyond their growing proximity.

But part of him wanted to.

A little, at least. But it was also stupid. If he'd had a dice with him, he might have rolled it. Ten or below, say, and he would speak; anything above and he would mind his own business. Leave it up to chance, in other words – albeit heavily weighted towards maintaining the status quo.

But the thought reminded him of a conversation he'd had with Hobbes a couple of nights before. The old man had been intrigued that Chris had enjoyed role-playing games when he was younger. Chris wasn't sure how the subject had come up, but Hobbes had a way of doing that – of steering the conversation round to whatever he wanted to talk about – and they'd ended up talking about what it meant to leave decisions and repercussions to the roll of a dice.

It's just chance, isn't it? Chris said. *That's what makes it fair.*

Hobbes had inclined his head, as though only considering the matter for the very first time. He had a way of doing that too. It could have been annoying, but Chris quite liked it. The old man would have made a good father, he thought.

But is it chance? Hobbes said thoughtfully. *And does it really make it fair? Because the number you roll was the number you were always going to roll. And it's still* you *making the decision, isn't it? The angle of your arm. The flick of your wrist.*

Chris couldn't think of an answer to that.

It just seems to me, Hobbes said, *that you'd be better off making the decision with your head instead. Or trying to.*

And so.

'What are you doing?' Chris said.

'Jesus!'

By that point the man was crouched down barely a metre away, and the surprise made him wobble off balance; he had to put one palm on the grass to steady himself. When he'd recovered and looked round, Chris held his hands up.

'Sorry,' he said. 'Didn't mean to startle you.'

'I didn't realize there was anyone else here.'

'Yeah, clearly. What are you doing?'

The man gestured across the park with the camera,

as though the device was his primary means of communication.

'I'm taking photos of the trees.'

'Yeah, I know.' The trees didn't appear to be anything special to Chris. 'I was just wondering why.'

The man looked at him curiously. Up close, he was much younger than Chris had been expecting. He wasn't sure why – maybe it had been the coat. But now he registered the jeans the man was wearing, along with what looked like a waistcoat over a . . . was that a band T-shirt of some kind? He had grandfather glasses that should have been ridiculously uncool on someone their age but actually suited his face. All in all, there was something *out-of-time* about the man, Chris thought. It was as though he'd travelled hurriedly through different periods of history and fashion, grabbing a single item at random from each to dress in, and somehow got lucky.

'To sketch from,' the man said. 'I need something to use as a study.'

'A study for what?'

'A painting I'm working on.'

The man explained he was an art student at the university, and that he often took photographs to use as the basis for parts of his paintings. Chris had a hard time wrapping his head around the idea. Surely art was meant to come from your own imagination? James – Chris learned his name quickly – disagreed with him, arguing that most artists worked from models or reference material.

It felt like a cheat to Chris, but he wasn't sure why. He stared across at the drab little cluster of trees. If you based a painting on a photograph, surely that meant

everything was there already? You weren't creating anything in the present; it was all just snapshots of the past
arranged in different formations.

James took the points well, but grew exasperated with
him nevertheless.

'*Everything* builds on what's come before.'

'Does it really, though?'

'Yes.' James sighed. 'Do you want to go for a coffee?
I'll try to explain a bit better. We can even talk about
something else if you like. You maybe?'

Chris sensed the shutters coming down inside him.

'I'm not interesting,' he said. 'And I've already got a
drink.'

'OK.' James looked disappointed. He took a step
back.

Chris found himself fighting a familiar sensation in
his chest. He was so used to protecting himself –
pushing people away. Keeping safe. But that wasn't how
he had to be, was it? He could be free to make choices
with his head. And when he looked at James, he realized
what he wanted to do was talk to this person some more.

So Chris held out the carton of coffee. 'But I'm happy
to share,' he said, 'if you are?'

This had become something of a joke between them after
that.

Whenever Chris made coffee in his flat, he only made
one and they had to pass it between them. Takeaways
from cafés always consisted of just a single order to
share. It was ridiculous on one level – not to mention
impractical – but it had become part of their life together.
A ritual neither of them was willing to break.

Chris sipped his coffee now, weighed what was left, then held it out to James.

'You finish it,' he said.

'You sure?'

'Yeah. It's pretty much gone anyway.'

James took it.

Chris looked across at the stand of trees. At that moment the clouds broke a little and a flood of sunshine passed over the park. The light caught the edges of the branches, creating a glistening web of complexity. And, just for a moment, it was as though he could see a pattern there. The leaves drifting down became black notes fluttering through a mesh of broken musical staves, and as he tried to follow them, there were a few seconds when he could *almost* hear the music they made.

'What are you thinking?' he said.

James frowned.

'I'm thinking I'm tired,' he said slowly. 'I'm thinking that my back hurts.'

'Yeah, mine does too.'

They had been sleeping on the floor of James's art studio for a few days now. Out of the handful of places available to them, it was the only one that felt safe – the only one where it felt like they wouldn't be found by whoever was hunting them. It wasn't great, but he was used to sleeping rough. You were cold and uncomfortable, but you knew you would be and so you accepted it. It was an endurance test. Chris had lived with the mentality that required for a long time, and the mindset had come back to him easily, like an old T-shirt that still fitted when he tried it on.

But the fit was far from a welcome one.

Since leaving the clinic he'd become accustomed to the luxury of having a roof over his head. A hot shower first thing. A comfortable bed. He had even started to take those things for granted. And there was a small unwelcome voice in his head now – one that had been with him to some extent his whole life – that was telling him he had never deserved any of it.

That a happy life was not for the likes of him.

James passed the coffee back to him. 'Here.'

'I said you could finish it,' Chris told him.

'Yeah, I know. But there's still enough left for both of us.'

Chris smiled and accepted the carton.

Rituals were important. You had no choice but to go along with them.

That made him think of Alan Hobbes again. The old man had always liked to talk, but in recent months his thoughts had become increasingly detached from reality. There had been more and more moments when he was barely lucid.

It feels like a journey at the time. Step by step.

Oh?

Yes, Hobbes said. *But the reality is that all the steps are there at once. Beginning, middle and end – they're all the same. From above the whole journey is there.*

That had been inscrutable, but other occasions had been worse. A few weeks ago, Hobbes had sat up suddenly and grabbed Chris's wrist, all but screaming into his face.

Oh God, it's under the bed. It's under the fucking bed!

Then he had collapsed back down and started to cry.

I miss you so much, Joshua. So much.

Beside Chris, James sighed now. 'What the fuck are we going to do?'

Chris didn't answer. He just sipped the coffee carefully. Because while there wasn't much left of it now – and the dregs were almost too cool to drink – he thought there was still *just* enough to pass back to James. And that was the deal. They might not have much, the two of them, and it might not be great. But it was theirs. And the reassurance of that had been right there in James's question.

What were *they* going to do?

'I don't know,' Chris said. 'But it's going to be OK.'

'Is it?'

'Yeah,' he said. 'Of course.'

He smiled at James, wanting to believe his own words, but then he looked down at the rucksack on the ground in front of him. It was packed well and tied tightly – another old habit – but he could sense it inside there.

The book he had taken from Alan's private room.

It might have been out of sight right now, but he could feel the throb of it anyway – it was as though the thing had a pulse or was somehow breathing. It seemed like the thought of it made the sun disappear behind the clouds.

What are we going to do?

He didn't know.

And then the phone Alan Hobbes had given him began to ring.

15

When Laurence was a child, he had learned how to draw a maze.

While they had arrived in the country with little, his father had gradually accumulated a library's worth of books, and encouraged his son to read whatever he fancied. Many had been too dense and esoteric for a child – although that had not stopped him attempting them – but there had been one particular book, an old tome on mysteries and ancient civilizations, that he had always loved, and he had found the method for drawing a maze concealed in there.

You started by drawing a cross. You added a dot in each of the four open squares that created, and then a curve on the top, like the end of a shepherd's crook. Finally you drew a series of curling lines that ran around the whole shape, joining this dot up to that point of the cross, and so on. The lines became increasingly complicated, weaving between others, but were always guided by the endpoint they were curving inexorably towards. If you followed the instructions carefully, you created a simple maze.

As a child, that had felt like magic. It was only when he was older that he had realized it wasn't a *proper* maze. Because there was no way of going wrong or losing your way. There were no choices to be made. No possibility of making a mistake. It offered the illusion of complexity at first glance, but in reality it was simply a single path that swirled elaborately around, turning bewilderingly back and forth on itself, before ending inevitably at the centre.

Talking to Professor Nelson had brought that memory closer to the surface, and he was reminded of it properly a short while later, as he drove through the network of streets around St William's Church.

From above he imagined this leafy suburb would look like one of those mazes. A single road led in, then coiled around between endless rows of expensive retirement bungalows and detached family homes. The neat grass verges were dotted with apple trees, and every hedge in sight was carefully trimmed. Everything was tranquil and quiet, the atmosphere outside the car almost soporific. It made it easy not to notice that there were few turnings on this road at all, and that it led almost inescapably to the church at its heart.

Upon reaching it, Laurence parked up on the kerb and then walked up the wide driveway. St William's loomed overhead, the brickwork brown and clean, and the colours in the stained-glass windows so bright and vivid that it was as though light was somehow streaming out from inside.

At the top a black hearse was parked, a smaller car beside it. The entrance to the church was an enormous arched doorway that reminded him of the entrance to Hobbes's mansion. One of the doors was open, and the sound of organ music drifted out. He stepped inside, then followed the trail of music down a short corridor and into the main body of the church. The vaulted ceiling was supported by massive stone columns above rows of wide pews. The air smelled of dust and wood, and a hint of wax from the racks of flickering candles that lined the walls.

In the far corner an ancient man was working away slowly behind the vast brass pipes of an organ, his thin shoulders rolling along with the solemn music. Two men were before the altar. A priest, who was standing straight and formal, listening attentively, and Richard Gaunt. The lawyer was holding a clipboard and talking quietly.

Laurence coughed loudly.

The sound echoed around the church. The man at the organ continued playing, but Gaunt and the priest looked up. And was the lawyer startled to see him? Laurence wasn't sure. He had called the man's office after leaving the Philosophy department and been told he would find him here. It was official business apparently, and so it wasn't like Gaunt was hiding from him. And yet from the expression on his face it would be easy to believe he had been.

Laurence nodded and gestured behind, and then walked back out of the church without waiting to see if the lawyer would follow. Perhaps he would make a show of turning a few more pages on his clipboard first in order to refute any suggestion he had been summoned. In the meantime Laurence stepped back out into the light, and then followed a path that led to the rear of the church.

He found himself on the edge of a graveyard. An area of grass the size of a small field lay ahead of him. The ground was uneven, and so the mass of headstones stuck up at odd angles, like teeth grown crooked out of the earth. There was nobody else in sight, although a rusted yellow digger was parked, still and silent, by a hollowed-out plot.

Laurence made his way between the headstones.

When he reached the open grave, he peered in. The hole was deep, the cut ends of roots emerging from the surrounding soil. Which he found curious. Looking around, there were no trees nearby. It was as though the tendrils were reaching out from the graves to the side.

Laurence stepped to the right and looked at the stone.

Charlotte Mary Hobbes
9 August 1952–29 June 1985
Sleep Well, Beloved Wife

And then the one beside it.

Joshua Charles Hobbes
29 June 1985–13 April 1986
Sleep Well, Beloved Son

He stared between the graves, reading the dates once again in order to be sure. A shiver went through him.

'Detective Page.'

He turned to see Gaunt approaching, picking his way awkwardly between the graves. He seemed unsure of his footing, and younger than he had during their previous meeting. A little of his confidence had faded, and it didn't look like he was going to recover much of it any time soon.

'Mr Gaunt,' Laurence said.

'Might I ask why you're here today?'

'By coincidence that was going to be my first question to you as well.' Laurence smiled politely and waited.

Gaunt relented. 'I'm here to make arrangements for Mr Hobbes's funeral,' he said. 'He left a very specific and detailed list of requirements for the ceremony with my company.'

'But his body hasn't been released yet.' Laurence checked his watch and frowned. 'In fact, the post-mortem is still taking place even as we speak. It seems premature to be planning anything yet.'

'I'm just doing what I'm told.'

Gaunt looked a little helpless, as though he wanted to have a better and more authoritative answer but didn't.

Laurence angled his body slightly. 'When were these *requirements* given to your company?'

'A few weeks ago, I think.'

'You think or you know?'

Gaunt thought about it. 'Actually, perhaps more recently than that.'

'Interesting.'

'Well, you have to remember that Mr Hobbes was very old. He was in poor health. It isn't strange that he was making those kinds of plans.'

Laurence nodded to himself, resisting the urge to point out to Gaunt that it was not for him to suggest to a police officer what was strange or needed to be remembered. But it was possible the lawyer was correct.

'I have an understanding of Mr Hobbes's work and finances now,' he said. 'But I know very little about his private life. For example, I had the impression he had no family.'

'He didn't.'

'Except he did.' Laurence pivoted at the waist and gestured at the graves. 'And here they are.'

Gaunt looked past him at the two plots.

'Well, yes. But that was a long time ago.'

'Even so. Do you know what happened to Professor Hobbes's family?'

'I know that his wife died in childbirth.' Gaunt smiled. 'Hard to believe in this day and age, right?'

'No,' Laurence said.

Gaunt put the smile away quickly.

'What happened to the child?' Laurence said.

'There was a fire. Mr Hobbes was away from the estate at a conference. The fire broke out in the room his son was sleeping in. There was staff there at the time, and they managed to raise the alarm and contain the blaze, but not in time to save Mr Hobbes's son. You might have noticed the damage it caused when you visited yesterday?'

Laurence thought back to arriving at Hobbes's house and recalled the charred, collapsed section he'd seen at the centre of the building.

'What was the cause of the fire?'

Gaunt hesitated. 'I can imagine what you might be thinking,' he said. 'But my understanding is the incident was fully investigated at the time. It was an electrical fault. It's an old building, and parts of it have been in a state of neglect for quite some time.'

'Why would I be thinking anything else?' Laurence wondered.

'Sorry?'

'It just seems odd you would say that.'

'I—I'm not sure.' Gaunt shook his head. 'What does the fire have to do with anything?'

'Nothing, I'm sure.'

Which was most likely the truth, and yet Laurence realized his thoughts kept running off on these strange tangents. Perhaps that was just a result of his natural curiosity, but whatever might be *most likely* here, he couldn't quite shake the sensation of there being a complicated network of cogs turning below the surface of this case. But again he stored the information away for now.

'You told us yesterday that you had some knowledge of Professor Hobbes's possessions?'

'Yes. He had an extensive library. Some of the philosophical texts he'd collected over the years are intensely valuable. Your DCI has kindly allowed us to begin removing them for safekeeping.'

'Yes, DCI Barnes is renowned for his kindness. Is anything *missing*?'

'Not from there.'

'From where then?'

'Mr Hobbes was a very rich man.' Gaunt looked awkward. 'Over the years, he had amassed an additional collection of . . . I don't know how to describe it. Shall we say *artwork*?'

'I don't know. Shall we?'

'Well, it's all just money in another form, isn't it? Some of the items in this collection were also valuable. Very valuable indeed. As far as I've been able to tell, most of it's there. But there might be a couple of things missing. Although one of them in particular – potentially the most expensive – there's no way of knowing if it's actually missing, or if it's stored elsewhere, or if it even –'

Laurence lost patience. 'What is this item?'

Gaunt gave a humourless laugh. 'A book,' he said.

Laurence was quiet for a moment. He thought back

to the footage he had watched, picturing the object that Christopher Shaw had brought out from the archway. It was about the right size and shape for a book. It had glinted in the light, but he presumed a valuable book would need to be wrapped in something to protect it.

He was about to press Gaunt for more information when his phone rang. He held up a hand to signal their conversation was far from over and the lawyer must wait, and then stepped away and took the call.

It was Pettifer with an update on the search for Christopher Shaw. She and another officer had gone to Shaw's mother's house and spoken to her, but the woman insisted she hadn't seen her son in two years. Laurence detected in his partner's frustrated tone that the woman had not been particularly easy to deal with. Regardless, Pettifer had managed to excuse herself for the bathroom, at which point she had ducked her head quickly into the various rooms and found no evidence of Shaw's presence.

'Did you believe her?' Laurence said.

'I don't know,' Pettifer said. 'But given what happened two years ago, it wouldn't surprise me if Shaw really was keeping away.'

'Anything else?'

'Post-mortem's just finished; we'll be getting a provisional result from that shortly. And we might have visuals on Shaw. I've found a bank account registered to him, and he's made various withdrawals from cash machines over the last few months. The most recent was yesterday. I'm waiting on security footage from that now.'

'That's something,' he said.

Silence on the line.

'Sorry,' he said. 'Of course what I meant was that's *excellent work.*'

'That's better. And how are you doing?'

Laurence glanced at Gaunt. 'I'm not sure yet. I'll let you know shortly.'

He ended the call and then stepped back over, joining the lawyer by the graves, and staring down at them for a moment. Two were filled with the victims of terrible tragedies. One was waiting to be with the victim of an equally horrific murder.

And all because of what?

Laurence looked up at Gaunt.

'Tell me about this book,' he said.

16

Katie had time to kill after she left James Alderson's art studio.

She couldn't go home without letting Sam know she hadn't been at work that day, and yet she had no obvious further options in terms of finding Chris. All she could do now was hope he would see the message she'd left and call her. Unable to think of anywhere else to go, she drove at random, ending up in an area of the city she didn't know well, and then found an anonymous cafe, in which she did her best to make a sandwich and two cups of coffee last as long as she could.

It gave her an opportunity to think.

Which was not necessarily a good thing. Her phone was on the table. There had been no contact from Sam all day, and part of her was relieved about that. After all, he thought she was at work; if he texted her now, then any reply she sent would be a lie. And, of course, she *had* ended the call that morning brusquely. At the same time, he often texted her during the day – just little connections, perhaps even especially after arguments – and so a different part of her was upset not to hear from him. Even if there was no reason for it, it felt like the events of the last twenty-four hours had exacerbated troubles that had been lying just beneath the surface of their relationship for a while now.

Money, of course.

She usually tried not to think about that, but she forced herself to do so now. She knew how important music was to Sam – in all the forms he pursued it – but increasingly it felt like he was chasing a dream they both knew was unrealistic. Of course, there was much more to a relationship – a life together – than the money you brought to it, but there had been lean times recently, and perhaps she didn't always reassure him as convincingly as she should.

And yet neither of them was able to acknowledge that openly, and so instead the tension had started to come out in little asides and oblique references, never resolving itself. Sometimes she thought he was ashamed, which she hated. But at other times he would overcompensate almost bullishly, so that she'd come home to find he'd effectively done nothing all day, and all the chores and housework were waiting for her. At times like that it was almost as though he was trying to provoke her.

But she never took the bait. And while it bothered her that they were keeping things from each other right now, perhaps the worst thing was that it didn't bother her as much as it *should* have. Part of her accepted that it was just who they were now. That they had started sleepwalking in different directions, and if they weren't careful, then one day they were going to wake up in different rooms.

Katie looked at her phone. She could have texted him *herself*, of course.

But she didn't want to, and that was part of the

problem. Instead, she took the newspaper clipping out of her pocket and put it on the table, smoothing out the creases and then looking down at the little boy in the picture.

Nathaniel Leland, 7 months, remains missing.

This child was a mystery to her, but he was in the composite painting and so clearly Chris considered him part of his history – as important on some level as the photographs of her and their parents. She picked up her phone and opened the internet, and then searched for variations on the name. There were plenty of hits, but none seemed obviously relevant. There was nothing about a missing child.

But in the afternoon light the paper appeared even older than it had before. Whatever had happened to Nathaniel Leland, it had obviously been a long time ago. And while every missing child was newsworthy to someone, the sad truth was that people could disappear from history just as easily as they did from life.

She closed the browser and put the phone down. Just as she did, it vibrated and the screen lit up. She was picking it up when the waitress approached.

'Another cup of coffee, love?'

Katie checked the screen. A text from Sam.

Hi there. Just a reminder I have a gig tonight in case there's a danger of you 'working late' again! Love you.

She stared at the message for a couple of seconds, breathing slowly, wondering what it was about it that annoyed her the most. The exclamation mark? The quotation marks, which seemed designed to diminish her concerns about her students? The lack of the usual kisses at the end?

Perhaps it was all of these.

She put the phone down and smiled flatly at the wait-ress. 'Yes,' she said. 'Another coffee, please.'

Not that she *was* late home, of course.

She actually arrived a few minutes early – although whether that was to show willing or to maintain the high ground was open to interpretation. She walked inside to find Siena seated in front of the television – again – and Sam's guitar and equipment leaning against the wall of the front room. He emerged from the kitchen as she closed the front door, already pulling his coat on.

'Can I grab the car keys?' he said.

Not even a hello.

Katie handed the keys over but checked her watch.

'I thought the gig wasn't until . . . eight?'

'It isn't. But I want to get there early to set up. Say hello to a few people and have a catch-up. Plus, we've not had a chance to practise much recently.'

'Right.'

He hesitated. 'Is that not OK or something?'

'No,' she said. 'Of course it's OK.'

He hesitated again, then gave her the look that pissed her off more than any of the others in his arsenal. It was an expression that said: *I can see you're in a bad mood for no reason, and I'm going to be the bigger person and not rise to it.*

OK,' he said. 'Fine then.'

Katie sat down with Siena while he made a couple of trips to the car with his gear. Then she made a point of getting up and beginning to prepare Siena's dinner just before it was obvious Sam was ready to leave.

'Bye then,' he called through.

'See you later,' she called back. 'Break a leg.'

She finished making Siena's meal, and then sat with her on the settee while she ate it. Normally Sam insisted on them eating at the table, but Sam wasn't here, and so she let Siena balance the plate on her knees, occasionally helping her manoeuvre the food with her fork and spoon. There was the predictable amount of spillage, and she made a mental note to add Siena's T-shirt to the washing that still needed to be done that evening.

Eventually it was time for bath and bed.

Katie washed her daughter's hair slowly and carefully.

'Everything go OK today, Snail?' she said.

'Yeah.'

'Tilt your head back.'

She rinsed out the shampoo, making sure to keep the foam away from Siena's eyes.

'Nothing weird happen at nursery?'

'No.'

She squeezed out the sponge, wishing she was more relieved by her daughter's answers. She didn't want to alarm her over what had probably been nothing. But she also knew from experience that, while Siena had an astonishing memory when it came to pictures in a book, or the exact number of treats she was entitled to, a bomb could have gone off at the nursery today without her feeling it necessary to remember and relate.

Once Siena was in bed, Katie read a Julia Donaldson book to her, and then spread out her beloved flag on top of the sheet. The flag was a relic from her and Sam's past. They had been together since their teens, but that first year apart, studying at separate universities, had tested them a little. They had emailed constantly, visited each other as much as they were able, and then, in the summer holidays at the end of that first year, had gone backpacking together.

Their trip had begun in Italy, with a few days spent in Siena. Even now, she could still remember the oppressive heat of its narrow sandy streets, and all the districts, with their lanterns and fluttering flags. The experience had felt magical on every level. The flag was a souvenir she'd bought from the Snail district, and it had spent close to two months that summer tied casually to her backpack as she and Sam travelled around. While the city was not where they had fallen in love, it was the place their relationship had been cemented after what felt like a period of both tragedy and uncertainty. It was where both of them had decided: *Yes, I really do want to be with this person for the rest of my life.* And so they had given its name to their daughter when she was born, and Katie had passed the flag on with it.

When she had finished reading, the two of them walked over to the window together and Katie opened the curtains. The sky was black with cloud.

'Moon?' Siena said.

'Too cloudy tonight, kid. In fact, I think it's going to pour down. But here's the thing. Even if you can't see it, the moon's there somewhere. So I'm sure it will still hear you.'

'Goodnight, moon.'

'That's the ticket.'

Katie tucked her into bed. 'I'll be back up to see you in a minute. Sleep well in the meantime, Snail. I love you.'

'Love you too, Mummy.'

She put the washing on downstairs, then went up to check on Siena a few times until she was sure she was safely asleep. Then she made herself some dinner and sat at the kitchen table, eating slowly, the glass of wine beside her plate more appealing than the food. She was facing the window that looked out over the cottage's small back garden. Her reflection stared back at her from the black world outside, chewing thoughtfully.

When she was done, she put the plate in the sink and then got both a second glass of wine and her laptop.

She wasn't sure if she'd really expected Chris to phone her, even if he'd seen the message she'd left at the studio, but she had hoped he would. Perhaps she hadn't exhausted *every* avenue, though. She opened up a browser on the laptop and did a cursory search for James Alderson. The name was so common that it was hard to find him on social media, but she stumbled on a couple of accounts that might have been him, and an Instagram account that certainly was. None of them were helpful. The Instagram was exclusively photographs of his artwork, and he seemed to have only a handful of followers there. The other accounts, assuming they even were his, didn't appear to have been used much in years.

So what else?

Katie took a sip of wine, watching her reflection in the window do the same. She was at a loss for a moment. But then she remembered the sheet of paper she'd seen briefly in the drawer at Chris's flat.

What had the headline been?

THE DESPICABLE HISTORY OF JACK LOCK.

Probably nothing.

But she typed *Jack Lock* into the search bar anyway. When she pressed return, she was met by numerous links, and clicked on one at random. It took her to what appeared to be a biography of the man.

OK then, Jack, she thought. *Let's see how despicable you really were.*

17

JACK LOCK

<u>Introduction</u>

Jack John Lock (2 July 1908–28 September 1956) was a mid-twentieth-century serial killer who is also known by the name 'The Angel Maker'. Following his arrest on 6 March 1956, Lock was charged with the murders of four children and his wife, Elaine. The remains of his younger victims were found buried in the garden of his manor house in Dree, while Elaine's body was discovered inside.

Lock was found guilty of all charges and sentenced to death on 8 May 1956. While he was scheduled to be executed by hanging on 28 September 1956, he was found unresponsive in his cell early that morning and pronounced dead shortly afterwards. His death was recorded as suicide. There was a great degree of speculation at the time as to how Lock had obtained the item discovered in his cell that facilitated his death. While Lock was convicted for his involvement in five murders, the precise number of his actual victims has never been ascertained.

OK, Katie thought, taking a sip of wine. *Fairly* despicable, then.

Beside the introduction was the same photograph she remembered seeing at her brother's flat: a sepia print of a man from a different age, one which appeared to have been taken even further back than the dates referenced

in the text. There was something of the Victorian aristo-
crat about him, with his neatly styled hair and enormous
moustache. The smart black suit with the flower in the
lapel. His expression was stern but, looking more closely,
she thought there was also a slight glint of amusement
in his eye.

I know something you don't.

She scrolled down slowly, continuing to read.

Early Life

Jack Lock was born on 2 July 1908 to Mary Anne Lock (née
Williamson) and Gregory John Lock. His parents were
active members of an obscure religious chapter known as
Deus Scripsit, which was based around a number of close-
knit local family groups.

The beliefs of Deus Scripsit – 'written by God' – involved
contested readings of the Bible and more esoteric aspects of
theology. These revolved around the notion that God is eter-
nal (i.e. situated outside time itself) and therefore sees the
past, present and future of our world simultaneously. Since
every moment already exists before God, it follows that
whatever we do is preordained and inescapable. Moreover,
to attempt to do otherwise should be viewed as a terrible sin.
The sect was notable for its extreme puritanical leanings and
strict physical punishments.

The family of three left the community in June 1915 for
reasons that remain unclear, and moved several miles away
to a cottage close to the village of Dree, where it is believed
they continued to practise the religion in which Jack was
raised.

Contemporary accounts of Jack's early life describe an
odd, neglected child. He would often be seen walking alone
during the night, wearing ragged clothes and talking to

himself. During his brief time at a local school, there were incidents where Jack entered what appeared to be a fugue state, during which he spoke to someone or something not present. Following these incidents, he would be seen writing furiously in the notebook that rarely left his side. Teachers expressed concerns over both his behaviour and marks on his body that appeared consistent with beatings and whippings, at which point Jack was removed from classes and home-schooled. No further interventions by authorities were made.

As a grown man, Lock showed little aptitude for pursuing a particular career. He was unemployed for several years, although he had notable success as a gambler. During this period he also became notorious for the sermons he would deliver on the streets of Dree. No record of the speeches survives, although second-hand accounts suggest they were performed with a degree of fervour and conviction that listeners found disturbing.

Elaine Bell

Lock married Elaine Bell on 16 July 1932, following a whirlwind romance. According to Bell's acquaintances, Lock courted her with a confidence that belied his standing, claiming the two were destined to be together. Bell was the daughter of a wealthy industrialist, and the union was frowned upon by her family, who viewed Lock as being an eccentric of poor character and low social status, although they continued to support the couple financially.

Known Victims

The first known victim of Jack Lock was Winnie Bowers, eight, who disappeared from her street on 13 April 1949. The girl's older brother gave an account of a man he had seen speaking to his sister, whose description was later matched to that of Jack Lock.

Three further abductions followed, this time without witnesses. The remains of Winnie Bowers, Joan Lessing (seven, abducted 15 June 1951), Maureen Godling (eight, abducted 11 May 1953) and Jean Kilner (nine, abducted 19 October 1954) were discovered buried on the Lock property.

Arrest

The attempted abduction of Ann Harrison, ten, occurred on 6 March 1956. On this occasion, Jack Lock's attempt to kidnap a child was interrupted, culminating in him fleeing and being chased down by a mob. Lock was savagely beaten by the crowd before being taken into custody. Upon arrival at Lock's house, officers discovered the body of Elaine Bell in the kitchen, and then the remains of the previous victims.

According to contemporary accounts, two boys were found alive in the property. While there was no official record of their births, they were believed to be the sons of Jack and Elaine. The children were rehomed and due to the nature of their upbringing their subsequent adoption records were ordered to be sealed.

Katie leaned back in her chair, considering what she'd read so far.

Dree was an area just north of the city. Given the number of victims, she was surprised not to have heard of Jack Lock before now. She would have expected him to be well known locally, even if spoken of in hushed tones and whispers. Then again, it was possible these crimes had been committed too long ago to have resonance in the modern day. Or perhaps the explanation was even simpler than that – that some people were so terrible that they needed to be forgotten. That for the community to hang on to Jack Lock's memory would leave it bruised and traumatized, locked in a state of horror from which it was impossible to move on.

Which begged the question: why had Chris been interested in him?

While her little brother was a stranger to her in many ways, one thing Chris had always been was sensitive, and she couldn't imagine that changing. That sense of fragility and vulnerability was baked into his DNA, and this was exactly the kind of real-life material she thought he would recoil from. So what was the interest here?

Was there even any connection at all?

But she was only about halfway through the article. She turned her attention back to the screen and scrolled down, reading further.

Trial, Conviction and Death

Jack Lock laughed openly during his trial, in a display that attracted disbelief and derision from the men and women assembled in the courtroom. Lock claimed that it had been revealed to him he would commit the murders, and that he had been compelled to carry them out, as to do otherwise would have been to refute the orders of God. 'My life was set in stone before my birth,' he told the court. 'As was yours. The difference between us is that I have been purified and my path has been revealed to me.'

A number of pieces of writing were discovered at Lock's manor house that gave a full account of each child's murder, including descriptions of their abductions and graphic details of their deaths. Lock's contention in court was that he had written these passages in advance, when the future had been revealed to him.

The prosecution offered the more obvious explanation, which was accepted by the court. The accounts had been written after the murders had been committed and were now being used by Lock to justify his vile crimes.

Lock was found guilty of the murders on 8 May 1956 and sentenced to death. At the conclusion of the trial the judge in charge of proceedings was visibly upset, and ordered the post-mortems on the children to be sealed due to 'the unrivalled depravity' of what had been done to them.

Lock laughed again during his sentencing – 'so hard that his body shook' – and appeared indifferent to the judgement of the court. 'God has tested my faith,' he called out. 'Through His tongue He revealed my path – all of our paths – including the monstrous things He intended for me to do. He expected me to falter and fail. But my faith is strong. I knew I had to carry out His plans. To disobey Him would have been a blasphemy far worse.'

On the morning of 28 September 1956 Jack Lock was found unresponsive in his cell. He was pronounced dead later that day. He had slashed his wrist with the nib of a fountain pen. Despite a comprehensive investigation, it remained a mystery how the item came to be in his possession.

Posthumous Legacy

Although Lock's crimes are mostly forgotten in the present day, traces of them can still be found in the curious field of murderabilia. Modern-day collectors of the macabre have sometimes been known to trade objects associated with Jack Lock.

A sewing machine and needle set, believed to have belonged to Elaine Bell, attracted low five-figure bids during an auction in June 1982. The knife Jack Lock used to commit his murders is alleged to have been sold to an anonymous buyer in January 1987 for an undisclosed sum. Reports have also circulated of pages of Lock's writing changing hands for considerable amounts of money.

More broadly, rumours persist that Lock spent a substantial portion of his life compiling a much longer piece of writing – a 'masterwork' – that filled the notebook he had carried since childhood. The existence of this item has been debated and contested over the years. The exact contents of the notebook, should it be real, remain unknown, although some believe, as per Lock's claims, that careful study of it might be used to divine the future and reveal God's will.

That was the end of the article.

Katie leaned back, feeling uneasy. While the murders had occurred several decades ago, and Lock himself was long dead, what she'd read had disturbed her.

My life was set in stone before my birth.

It made her think of the portrait Alderson had created of himself and Chris – a snapshot of the present, constructed from all the moments in the past that had brought the two of them inexorably together in that time and place.

She scrolled all the way back up, and looked again at the photograph of Jack Lock at the top of the page. Again, there was that knowing look in his eyes.

God has tested my faith . . . But my faith is strong.

Katie picked up her wine and took another sip – a larger one this time – and watched as her pale reflection in the window did the same. She squinted at herself there, as though she might be able to read her own thoughts.

Her reflection grinned back at her. And then part of it disappeared as whoever was standing outside stepped away from the glass.

She stood up too quickly.

The chair screeched and clattered over backwards, and the glass she'd been holding shattered loudly on the floor at her feet. She stood very still for a few seconds, staring at herself – just herself now – with her heart pounding. Then her gaze moved slowly over to the black glass of the back door. And then down to the handle.

She saw it move slowly before the lock stopped it.

Click.

And then once more.

Click.

'Mummy!'

Katie whirled round. Siena's voice – calling out from upstairs. It set her moving. She glanced back as she reached the bottom of the stairs, and then thudded up them as fast as she could, desperate to reach her daughter, to make sure she was safe, certain somehow that she was not, and –

Siena was standing by the window as Katie flicked the light on. She had the flag pulled round her like a safety blanket, but she let go of one corner and shielded her eyes against the light.

'Ow.'

Katie moved quickly over and hugged her daughter to her. She could feel Siena's heart beating hard against her. Then she leaned back and took hold of the sides of her arms.

'Siena?'

'I heard a noise. Did something break downstairs?'

'Yes,' she said.

'Is it OK?'

No, Katie thought. *It's not OK at all.*

From somewhere outside she heard a car revving its engine. A moment later, there was the screech of tyres as a vehicle sped away down the street. She needed to call the police. But first of all she had to make sure her daughter was safe.

'It's fine,' she said. 'Are you OK?'

'Yes.'

'Why are you up?'

'Moon.'

Siena smiled happily and turned to the window just as rain began pattering against the glass.

'Moon came to say hello again.'

18

It was raining heavily as Laurence and Pettifer drove north out of the city, retracing the journey they had made yesterday afternoon. This time he was driving. When they left the department, Pettifer had moved straight to the passenger side without discussing the matter, which Laurence had taken as a subtle reflection of their respective levels of enthusiasm for the journey ahead.

Water lashed the windscreen, growing in intensity as they went. By the time they were into the countryside, it felt like angry fistfuls of rain were being flung at the car, blurring the glass in front of him faster than the squeaking wipers could clear it away.

'We could have sent someone else to do this,' Pettifer said.

'And miss this delightful view?'

'When you put it like that, I become even more right.'

She left it at that, the grumble more what was expected of her than a genuine complaint. A lot had happened that afternoon, and they both knew that, wherever else they might be right now, relaxing at home with their feet in front of the fire was not one of the options. But Laurence was aware Pettifer was doubtful about their pursuit of this particular angle.

She took out her phone and scrolled the screen with her finger.

He gave her a moment. 'Anything?'

'Just more fucking security footage.'

He understood her frustration but took a slightly different perspective on matters. They wanted to know where Christopher Shaw was, of course. But Laurence thought knowing where he was *not* might also be useful in its own small way.

Pettifer had done good work today. Tracing Christopher Shaw's bank account had granted them a handful of glimpses of him, the footage all taken from cameras close to the cashpoints he had used. Until recently that had mostly been confined to an area west of the city, and Laurence was willing to bet that was close to wherever Shaw had been calling home. But his behaviour had changed last week. Subsequent footage came from cameras in apparently random streets in the city centre. The coverage was better there, and they had been able to follow him from street to street, even if they always lost him eventually.

For some reason Christopher Shaw had altered his routine.

Even better was the footage they had from the last withdrawal yesterday morning, which showed Shaw and another young man walking down the street together. They looked a little unkempt, and both were carrying heavy backpacks. While they disappeared off grid quickly – annoying Pettifer immensely – the sighting had made Laurence happy because it provided them with more information. They now knew that Shaw had a companion. And that the two of them appeared to be on the move.

Pettifer sighed. 'What do you make of this?'

He risked looking away from the rain-drenched road for a second and realized she had the results of Alan

Hobbes's post-mortem report open on her screen. Upon first viewing the body yesterday, Laurence had imagined it obvious that the savage injury to the old man's throat would be the cause of death – and indeed the pathologist had confirmed that was the case.

But the story had turned out not to be so simple.

Not so simple at all.

Laurence looked ahead again, turning the wheel gently. 'I don't know yet,' he said. 'We will see.'

The trees packed tightly on either side of the dirt road that led to Hobbes's house provided some respite from the weather, but the car tyres rolled and squelched in the mud, and then the rain redoubled its fury when they emerged into the clearing at the end. Laurence heard a sound like snapping kindling as he parked up on the pebbled area by the front doors. The scene was due to be released tomorrow morning. For now a single police car remained in place, an officer sheltering against the elements within it.

Laurence stared out of the window at the house. The building had appeared grand to him yesterday, but he found himself re-evaluating this in light of what he had learned since. Those enormous wooden doors seemed smaller now, and the empty wings to either side appeared desolate and sad. But most of all there was the stretch of charred, fractured brickwork high above – the room where Alan Hobbes's infant son had perished in a fire, and which had not been repaired in the three decades that followed. Right then, the house seemed as saturated by grief and sorrow as it was by the downpour.

Alan Hobbes had been wealthy. He could have lived wherever he liked. And so Laurence found himself thinking about his own flat – carefully organized to reflect his needs – and wondered what choosing to remain in this property said about Alan Hobbes.

After showing their IDs to the officer in his car, they hurried into the house. Laurence turned on the torch he'd brought, illuminating the chessboard-patterned floor and the twin staircases that lay ahead. The officer had taken them up the stairs on the right-hand side yesterday, and so for some reason he chose the left-hand side this time. It led them to the same landing, of course.

As they ascended further, he breathed in and noticed odours he had missed upon their first visit: damp and mould; old wood and spilled ink. When they reached the first landing, he heard a noise behind them, and turned quickly, swinging the torch's beam round to point back down the staircase.

Nothing but mist swirling.

Beside him, Pettifer flicked her own torch on under her chin and pulled a frightening face at him.

'A genuine improvement,' he said.

With their torchlights bobbing, they made their way up the rest of the stairs, and then down the corridor that led to Hobbes's flat. The door at the end was closed but not locked, and when Laurence opened it the space beyond was filled with a darkness the beam of his torch seemed to disappear into. Pettifer stepped past him and reached round the frame, her fingers groping across the wall until they found the light switch.

Laurence blinked at the sudden brightness, then clicked off the torch and followed her into the flat. The main room was more or less as he remembered it but felt emptier than before, in a way the lack of people did not fully account for. The bed had been stripped and resembled a hospital gurney now, the bloodstains on the wall somehow uglier in contrast to its bare metal frame. He glanced behind him and saw the camera above the door, hanging limply from its broken plastic casing.

Then he turned his attention to the archway at the end of the room.

Once again, the light in the room didn't penetrate much further than a metre or so into the old stone corridor. Beyond that there was just a green-black darkness.

But he could feel the same cold breath coming from it as he had yesterday.

A light flicked on to his left.

Pettifer had already moved into the small bathroom that led off from the main room, and he followed her in. It was a small, utilitarian area – just enough space to fit the basic necessities. Pettifer put on a pair of gloves and opened the cabinet on the wall above the sink, and then began working methodically through the various plastic bottles that were lined up inside. Hobbes had been on a great deal of medication. Some of the bottles rattled as she picked them up, but others did not, and it was those she paid closest attention to, holding them up to the light and peering at the labels. Some she returned; others she placed on the back of the sink. By the time she finished there were six of those.

'So,' she said. 'There we are.'

Laurence bent at the waist to read the labels.

Here was the anomaly the pathologist had noted in his report. The severe blood loss indicated Alan Hobbes's heart had still been beating when the knife wound was administered to his throat, and that was judged to be the cause of death. But Hobbes had already swallowed enough prescription painkillers to euthanize a horse. Had he not been murdered, he would have been dead within an hour regardless.

'I assume,' Pettifer said, 'we're not suspecting the killer force-fed him?'

'Alan Hobbes was not Rasputin. He only needed killing once.'

'Self-administered then.'

'I suppose we can't be certain,' Laurence said. 'But, yes, I think so.'

He leaned back up again. 'We thought it was strange, didn't we, that Hobbes would dismiss all his staff – as though he knew his killer was coming and had resigned himself to his fate. And so perhaps this is our explanation. He wasn't expecting to be murdered at all. He was planning to take his own life and did not wish to be disturbed.'

'But then he was.'

'Yes.'

'Which can't be a coincidence.'

Laurence considered that. Coincidences did happen, after all, and perhaps there really was an element of that here. But he, too, suspected there were connections they weren't seeing yet and that, when they did, they would revolve around Christopher Shaw. Because while Laurence still didn't understand why, he was sure that the man's presence here would turn out to be key.

And also the item Shaw had removed from the property.

Tell me about this book . . .

Laurence turned away and headed back into the main room.

Close to, the air that seemed to be breathing steadily out from the archway felt colder, and the darkness before him seemed even more impenetrable. Both sensations were unpleasant, but the latter could be dealt with. Laurence reached out, searching for a light switch on the wet wall beside him, and found what felt like one. He flicked the switch and pale light flared from a bare bulb hanging down. The rush of air was joined by a humming from above.

The corridor ahead was made of old rough stone, dotted with green in places. It reminded him of a narrow passage below the ground in some ancient castle. But it was short. It ended in another archway only a short distance away, which appeared to open out into another room that was lost mostly in darkness for the moment.

Laurence stepped into the corridor.

When he reached the second archway, the breeze became much stronger, and he could hear something now. The noise was familiar on some level, but he couldn't quite place it – it sounded a little like chattering teeth. He reached round the archway, searching for a light switch again, this time without success. Instead, he clicked the torch on and stepped forward.

The floor was made of stone, and from what he could see the room was large and mostly empty – but not entirely. While the centre was clear, a series of bookcases was bolted to one wall, their shelves entirely cleared of all the valuable philosophical texts Alan Hobbes had amassed over the years. Laurence turned his body slightly, moving the beam to the wall beside the empty bookcases. There was a desk and chair there, and a wide wooden display cabinet. Framed prints of some kind hung from nails that had been driven into the stonework above.

He played the torch's beam over them, but was unable to make out the details from where he was standing. And he found himself reluctant to move closer, as though the air itself had formed a wall that was pushing back at him.

'Laurence?'

Pettifer arriving behind him broke the spell. He shook his head and then walked across to the cabinet. It had drawers and glass panels, a padlock securing each. He could tell there were objects behind the glass, but it was hard to make them out. A pen. An ancient sewing machine. What appeared to be a cat's collar. An old black suit, folded carefully, with the brittle, desiccated remains of a flower resting on top.

Pettifer joined him, moving her torch's beam over the items on the wall above. He raised his own torch, illuminating the prints hanging closer to him. They were not pictures but pages of notepaper, small enough to fit four to a frame. The handwriting was smaller still. Even peering closer to the glass, Laurence found it almost impossible to decipher, and all he received for his troubles was the sensation that he was in the presence of evil.

'Jesus,' Pettifer said quietly.

'Would not feel at home here,' Laurence agreed. He leaned away.

It appeared that Alan Hobbes had been many things. A professor of philosophy. An astute investor and businessman. A philanthropist. And yet behind that facade he had also been *this*. A man obsessed with the crimes of the serial killer Jack Lock, and who had dedicated his life to seeking out and purchasing – often illegally – every horrible artefact he could find that was connected to the Angel Maker.

Laurence became aware of the cold breeze again. The sound of chattering teeth.

'Here,' Pettifer said.

She was holding her torch steady this time, revealing the open front of one of the display cases. The inside was lined with what appeared to be dark velvet, a patina of dust surrounding a pristine rectangular impression.

'About the right size and shape for a notebook,' Laurence said.

According to what Gaunt had told him at the church, legend had it that Jack Lock had spent his life writing down the future as it had been revealed to him. And that the book he had left behind could effectively be used to see into it.

Pettifer kept the beam on the empty case. 'You don't really believe in all that, do you?'

Laurence considered the question.

'Not at all,' he said.

Jack Lock had not been a prophet; he had simply been a deluded child-killer. At the same time, Laurence *did* believe that Lock was also the product of a terrible household. That he had been a child saturated in religious dogma and subjected to physical and emotional abuse by his parents. And to the extent that the writing in his notebook had detailed these early traumas, he supposed that in some ways it *did* predict the future – because the initial seeds of Lock's atrocities must always have been visible in its pages.

And there was another consideration.

'But it doesn't matter what the two of us believe,' he said. 'What matters is what *other people* believe – and what they might have been prepared to do to obtain such an item.'

'For example, commit murder.'

'Indeed.'

Chattering teeth again.

Pettifer seemed to notice it at the same time. 'What the fuck *is* that?'

They both turned round, aiming their torches at the darkness at the far end of the room.

In the corner of the room strips of charred, soot-stained wallpaper still clung to parts of the stone wall. The brickwork there was shattered, the surrounding plaster scorched and bubbled by the fire that had ripped through this room decades before. The ceiling above and part of the wall were open – the source of the breeze. A span of charred timber formed thick, blacker lines across the dark sky above, and the rain was pouring in past them.

Laurence froze slightly. This was the room in which Alan Hobbes had kept his macabre collection.

But it had once been something else.

The rain spattered down, tapping incessantly against the item that still rested by the base of the wall.

The half-melted metal frame of what had once been a child's bed.

Bolted tightly to the stone floor.

19

Edward Leland approached the door.

His father had taught him many things as a child, and one of his most important lessons was this: every man should have a private place in their house. A space that was solely theirs, in which the contents of their hearts could be on open display.

And this was his.

He unlocked the door and stepped forward into the dark. The room was large and almost entirely empty. He stood a little way past the threshold. The light from the corridor behind cast his shadow over the polished wooden floor but failed to reach the blackness at the far end. There was a window there, but it was boarded over with planks. It had been a long time since this room had seen daylight.

Almost swallowed by the dark, a large plasma screen was mounted about halfway along the wall, surrounded on either side by rows of shelves. The shelves contained his personal collection, amassed over many years. It spanned decades and was probably the largest of its particular kind in the world. There were old reels of film here; spools of slides; VHS tapes; CDs and DVDs in clear plastic cases. The footage they contained had been gathered from war zones and security cameras and police lockers.

And some of it he had created himself.

He closed the door behind him. The room became black, and he stood still for a few seconds, enjoying the dark and the silence. The sensation was like being in a void. Closing his eyes made no difference, and his body felt weightless and unreal, more spirit than flesh. He walked across, his shoes tapping on the floor, taking precisely measured steps that left him close enough to the screen that, when he reached down, his hand found the controller on the floor by his feet.

A press of one soft button and the screen came to life.

He put the controller down again, turned round and walked towards the centre of the room. The footage behind him was silent and grainy, but bright enough to cast a deformed shadow against the opposite wall. He stopped in the centre then turned to face the screen. Flickering light played over his face, as though the images were being projected directly on to his skin. In his head – either despite the quiet or because of it – Leland imagined he could hear the same rattle of old film that sometimes accompanied the nightmare about Nathaniel.

After a moment, he held his left hand up before him, then reached forward with his right, turning it at the elbow, as though to cup a ghost standing before him. He took a long, slow breath. And then he moved.

Left foot stepping a short, elegant distance forward.

Right following it, but out to the side.

Left sliding in to join the right.

In the absence of music to guide him, he counted the beats in his head. *One, two, three.* Then he switched his weight, sliding his right foot back and reversing the process – *one, two, three* – his body moving gently up and down with the motion, keeping his elbows up and maintaining the frame that held his invisible partner.

He had learned to dance when he was young. Due to Giles Leland's wealth and standing – the circles he moved in – it was something that had been expected of Edward, alongside the usual piano lessons, tutorials on the correct use of cutlery, and all those other matters of meaningless social etiquette. He remembered the childhood sessions with the private tutors Giles Leland had paid for. The women who had avoided his gaze and always felt stiff in his arms, as though he frightened them in some way.

The angels he had danced with in the years since.

But mostly he danced alone.

Left foot forward again.

He kept the plasma screen as his line of focus for several repetitions, and then began waltzing slowly and methodically around the empty room, his feet sweeping over the floor, the light from the screen flickering across him.

One, two, three.

And then, as he turns once more, the darkness of the room swirls into ribbons of golden light, and he feels a presence in his arms.

It is 3 July 1976.

Edward Leland is dancing in the gilded ballroom of a hotel. It is a random event in the social calendar, held because it is always held, but it is attended by the kind of politicians, businessmen and low-ranking royalty that it pays to share space with. The chandeliers above are bright and glittery, and the air is filled with music and the tinkle of crystal glasses. Around him a sea of black suits and expensive gowns.

One, two, three.

Or at least that's the idea. Except that the woman he is dancing with – a rather plain woman named Eleanor – cannot dance. She keeps misplacing her feet, and he isn't sure whether that's from a lack of training, too much champagne, or a combination of both. She has been displaying an interest in him that, at least right now, is not reciprocated, but when she asked him to dance he found himself unable to say no.

One, two –

'Ow,' Eleanor says.

He has trodden on her toe. They pause for a moment, then she pats him reassuringly on the arm, as though it is him who made the mistake. A few seconds later, they resume, falling back into synch with the men and women dancing more effortlessly around them.

'Are you OK?' she says.

'Of course.'

'You seem distracted.'

'Not at all.'

He *is* distracted, though. As they dance – the *one, two, three* in his head now also a silent, teeth-gritted countdown to Eleanor's next misstep – he is looking around the room and scanning the crowd.

Searching for the other reason he is here tonight.

Charlotte Mary Cooper.

The first time Leland had seen her was at a black-tie dinner. Charlotte had been in her early twenties at the time. She had arrived wearing an elegant red dress in which she seemed slightly ill at ease, as though she had not yet grown fully into her skin. But there had also been a confidence that belied her years and lack of social polish, and it was that, along with the more obvious fact of her beauty, that had quietly bewitched every man at the table that night. Leland had not spoken to her, but he had been unable to take his eyes off her. And as he had stared at her, he had felt something click into place inside him.

Charlotte Mary Cooper didn't know it yet but she belonged to him.

In the weeks that followed Leland had courted her patiently and casually. There was no need to hurry. Brief interactions; occasional conversations. When something was inevitable, such approaches were more than sufficient. Even so, Leland had fallen more deeply in love with her each time they met, and although he registered her apparent indifference – the way she might be looking over his shoulder when he spoke, the slight disdain in her voice when she replied – it was of no importance to him. What was meant to be was meant to be. Charlotte Mary Cooper was meant to be his, and so she would be.

As God has written.

And now he sees her.

Charlotte is on the far side of the room, not dancing but standing by one of the buffet tables, a glass of champagne pressed to her chest. By chance, she is wearing the same red dress as the first time he saw her, and she glows so brightly that it seems impossible it took him so long to spot her.

She throws her head back in laughter at something someone has said –

One, two, three.

– and then she is away to one side of him, out of sight now.

He tenses slightly. She has never responded to *him* like that. Who is she talking to?

One, two, three.

He finds himself resenting Eleanor's hands on him now, not just because she is not Charlotte, but because it feels as though she is leading him away – holding him back – and he has to resist the urge to turn his head and stare across the room.

One, two, three.

And then there Charlotte is again.

She is still laughing. Beside her is a handsome, smartly dressed man, who is leaning in closer to her than is appropriate, smiling at the reception his remark has received. Leland's gaze moves to the man's face – and then he freezes.

Because even after all these years, he recognizes his brother.

'Ow!'

Leland releases his grip on Eleanor, and the two of them come to a halt in the middle of the room. The sea of dancers continues to swirl around them, obscuring his view of Charlotte and Alan. But Leland can *sense* the two of them over there, and for a moment he feels as powerless as he did as a child, watching Alan disobey their father and disappear down that corridor.

Eleanor is looking at him.

'I apologize,' he says.

'It's all right.' She hesitates. 'Maybe we should get a drink?'

Leland considers it. He can feel fury building in him. 'Yes,' he says. 'I think so.'

He takes Eleanor home with him that night, but feels absent during the sex and then lies awake in the darkness afterwards. She snores gently. It feels out of place having her beside him in the bed, to the point that he has to keep reminding himself of her name. It is as though he has woken up in a place he doesn't recognize and which he has no recollection of arriving at. Something has gone wrong.

For a while the sight of Alan – rich, successful and dressed to the nines in finery – is impossible for him to process. It makes no sense. Alan was destined for nothing; Edward for everything. The world has tilted off its axis somehow, and now everything is crooked and sliding. Alan had no business being there at all – and especially no right to be talking to the woman who belonged to Leland. And yet there he had been. And there had been Charlotte, laughing with pleasure at his joke.

Leland rolls on to his side.

It is unacceptable.

It is *wrong*.

And it is in the early hours of the next morning that the only possible explanation for this wrongness occurs to him. The understanding makes him shiver. He remembers the last time he saw his brother.

You can't do this. It's not allowed.

And yet Alan had. He had gone into their father's study and taken his sacred notebook. In doing so he had stolen teachings and revelations that belonged to Leland by right. And while the thought is almost too abhorrent to comprehend, he realizes now that a man prepared to transgress so shamelessly in one way is surely capable of doing so in others too.

First against his father.

And then against God Himself.

It is 6 October 2017 again.

Leland turned and stopped.

Lost in his memories, he had not noticed the slight change in the light. The door at the far end of the room was open now, and Banyard was standing there, waiting patiently. The man's face was illuminated by the images flashing across the screen on the wall. The footage was an old black-and-white recording plagued by static, but that was standard for the quality of home video available when it had been filmed, and the quality was still good enough to see what was happening to the woman.

Leland maintained his frame, his arms extended.

'Yes?'

Banyard remained impassive. 'He has just left, sir.'

One of Leland's lawyers.

'And what did he have to say?'

'He can arrange the withdrawal of the funds you requested, but for such an amount it will be tomorrow afternoon.'

It never ceased to surprise Leland how cautious these people could be. They had their checks and their procedures to follow, of course, but the money was such a small amount – next to nothing in the grand scheme of things.

In fact, he had almost felt embarrassed for Christopher Shaw when the boy had named his price for the book. On the other hand, he supposed that made Shaw clever. A reasonable offer was likely to be accepted quickly. And, of course, money had volume. Leland knew from experience that the amount Shaw had requested was the approximate limit of what could be packed into a large briefcase. Bank transfers left tracks and traces, after all; Shaw wanted to be able to sell the book and disappear.

But Shaw did not know the true nature of the transaction. He had no understanding of what had gone wrong.

And no idea what was necessary to put it right.

'That will be fine,' Leland said. 'Will you take care of the other matter?'

'Of course, sir.'

'Thank you, Mr Banyard. Please close the door on your way out.'

The man gave a curt nod and did so.

One, two, three.

With a thrill running through him, Leland began dancing again. And as he continued to waltz around the empty room, bathed in the flickering light of the atrocities playing out on the screen, his arms no longer seemed quite as empty as they had before.

It felt more than ever like a ghost was there dancing with him.

PART THREE

20

Light from the old projector flickers around the lecture theatre. Ahead of him, curved rows of seating rise towards the door at the back of the room. The black shapes of students are dotted here and there in the darkness.

It is 26 October 1984 and Alan Hobbes has the Devil at his back.

He glances behind him at the painting displayed on the screen: *Tartini's Dream* by Louis-Léopold Boilly. It depicts Giuseppe Tartini in his bed, asleep but responding with visible reverence to music played by the Devil, who is perched half on the bed and half on a plume of smoke. When the composer woke, he was inspired to write his Violin Sonata in G minor – the Devil's Trill – and then spent his life frustrated by the disparity between his own composition and the perfect music he had once heard in a dream. Hobbes always uses the picture for this lecture.

He turns back and his voice echoes around the auditorium.

'There are many objections one can raise to Laplace's demon,' he says. 'We have already discussed possible difficulties created by quantum theory and thermodynamics.'

He pushes his glasses back up his nose. '*But* . . . we should note that neither objection helps with the problem of free will. On that level you are still – and forgive me for using obscure scientific terminology here – *completely screwed.*'

A ripple of laughter goes through the theatre. Hobbes pauses to allow it, enjoying it, but a moment later his attention is drawn to the back of the room. He watches as the door opens and a figure enters the room, silhouetted against the light there for a few seconds before quietly taking a seat in the back row.

There you are.

Hobbes realizes his mouth is dry. There is water on the table and he takes a sip.

'*However,*' he continues, 'we have ten minutes left in which I want to explore the problem from a different angle. Because there is another reason Laplace's demon is impossible.'

The notion is a complicated one, but he has given this lecture many times now, and has done his best over the years to refine the explanation and make it as clear as he can.

'As we know,' he tells them, 'Laplace's demon theoretically knows the exact state of everything in the universe, meaning that it can see – laid out before it – everything that will come to pass.'

However, he explains, the problem is that if Laplace's demon were part of our universe, then its thought processes would *also* be part of the universe. It would need to take those into account. Which means that the experiment would become endlessly self-referential, with cause and effect crumpling in on themselves the way a star collapses into a black hole.

'The only way it could work,' he says, 'is if Laplace's

demon existed *outside the world* – somewhere completely distinct from the space and time we occupy, and yet somehow capable of observing it. And if that were the case . . . well, I believe we already have a different word for such a being.'

He pauses again, taking the opportunity to look around the theatre. Even in the darkness he has become attuned to signs of confusion and misunderstanding in his students, and he checks for them now. His heart is beating a little faster than it normally would, and he's aware he's fudged a few of his lines.

He avoids looking directly at the shadowy latecomer in the back row.

Another sip of water.

'*Right*,' Hobbes says. 'We have also talked about one theological argument for determinism – that God's omniscience requires the past, present and future to be set in stone. *But* . . . that also creates problems for theology. For one thing, if it were true, how can anyone be praised or blamed for doing something they had no choice in? And as we all know from the lady who rants in the square by the refectory every Sunday, God is famously *very keen* on right and wrong.'

Another ripple of laughter – albeit this time with a slight undertone of relief. Hobbes knows that talk of God leaves many of them cold.

No matter.

Just get through this.

'But what if we look at these problems together?' he says. 'Imagine God as an artist. He can always see the whole canvas – yes, of course – and in that sense His knowledge is complete. But He is not finished. He keeps

181

dabbing bits of paint here and there, making the picture deeper and more meaningful to Him. Seeing what happens. And if some of those dabs were Him giving us glimpses of the picture as it stood, wouldn't the choices we made as a result *then* have weight in His eyes?'

A final pause.

At this point in the lecture he almost always loses several of the students, and today is no different. Philosophy is meant to be a dry, logical discipline, and these flourishes of colour have no real place in the discussion. But the hour is nearly over and he has already covered the necessary components of the syllabus; he doesn't mind so much if he leaves a few of them behind. Especially because he's not really talking to them right now anyway.

Hobbes focuses his gaze on the shadow in the back row.

'And so the question then,' he says, 'is whether God would *want* us to act on those revelations. Some might argue we should never go against God's knowledge – that our duty is simply to carry out His will, whatever terrible things it compels us to do. *Deus scripsit.* But I would ask you this. If you were a father, which would you prefer? A child who always did as they were told, or a child who disobeyed you and tried to forge their own path – to do the best they could for themselves and for others?'

There is a moment of silence in the room.

The black figure at the back remains still and implacable.

And then the bell on the wall rings loudly, jarring almost everyone.

'I'll leave that as a rhetorical question then,' Hobbes says.

The students are already gathering their things together, shuffling along the rows, eager to escape into what they are correct to believe will be one of the last warm afternoons of the year. Hobbes can't blame them. This is his final lecture of the day, and he is anxious to finish up some administrative work and get home to Charlotte. The thought of her makes him look again towards the far end of the hall.

The figure is gone.

Hobbes stares blankly for a moment, watching the other students filing out.

I had to protect her, Edward, he thinks. *Because you were going to kill her.*

I know you don't understand that, but you were.

Then he turns back and begins collecting his paperwork from the table by the projector. While above him, the Devil – perched there with his violin – continues to play.

It is 4 October 2017.

Hobbes opens the door of the bathroom cabinet and selects the various bottles he will need, lining them up one by one at the back of the sink. He does not swallow the pills yet; that moment comes later. They will not take action quickly enough to save him, and he will still be drifting in and out of consciousness when he is killed, but they should at least dull him to the worst of the pain. And after everything he has done, perhaps all he has earned is the right to shave the edges off the suffering due to him, not avoid it altogether.

He walks stiffly back through to the main room, which has been pared down to essentials over the years, a few personal items excepted. He moves over to the bed. On the table beside it, positioned so he can see it if he turns his head when lying down, is a photograph in an old silver frame. He picks it up and brushes a sheen of dust from the glass, revealing a picture taken of Charlotte and him on their wedding day. They both look so young. So happy.

So long ago.

But, of course, there is really no such thing as *long ago*, and for a few blissful seconds he can feel the warmth of the sun that day and the pressure of her hand in his. He doesn't need to remember the love he felt for her, though, because it has never left.

I love you so much, he thinks.

Then he takes the photograph into what had once been Joshua's room and stands by the desk. He looks up at the books on the shelves. In a day or two they will all be gone. The instructions he has given to Richard Gaunt are detailed and specific. In the event of his death most of the titles here will be kept in storage, but several of the titles will be donated to the university, while a few have been selected with care and affection to be sent to former colleagues and others who have become dear to him.

Hobbes picks up one in particular and rubs his hand tenderly over the cover. Then he takes the photograph out of the frame. The clasp is small and his hands have been betraying him for months now, but when he finally manages it, he places the photograph face down on the desk, and then picks up the pen and adds a message on the back.

He turns it back over and looks at himself standing with Charlotte.

I love you, he thinks. *I always have. I always will.*

Then he places the photograph on top of the book and selects an envelope.

And I'm sorry.

It is 26 October 1984.

On his way back to his office after the lecture about Laplace's demon, Hobbes stops into the office to collect some paperwork from his pigeonhole. Before he can extract the pile waiting there, Marie – one of the secretaries – comes round from her desk.

'This was just dropped off for you, Alan.'

'Thanks.'

He takes the envelope she is holding out and begins to tear it open. Inside, he finds a single piece of expensive paper, and when he unfolds it he sees a short message there, written elegantly by hand in black ink.

You have committed blasphemy and it will be corrected.
~ Edward

Hobbes stares down at the message for a few seconds, a trickle of ice in his chest. That dryness in his throat again too. But, of course, there is no water at hand here to save him.

Marie notices his discomfort. 'You OK, Alan?'

He forces a smile. 'Yes. It's just another *complaint*.'

There have been several of those over the years – students, perhaps overly sensitive, who have handled certain aspects of the course material badly – and his usual practice has been to reach out to those he feels he can help while disregarding the others. But he folds this particular piece of paper and hands it back to Marie.

'Can you make a note of this one and keep it on file, please?'

'Of course.'

Hobbes heads off down the corridor. When he reaches his office, he closes the door quickly and then leans his back against it, closing his eyes. The window across from him is bright, and he can see the map of red blood vessels in his eyelids, and feel his heart beating hard against his chest.

You have committed blasphemy and it will be corrected.

His brother's words have landed. Hobbes truly believes what he told his students at the end of his lecture – that if *he* were God, he would neither want nor expect blind obedience from his children – and yet there is something in Edward's note that has conjured up a sense of dread inside him.

It is that notion of *correction*.

Because while he has made sure to keep his influence upon the world small, he has still undoubtedly made changes. He has gone against what was written. And because of this, there have been moments when he has experienced a sensation of being off balance, as though he is attempting to steer a ship listing on a turbulent sea, and all the old timber around him is creaking and straining in an attempt to correct its course.

As though perhaps he has misjudged what is expected of him.

Deus scripsit.

Three sharp raps at his back.

186

Hobbes jumps slightly and steps away from the door, his heart beating faster as he turns to face it. For a moment he's convinced it must be Edward on the other side . . .

But when he opens it, Charlotte almost bursts into the room.

His wife has her arms round him so quickly that Hobbes barely has time to register his confusion – she should be at home when he arrives back an hour or so from now – but he returns the embrace, grateful to see her. Part of him realizes he *needed* to after receiving Edward's message. Because there is a different version of this day – a worse one, in a more badly painted universe – where the woman who has become the love of his life is already dead by his brother's hand.

'This is a lovely surprise.' He steps back a little while keeping his hands on her upper arms. 'But aren't you supposed –'

'*I just couldn't wait.*'

She smiles then, staring at him with those eyes that captured him the first moment he saw her. Good God, there is so much vitality to her, he thinks. She is so exceptional – so *vivid* – that he can almost feel her body fizzing with warmth and energy beneath his hands.

And yet as she puts her hands over his own and leans in to kiss him, that sensation of the world *creaking* around him is stronger than ever.

'We're going to have a baby,' she whispers in his ear.

21

Katie remembered how it had felt to wake up the day after her father died.

His death had been sudden and peaceful – a good death in many ways. He and her mother had both been home, her father reading in the armchair in the front room while her mother bustled about the flat. They had been talking only minutes earlier. And then her mother had walked back through to the front room and found her husband unresponsive. He was still sitting just as she'd left him, with a book splayed open on the arm of the chair beside him, as though he'd put it down carefully there before deciding to take a nap. She called Katie while she waited for the ambulance, and, even then, she still wasn't sure if he was just sleeping and if she might be bothering everyone for nothing.

That afternoon and evening had been too busy for Katie to take it in properly and for the grief to hit. It was a state she took to bed with her. When she had woken up the next day, there had been a moment when everything was normal. She was in her bed with Sam asleep beside her, and the morning light in the room was exactly as it always was. There had even been a few seconds spent drifting. But then her mind began prodding her. Something was different. Something was *wrong*. And then she remembered. The knowledge that her father was gone arrived as a horrible clench inside her chest, and it felt like the world suddenly upended around her. This was not how it was meant to be. Rather than emerging from a nightmare, she had somehow woken up in one instead.

She experienced a similar sensation when she woke up the morning after seeing the face at the kitchen window. The night's sleep had brought a degree of peace that remained for a few seconds before it was replaced by the nagging sensation that something was wrong. Then she remembered what had happened, and a feeling of dread ran through her and snapped her awake.

Someone had been watching the house.

She rolled over quickly. Sam was there, lying with his back to her. She assumed he was asleep. *Not a care in the world*, she thought. She slipped quietly out from beneath the sheets. In the hallway she leaned round Siena's door and saw that she was still asleep too. The whole house felt silent and *safe*. And yet a thrum of fear was running through her.

Because it wasn't.

Katie padded softly downstairs and made herself coffee.

Then she stood by the back window, staring out at the bedraggled garden.

The police had arrived quickly last night. Two officers – both male – had turned up within twenty minutes of her call, listened to her, and seemed to take the matter seriously. One had stayed with her in the kitchen, taking notes, while the other investigated the garden, a torch beam moving here and there in the rain, occasionally settling on something and pausing before moving on.

Her mother had insisted she not talk to the police

about her brother, and she decided to leave him out of it for now. Regardless, they had been interested in the car that had been spotted at Siena's nursery and said they'd follow up on that, which was something. There had been a sense of relief that her concerns weren't just being dismissed.

And then Sam had arrived home.

There had been relief at that too – at first. Obviously he was surprised to find her in the kitchen, rocking a dozing Siena and talking to two uniformed police officers, but the fact he was back meant she wasn't going to be alone when they left. She explained what had happened, and the two officers repeated some of the things they'd said to her. But then something strange happened. Sam didn't appear as worried as he should have been. He nodded here and there, a serious expression on his face, but he didn't say much, and he didn't seem particularly alarmed either. When he saw the shattered wine glass, his gaze lingered on it for longer than she liked.

And she sensed the two officers picking up on that.

She registered the glances between them. A slight shift in their body language and tone. Nothing overt. But she became aware that she was in a room with three men, and that they had all started taking their cues from one another rather than from her. While the officers had been treating her seriously before Sam got home, the dynamic had changed now. She felt anger rising inside her. It had been *her* this had happened to, and *her* who had called them, and yet it felt like she had suddenly become the least important person in the room.

By the time they left she wasn't sure they were taking her seriously at all.

Afterwards, Sam had listened to her without giving the impression he was hearing her. Any concern he had seemed muted and qualified, an underreaction to what she was telling him had happened. *You don't believe me*, she found herself thinking but not saying out loud – not yet – because she couldn't quite accept it was true. In the end she'd gone to bed. Sam had stayed up for a while. She had no idea what time he'd finally joined her.

She made another coffee now.

A few minutes later, she heard the telltale sound of movement overhead. Siena was up. At least that would occupy her for the next couple of hours.

Katie got her dressed and downstairs, and then set about entertaining her for the morning while attempting to pretend everything was normal. And to Siena, of course, it was. She didn't mention the police at all; Katie wondered if she even remembered them coming. And while she knew she should be pleased Siena hadn't been scared by what had happened, it felt like her daughter's reaction minimized it in the exact same way that Sam's had.

As though everything was fine.

Her husband emerged mid-morning, bringing a cloud of tension downstairs with him. He looked like he'd actually been awake for a long time, pondering a difficult problem – more in sorrow than anger – and he and Katie barely glanced at each other. Without discussing the matter, they tag-teamed the childcare. He took over with Siena while Katie went up to shower and dress, making sure she took her time doing both.

It was nearly lunchtime when they finally spoke.

Siena was in the front room, while Sam was in the

kitchen, staring out of the window the way she had first thing. Katie stood in the doorway and leaned against the frame. He had his back to her. It occurred to her that was often the case these days.

'You don't believe me, do you?' she said.

She found it hard to say the words out loud; it was almost shocking to give voice to them. But it was like he hadn't even heard her.

She leaned away from the door frame and stepped into the kitchen.

'You actually don't care that we aren't safe.'

'Oh God.' He sighed. 'That's exactly it. We *are* safe, Katie.'

'You don't know that.'

'What I care about is why you never *feel* like we are.'

'Wow.'

He turned slightly, side on to her now. 'Can we not do this in front of Siena?'

There was a pleading tone to his voice that she found insufferable. Once again, it was as though she was the one being unreasonable while he was having to work hard to pacify her.

'It's not *in front of Siena*,' she said. 'And can you not patronize me, please?'

'I'm honestly not meaning to.'

'And yet honestly you are. Why would I make it up?'

'Jesus. I don't think you did.'

'So you think I imagined it?' She laughed. 'Yeah, that's actually worse.'

'I think you're putting yourself under pressure that you shouldn't. Maybe without you even realizing it.'

'Oh, really?'

He hesitated. Came to a decision. 'OK,' he said. 'Let's do this then, if that's what you want. Who's Nathaniel Leland?'

She opened her mouth to answer – but then shut it again. The question made no sense. How did Sam know about that? But then she looked at the chair by the kitchen table, saw her jacket from yesterday was still draped over the back, and remembered the news clipping.

The anger inside her intensified. 'You went through my pockets? How fucking dare you?'

She deliberately lowered her voice on the swear word, but it still caused Sam to turn round properly. He stared over her shoulder towards the front room, as though she'd screamed it in their daughter's face, and then he looked at Katie, angry himself now.

'What?' he said. 'Are you actually blaming me for that? A minute ago you wanted me to care. What am I supposed to do? You don't talk to me any more. And you *lied* to me, Katie.'

'What?'

'I know you weren't at work yesterday. The school called.'

Shit.

'Wow,' she said. 'At least you heard the phone over your music.'

'Oh, well done.' He pulled a face. 'For what it's worth I told them you were in bed.'

'Thank you so much for the favour.'

'You're welcome. So, where were you?'

'I'm surprised you don't already know, since apparently you're Sherlock fucking Holmes now.'

'Who's Nathaniel Leland?'

She looked away to one side for a moment and then back at him again.

'Why didn't you tell me about the nursery?' she said.

'What?'

'About the red car the children saw.'

He stared at her, momentarily confused. Then he shook his head. 'Honestly? Because I knew you'd be like this.'

'Like what?'

'Like *this*.' He sounded like he wanted to laugh. 'I mean, *listen to yourself*. You've already decided it was a red car. When the thing is – at least as far as I recall – nobody mentioned the colour at all. But *that's* what you zero in on, isn't it? And that is *exactly* why I didn't tell you.'

The anger inside her was almost too much now. She couldn't stand the way he was making himself seem so reasonable. So sensible. Especially because, yes, she'd slipped up there. But there was a lot he didn't know, wasn't there? She could have told him right now, but in the heat of an argument giving up secrets felt like giving up ground.

'You should have told me,' she said.

'Yeah, maybe. And perhaps I even *would* have done. But then there's all this stuff with Chris, and –'

'What?'

No swearing this time. No raised volume. But there was such ice in her voice – in just that one word – that it stopped her husband dead. He just stared at her for a few seconds, looking helpless.

'I know you, Katie,' he said finally.

'Do you, though?'

'Of course I do.' His voice was much quieter now.

'You worry too much. You jump at shadows. You're always scared that something terrible is going to happen. And I know why you –'

'No.' She held up a hand. 'We're not doing this.'

She stepped across to the chair, grabbed her jacket from the back, and pulled it on. Sam just stood there looking helpless. He took a single step towards her but the look on her face made him take it right back again.

'Katie, please,' he said. 'I know you blame yourself. But it wasn't –'

'We are *not* fucking doing this.'

And then she turned round and headed straight for the front door.

22

But Sam's question bothered her as she drove away from the house.

Who's Nathaniel Leland?

She hadn't been able to find out anything about the boy online yesterday, and not having an answer for her husband only increased her anger now. Because there *had* to be a reason the child had been incorporated into James Alderson's portrait of her brother with all those other images.

All those other images . . .

The answer hit her out of nowhere – and then she felt even more angry, this time with herself. While she might not know who Nathaniel Leland was, there was someone who might.

Her mother's house was quiet as she let herself in.

'Hello?' she called out.

There was no reply, and she stood in the hallway for a moment, staring down the corridor ahead, at the doors there, half hidden in the gloom. Each of them held memories. Because of the old-fashioned feel of the house and its furnishings, it had been easy to imagine this place was haunted while growing up here. Part of her still thought it was. It was just that as a child she hadn't understood what ghosts really were.

'In here.'

Her mother's voice, calling from the front room.

Katie stepped through. The room seemed darker than it should have been. The curtains were open, but the light from outside was occluded by the dirty glass of the window, and the air was the colour of stewed tea.

Her mother was sitting at the table. She didn't look up as Katie entered the room. The jigsaw was laid out on the table before her, and her hands were working at the puzzle. Katie walked across the room and looked down at it. The four of them were complete now, and her mother was working on the floor at their feet: a large patch of all but identical light brown pieces. Katie watched as she moved one around, turning it carefully, trying to find where it belonged.

'Have you heard from Chris?' her mother said hopefully.

'No.'

'I thought that might be why you were here. The police came to see me, you know. About him.'

'What?' Katie said. 'When?'

'Yesterday. They wanted to know if I'd seen him recently. I told them I hadn't. That I hadn't had any contact with him in years.'

'Mum –'

But she was interrupted with a sharp look.

'That's what he would have wanted. I'm not going to betray my own boy.'

Katie hesitated. 'Were they worried about him? Or did it seem like he'd done something wrong?'

'They wouldn't tell me.' Her mother looked down again. 'Both, I think.'

Katie tried to put things together in her head. What the hell had her brother got himself involved in?

And not just him any more.

'I spoke to the police yesterday too,' she said.

That got her another sharp look. 'About what?'

'Not Chris.'

She told her mother about what had happened last night – the face at the window – and how whoever had been outside had tried the back door. Her mother was slightly more concerned than Sam had been but, if anything, she seemed more relieved that they hadn't asked about Chris.

Katie bit down on the familiar resentment that caused.

'You told me Chris took some photos one time he came round?'

Her mother nodded. 'Yes. I've never thrown anything away.'

Katie took the piece of old, yellowing paper out of her jacket pocket.

'Who is this child?' she said.

Her mother peered at it for a second. Then she turned back to her puzzle.

'I can't possibly see in this light. Not with my eyes.'

'I think you can,' Katie said.

The jigsaw piece her mother was trying didn't fit. She placed it in a bag of discards by her side and selected another from the box. And then she sighed.

'He shouldn't have torn it,' she said. 'I'm a bit disappointed in him for doing that. If he wanted it, he should just have taken the whole thing.'

'The whole what?'

'The box is in your bedroom.' Her mother nodded towards the corridor. 'Go and see for yourself.'

'See what?' Katie said. 'Who is this?'

'Nobody. One of your father's fancies.'

The temperature in the room seemed to drop a notch. Katie wasn't sure that she'd heard her correctly, or what her words meant if she had.

'What did you say?'

But her mother didn't reply. She just kept moving the jigsaw piece around the empty space in the puzzle, rotating it methodically, trying it in every available position. Katie watched her for a moment, then put the photograph of the little boy back in her pocket and turned to face the gloom of the doorway behind her.

Go and see for yourself.

'OK,' she said. 'I will.'

It was not her bedroom any more, of course. It was a storage room now – filled mostly with rubbish. Her mother had indeed rarely thrown anything away. Broken bookcases and cabinets lined the walls, while folding tables were stacked on top of each other and slumped piles of bin bags stuffed with old clothes rested beneath the window. But the bones of the room were still familiar, and Katie felt a shiver of recognition as she stepped inside.

Her desk was still there.

She had loved it as a child: an old wooden school desk. There was a square black slate attached to the inside of the lid with a clock stencilled on to one corner. She walked across now and opened it slowly. The lid creaked up awkwardly on rusted hinges, releasing the sealed-away smell of chalk dust and chewing gum. The black slate was still there. The clock too. The ghostly marks of hundreds of chalk hands gave the impression it was telling every possible time at once.

Katie looked down. There was a cardboard box on the floor beside the desk. She kneeled down. At some point in the past the box had been sealed with brown parcel tape, but Chris must have cut it open. She opened the top to discover the box was full of material – old documents and paperwork; packets of photographs – but she found what she was looking for almost immediately. There was a collection of old newspaper clippings, and the one Chris had torn the photo of the little boy from was on top.

She picked up the yellowing paper and then took the photo of the child from her jacket pocket. It fitted into the corner of the clipping perfectly, and now that the photograph was back in place, the little boy seemed to be staring at the stark headline beside him.

SEARCH CONTINUES
FOR WHITROW'S NATE

Police and civilians today (12 Apr.) continued their search for missing infant Nathaniel Leland (pictured), combing the fields and woods around the home from which he is believed to have vanished last week. Their efforts were hampered by adverse weather conditions and the difficulties of the terrain.

One volunteer told them, 'It's boggy land, the trees are thick, and the rain has made progress pretty tough. It's just unforgiving out there. But each of us is one hundred per cent committed. If Nate is out there somewhere, we're determined to bring him back home, where he belongs. This is something that's affected us all.'

Local police are keen to emphasize that Nathaniel's disappearance remains a missing persons enquiry, but sources indicate that hopes of finding the child alive are now dwindling. Many are privately preparing themselves for the worst.

'We're determined to keep looking,' another volunteer commented. 'I think at this point we're all afraid of what we might find, but no child should be out there regardless. I know Nate's father. If nothing else, I want to find him for his sake.'

It is a view that has echoed throughout this tight-knit community ever since Nathaniel disappeared from his family home on Monday. Nathaniel was left in the care of a childminder, Peter Leighton, who is also missing. A tent believed to belong to Leighton was located in dense woodland nearby. As of today, his cottage remains sealed off while officers and forensic teams perform a fingertip search of the property. And, in the meantime, a shaken community continues to search.

Katie kept hold of the photograph but put the newspaper clipping down on the dusty carpet beside her. She was shaken by what she'd just read. Not by the contents, as such, but by the questions they raised. And by the implications she could feel gathering from her mother's choice of words.

One of your father's fancies.

What the hell could she have meant by that?

She turned her attention to the other news clippings in the box. There were several, and she took them out one by one – carefully at first, then more quickly – spreading them out on the carpet and then moving them round in an attempt to create an order – a narrative – from them.

Only part of one emerged.

It appeared that Peter Leighton had been a trusted childminder who had regularly been left in charge of Nathaniel Leland. But one evening Nathaniel's parents had returned home to find both Leighton and their infant son missing. An extensive search had ensued. While searching Leighton's cottage police discovered a collection of violent pornography that suggested he had long harboured a fantasy of killing and dismembering a child. The assumption was that he had finally done so. But – at least as far as these clippings went – no further trace of Leighton or the child appeared to have been found.

Katie sat back on her heels. The crime had taken place three decades ago and a hundred miles from here. And yet for some reason her father had collected and kept these newspaper cuttings. This child's disappearance had captured his attention. And then Chris had given a photograph of Nathaniel Leland to James Alderson to incorporate into his painting, which suggested her brother *also* believed the little boy's death was entwined with their lives somehow.

Who's Nathaniel Leland?

She had the answer now. But she still had no idea about his connection to her family.

Katie felt a presence behind her. Still kneeling, she shifted around to see her mother standing in the doorway, wrapped in a dressing gown and leaning on her cane. The expression on her face was tinged with sadness, as though something she had been dreading for a long time had finally arrived.

'Why?' Katie said. 'Why did Dad keep all of this?'

'He shouldn't have done, God rest his soul. It was a mistake. But then we all make mistakes, don't we? I shouldn't have let Chris look through the box – I'd forgotten all the things that were in there.'

Katie stood up. 'Why did he keep this, Mum?'

She started to answer but then stopped. She looked conflicted.

'It's not my story to tell,' she said.

'Please, Mum.'

But the conflict had been resolved and her expression had hardened.

The sadness remained, though.

'You need to find your brother,' she said softly. 'And ask him.'

23

Early afternoon and they still had nothing.

Or at least that was the way Pettifer was choosing to see it. They had spent the morning working in their office, taking separate calls and following up the small handful of leads they had. None were going anywhere, and Pettifer was making her displeasure felt. Laurence had no idea how ending a call or flicking through paperwork could be accomplished with such *violence*, but his partner managed it well. Every knock at the door was met with a look so angry it threatened to flay skin. Word had spread on the floor outside. Every officer delivering an action or an update to the office did so with the manner of a nervous zookeeper approaching a lion's cage.

Even Laurence had yet to tease her today.

He shared some of her frustration. They were now on the third day of their investigation – and the fourth since Alan Hobbes had been murdered – and seemed little further along than they had at the beginning.

Fingerprint results from the flat had come in first thing – a predictable smorgasbord from Hobbes's staff. They were still attempting to trace a couple of those, but most had been accounted for and interviewed, their whereabouts on the evening in question established. A number of Hobbes's business associates had also been investigated. To a man – and they were all men, Pettifer had made a point of noting – they had expressed shock at what had happened. All had alibis for the time of the murder. None appeared to have any motive whatsoever for harming Alan Hobbes.

Which left them with Christopher Shaw.

Or rather very much *without* him, because the boy had, to all intents and purposes, vanished off the face of the earth. There had been no further sightings of him. An analysis of his bank account had revealed money had been transferred there on a weekly basis by Alan Hobbes, but there were no outgoing payments that suggested rent or a mortgage. He appeared to have no social media accounts or internet footprint. And his fellow traveller – the young man spotted with him on the security footage – remained unidentified.

This all bothered Laurence greatly.

At the same time, it occurred to him that Christopher Shaw had lived a destitute life for a long time – that he had been a man without a safety net when he needed one – and so the fact he couldn't be netted so easily now might be considered a case of chickens coming home to roost. Regardless, they were at sea here. For all they knew, Shaw might be too.

His email pinged.

A message from Professor Robin Nelson, who had managed to compile a list of the handful of threatening messages received by Alan Hobbes that had been filed. Laurence resisted the urge to yawn as he read through the six notes – but then found his attention caught by the final one. According to the records, it had been hand-delivered to the office of the Philosophy department on 26 October 1984.

'Look at this,' he said.

Pettifer walked over and stood beside him, leaning down on the desk.

You have committed blasphemy and it will be corrected.
~ Edward

'What the fuck is that supposed to mean?' she said.

Laurence wasn't sure. The other notes on file were more obviously from angry students, but while this letter was quieter and less aggressive, there was still something about it that bothered him.

It will be corrected.

'I don't know,' he said. 'But Hobbes must have kept it for a reason.'

'This was over thirty years ago.'

'Even so.'

'Well, I mean, that's *brilliant*. Yeah, I vote we take this very seriously indeed. Get out the champagne – we have the first name of a suspect.'

'I agree,' Laurence said solemnly. 'We are halfway there.'

Pettifer glared at him, then walked back across the room and sat down heavily.

Laurence watched her go, then looked at the computer screen for a few more seconds before shutting down the message. Then he walked across to the whiteboard, picked up a cloth and pen, and began amending the provisional notes he had made yesterday based on the information they had discovered since.

A) Christopher Shaw attacked by Michael Hyde
(3 May 2000)

B) Katie Shaw reports CS to the police
(3 September 2015)
– CS disappears

C) Alan Hobbes murdered (4 October 2017)
– Philosophy lecturer (determinism)
– wife died in childbirth
– infant son died in fire
– dismissed staff on day of murder
– apparent suicide attempt (BUT killed anyway)
– collection of material related to Jack Lock

D) CS present at scene (4 October 2017)
– no record of employment by Hobbes
  (BUT paid anyway)
– disabled security camera
– theft from property (?)
– homeless (?)
– unidentified male companion

E) Jack Lock
– serial killer
– determinism / free will / will of God etc.
– valuable book now missing = motive for
  murder (?)

Laurence clicked the top back on the pen and studied his handiwork.

'There,' he said. 'Forget the message. These are all things we know – or at least *suspect*. Some are more speculative than others, admittedly, but for the moment let's say these things are all true and see where it leads us.'

Pettifer sighed. Then she walked over and stood next to him. 'OK. Where?'

He considered the board. It was like looking at a selection of jigsaw pieces. Some of them appeared to fit together, but for now he couldn't tell which ones even came from the same puzzle.

One thing was becoming clear to him, though.

'It suggests to me very strongly that Christopher Shaw is not our killer.'

'How so?'

'Think about it.'

Pettifer did not reply for a few seconds, and he could tell she saw it too. It was possible she didn't want to acknowledge it, given that Shaw was currently the only suspect on their radar, but the facts remained.

'All right,' she said.

'Because if we assume *the book* was the motive,' Laurence said, 'then Shaw had no reason to kill Alan Hobbes. For one thing, he would surely have disconnected the camera before committing the theft. But more importantly, by the time Hobbes was killed, the book was *already in his possession*. There would have been no need for him to murder Hobbes for it.'

'Assuming the book was the motive.'

'Which, as I said, is what we're doing for the purposes of this exercise.'

'No, I see a question mark next to motive.'

Laurence used the cloth to rub it away.

'That's better,' he said. 'Thank you. The book is now the motive for the killing. Ta-da. But not the motive for Christopher Shaw. For someone else.'

'Who?'

'I don't know.'

'Brilliant. Shall we call him "Edward"?'

'Not necessarily. But whoever murdered Hobbes, perhaps he arrived at the property *after* Christopher Shaw had already left. He discovered the book was missing, and then tortured Alan Hobbes in the hope of obtaining it. But, of course, Hobbes would not have known where it was because in the footage he appears to have been asleep when the book was stolen.'

'Which leaves us nowhere,' Pettifer said.

Laurence shrugged. 'If that is where we are, then it is better for us to know,' he said. 'And nothing is wasted. All the people we have spoken to needed to be investigated. And it still remains imperative for us to find Christopher Shaw. If any of this is right, then he is in possession of something people are prepared to kill for.'

'However ridiculous *we* might find the idea.'

'Exactly.'

Pettifer sighed again. Thought for a moment. 'Maybe Theo can help?'

Laurence considered that and then nodded. Detective Theo Rowan and his team worked in a small room in the basement of the department, spending their days trawling through the darkest corners of the internet. The people who might want to buy and sell Jack Lock's book were most likely to be found there.

'Better for you to do that, though,' he said. 'I don't think Theo likes me.'

'He doesn't like men very much in general. Nature of his work.'

'Indeed.'

'OK,' Pettifer said. 'I'll go and talk to him.'

'Make sure you stalk around *furiously* on your way down there.'

'Absolutely. Totally on it.'

After she left the office, Laurence sat down at his desk. But instead of turning to the computer he found himself staring again at the list on the board.

There were things missing.

The *house*, for example.

It continued to bother him. Even taking into account his charitable donations, Alan Hobbes had spent much of his life a multimillionaire. He had been a man with the means to live anywhere he chose – and yet he had spent the last thirty years in a dilapidated property far too large for his needs. He had never remarried. Aside from his teaching and his interactions with staff at the house, he appeared to have lived a hermitic existence. And even there, Laurence thought, the presence of staff would not have been required for the upkeep of a smaller property more suited to the size of the man's life.

So why?

With his elbows on the desk, Laurence closed his eyes and steepled his fingers against his temples.

His thoughts turned to the man's dead child. Joshua Charles Hobbes had been less than a year old when he died. Laurence had no children of his own, but he could imagine the depth of such a loss. He also understood – and there was no way of avoiding this – that Hobbes's grief over his son's death must have been compounded by the circumstances of his wife's.

Which made him think of his own father.

After Laurence was old enough to understand the truth, there had been times when he had blamed himself for his mother's death. He would look at the single photograph of her his father had brought with them – a pretty woman, caught forever in the bright light of youth – and, in his head, he would speak to the image of her.

I am sorry, he would say.

It was my fault.

I should not exist.

But his father had sensed that impulse within him and leashed it tightly, an animal that would not be allowed to roam loose in their house. And his father would speak to him too. *You have nothing to be sorry for*, he would say. *It is not your fault. You are a blessing, and every time I look at you I see her too.* And while the man only had a single photograph of his wife, Laurence understood that his father had come to this country carrying not just grief for her in his heart but also a part of her in his arms.

Every man was different, of course, but Laurence believed that Alan Hobbes had been a similar man to his father. The truth of that was etched on the child's headstone. Lost in his pain and grief, Hobbes had gifted a variation of his wife Charlotte's name to his son as a middle name.

But then the boy had died too.

In the face of such loss Laurence could imagine most men would wish to escape the scene of their trauma rather than be confronted with it every day. And yet not only had Hobbes remained in the house, but the injury to the property had never been repaired. Those were *choices* that had been made deliberately. They implied that Hobbes had felt tethered to the house for some reason and been reluctant to move on.

But why?

Guilt of some kind perhaps. Living there seemed a form of self-flagellation. As though Hobbes had blamed himself for everything that had happened and been determined to serve the sentence that warranted. Right up until the end.

How did Hobbes's apparent obsession with Jack Lock fit into that? The man seemed to have made a concerted effort to collect everything associated with the Angel Maker, gathering it together in a collection he had then kept in what had once been his dead son's bedroom. Why would he –

Laurence opened his eyes.

For a few seconds he sat very still.

It couldn't be that simple, could it? He would be forced to kick himself if so – or have Pettifer do it for him, he supposed, which would obviously be worse. He turned to his computer and set to work. The information was easier to locate than he expected and he had the report onscreen within minutes. The details were not specific, but there was enough information for him to read between the lines. And even if he did not quite understand it yet, he sensed it was as important as any of the other pieces of the puzzle he and Pettifer had assembled so far.

Alan Hobbes had owned the house for more than forty years. In the years leading up to his purchase, there had been a lengthy period in which the property had been empty and derelict. Potential buyers shied away. Investors made offers and then retracted them. Until Alan Hobbes came along, in fact, everyone involved with the property had seemed content to let it moulder away quietly, empty and forgotten.

Because two decades before Hobbes bought the house, its grounds were where the remains of four dead girls had been found, buried beneath the flower beds.

24

Leland picked up a pair of pruning shears from the bench in front of him.

When he clenched his hand to test the spring, the blades whispered against each other, as though the tool were sharpening itself. Rain pattered quietly on the greenhouse roof above him. The garden beyond the glass wall ahead of him was smeared and grey. But it was warm and dry in here, and there was a hum to the air.

A tray of roses rested on the bench before him.

He reached in and gripped a stem with a gloved hand, and then leaned down and snipped one of the petioles carefully away. It fell softly on to the tray of soil below, taking its cluster of leaves and malformed bud along with it. Leland picked up the clipping and tossed it into the bin beside the bench.

There were two roses in the tray, and both were exquisite. The reds were rich and vivid, with thin veins of blackness reaching out through the petals. The quality of the flowers was testament not only to his own skill and care but also to the quality of the soil they had been grown in.

And as he stared down at the flowers, Leland remembered helping his father make an angel.

It is 19 October 1954.

'How far is it?' the little girl says.

She is walking behind Edward. He glances back at her – but really he is looking past her. He is relieved that the road is out of sight now. But the field here is exposed; there is still a danger they might be seen, and his heart is beating hard. When he looks forward again, he sees the treeline in the distance. The approaching winter has stripped the branches of their leaves high above, and they stand out like thin black bones against the empty sky above.

A cold breeze is stirring the overgrown grass.

He picks up his pace.

'It's a little way in,' he says. 'I need to remember the way.'

That isn't true; the route he has to take is burned into his mind, as clear to him as all the other paths he must follow. And even though the treeline remains a little way off yet, he reminds himself that they will not be seen.

That is not what happens.

Because his father told him he would not be seen, and everything else he said has come to pass. The little girl was playing alone on the road exactly where Edward was told she would be. She was nervous when he approached her. There was a cat in the woods, Edward was to explain. It was caught in barbed wire, and he needed her help to free it.

Not a dog? he had suggested.

His father had smiled. *With this little girl it needs to be a cat. A black-and-white one.*

And, true enough, Edward had seen the doubt fall away from her face as he explained. He had watched it being replaced by hope. It was exactly what she had needed to hear to be persuaded to follow him.

Because his father knows everything.

They reach the treeline.

Edward moves more cautiously now, working his way carefully between the trees. The web of branches around him is sharp, the ground uneven. The world falls silent aside from the wet push of their shoes in the mulch of fallen leaves, and the air smells of earth and rot. It has been dismal all morning, but it seems to grow ever darker as they move deeper into the wood.

They are out of sight now, but his heart is beating harder than ever. There is a tingle of electricity running over his body.

They walk for a minute. He can hear her breathing behind him.

Then:

A *click* in the undergrowth off to one side.

'What was that?'

Edward looks back at the girl. She has stopped and is staring between the trees. Even more than back at the road, he notices how little she is. And also – now – how frightened. It is wild and dark here, and the expression on her face is like she has found herself in one of the fairy tales she probably reads in her bedroom at home. At the sight of that fear Edward feels a flicker of something inside himself. Some primal sense of pity. There is even a moment when he feels an urge to lead her out of here – take her all the way back to the safety of her village down the road, and then run as far and fast as he can.

Your faith is being tested.

And as soon as the thought comes, Edward recognizes the feeling for what it is. His father has warned him about moments like this. The path they have been tasked with following is a hard one, and there are times when he will need to be strong. The tingle of electricity he is feeling, the fast beating of his heart – these things are best thought of not as nerves but as the gentle touch of God, pleased that His word is being carried out as it has been written. That His children are doing what their Father intends.

And to do otherwise would be blasphemy.

Edward walks back to the little girl. 'It's nothing,' he says quietly. 'It's just the wood making sounds.'

'I'm scared.'

'Me too. I can take you back if you want. But I don't think I can save the cat on my own.'

She stares at him for a few seconds. She's still frightened, but he can tell she's weighing the fear against the desire to save the helpless creature she imagines awaits them. He can almost picture a set of scales in his head, and he feels that tingle on his skin again as he realizes he already knows which way they will fall.

'It's not far,' he says.

And without looking back, he turns and walks further into the wood.

A minute later, he hears something ahead. It sounds a little like someone crying, but it is too continuous for that, and he recognizes it as the quiet rush of water. They have arrived at the stream. He reaches out to the branches before him, and then holds them to one side to allow the girl to follow him into the small clearing.

The stream is a metre-wide string of shallow water rushing past, whispering against the sharp rocks at its edges. The clearing, such as it is, is surrounded by trees that press in on all sides. The trunks are thin and black, with countless white branches hanging down like ribbons.

Edward turns. The little girl has stepped to one side, her back to the trees. She is hugging herself and looking around in confusion.

'Where is he?' the little girl says.

For a moment everything is still. The only sound is the rush of the stream.

Then the tree directly behind the little girl moves.

'Here.'

And Edward's father steps forward, dressed in his black suit, his long white fingers splayed wide.

Six decades had passed since that day, but Leland still remembered it clearly.

Along with the night that followed. How *special* he had felt, sitting out behind the house in the darkness with his father. A lamp rested on the ground, illuminating his father's bright spidery hands as they worked over the earth, patting down the soil. They were the only visible part of him, the rest of him lost in the blackness of the night, but the murmur of his voice filled the air: a constant stream of language that was close to prayer, and which Leland could not quite decipher but found himself hypnotized by.

His father had reached back in the darkness. To one of the older graves.

When his hand returned to the light, it was holding a flower.

Standing in the greenhouse now, Leland looked down at the tray of roses. The lesson his father had taught him that night remained with him. It is not for us to question

God's will; however hard it is, we must simply do what our Father dictates. We must trust that He knows best, and that beauty will stem from the actions that have been set for us.

And so the roses before him now were exquisite not solely because of his care and attention, but because of the soil in which they had grown. The soil that had been drawn from his own garden, and nourished in turn by the angels that lay beneath.

A tap at the glass.

Leland looked up. A moment later, Banyard opened the door and stepped in out of the rain.

'The lawyer is here,' he said.

'He has the money?'

'He does.'

'Thank you. Tell him I'll be in shortly.'

Once Banyard had left, Leland picked up the shears again. He looked between the roses, trying to decide which was the most beautiful – which was the most appropriate for the meeting he had arranged with Christopher Shaw to acquire his father's book. Because he had waited so long for this moment. To receive His wisdom again after all these years.

And to put right what his brother had done.

Finally he clipped one rose off halfway up the stem.

And, feeling that tingle on his skin, he pushed it carefully into the lapel of his black suit.

25

Chris and James had spent most of the day in the tent. Much of it resting – or at least trying to. The rain had been torrential during the night, battering the canvas so incessantly that it had felt like being under attack. Even in the sleeping bag, with the warmth of James beside him, Chris had found himself shivering from the force of it, never quite able to fall properly asleep. He had spent a lot of time staring at the raindrops on the outside of the tent, some of them clinging stubbornly to the taut material, others trickling down it like tears.

It reminded him of Alan's house – the room with the broken-down wall and roof. Whenever it rained, the water spattered down in there.

Why don't you have it repaired? he'd asked once.

Alan had smiled sadly. *Because some things can't just be fixed like that.*

Dawn had brought a gloomy grey light only barely distinguishable from the night just gone. The side of his thin pillow was soaked through and cold, but Chris had hugged it anyway. There was nothing worth getting up for right then. Better to remain in a state of suspended animation as much as possible. To attempt to ignore the bursts of wind that still shook the tent, and the endless rattle of rain against it.

By the middle of the afternoon the weather had cleared a little.

But, God, he was still so *tired*.

He unzipped the front of the tent, crawled out into the dismal daylight, and then blinked as he looked around.

Along with so many others, they were camped on a vast square of tarmac, enclosed on all sides by abandoned office blocks from which black, broken windows stared sightlessly down. This had been a car park once, he remembered, and the buildings surrounding it had been bright and full of life. But now the offices were empty – the workers having long ago moved on to new, brighter premises – and what had once been a parking area for cars had been colonized as one for human beings instead.

A sea of tents stretched out around him, with webs of guy ropes criss-crossing the narrow pathways leading between them. The colours of the tarpaulins were drab and all but uniform in the weak light. He registered a few figures. Some were standing and stretching out their backs at the side of their improvised homes. Others were sitting half outside their drenched tents. A few were moving about, wrapped up in waterproof coats like fishermen. Here and there steam rose from boiling kettles. Everyone was frozen and bedraggled. But they were carrying on.

That was what people did, after all.

Chris stood up and stretched out his own back. Then he heard a rustle behind him and twisted at the waist. James, equally groggy, was emerging from the tent.

'Throw me my coat?' Chris said.

'What for?'

'Because it's cold.' He looked ahead again. 'And I'm going to the shop.'

There was a takeaway café a couple of streets away. Coffee available from the counter; rows of cheap sandwiches wrapped in cellophane in a lonely fridge humming against one wall. The bell rang as Chris walked in. It was nobody's idea of a fancy place, and yet he immediately felt the guy behind the counter's gaze following him, the expression on his face a familiar one.

Because even just one night on the streets was enough to mark you out.

This is all you'll ever be.

Chris did his best to shut the voice down. It wasn't true. After finding the note from Katie in the art studio, he had decided it wasn't safe for him and James to stay there any more. If she could find them there, then someone else might. The tent was only a temporary refuge, though. This was not his life again. If everything went to plan tonight, he and James would have enough money to stay wherever they liked from now on.

Why was Katie looking for him?

That made no sense, and the question nagged at him. Whenever he thought of his sister, there was a sense of shame so deep it was almost fathomless – a terrible and hollow emptiness that he could fall into for ever. When they'd seen the message she'd left, James had suggested calling her, but that was impossible for Chris to contemplate. Even the thought of doing it had caused a visceral reaction inside him. All his life he had been a failure. He had let people down at every turn. If there was ever a hope of reconnecting with Katie – *and there isn't*, he reminded himself; *there absolutely isn't* – then it could never begin like this, with him begging her for help the way he had always needed to.

Even so, he had stared at the message for a long time. *I love you.*

Written out of duty, of course. Or worse, out of pity. He refused to allow himself to believe she could possibly mean it – and if she did, she shouldn't.

Not after everything he had done.

He picked up a couple of sandwiches and took them over to the counter.

'A black coffee as well, please,' he said. 'Large.'

The man just stared at him, waiting. Chris fought down the anger inside him. He found his wallet, picked out the money required, and put it down on the counter between them.

The man looked at it, then back up at Chris.

'A. Black. Coffee,' Chris repeated slowly. 'Large.'

James was sitting in the entrance of the tent when he got back, wrapped up in his coat and hugging his knees. Chris handed him one of the sandwiches and the coffee.

'Here you go,' he said.

'Thanks.'

James shuffled over to make space for Chris to sit beside him, and then they both ate in silence, occasionally passing the coffee back and forth between them.

'Now what?' James said.

Chris screwed up the empty sandwich packet. There wasn't much they could do yet, but it felt important to take charge. James's spirits were down, which meant his needed to be up – that was one of the secrets to making a relationship work. They were like see-saws that way.

'Now,' he said, 'we get ready.'

Most of the belongings they'd brought with them had remained packed away in their waterproof rucksacks, but it still took them half an hour or so, either through lethargy or out of some desire they both had to keep themselves occupied. If you were busy, you didn't have to think.

Outside, he started removing the poles from the canvas.

'The tent too?' James said.

'Yeah.'

'What about tonight?'

'We're not going to need it any more, are we?'

James didn't reply.

As they worked, Chris noticed how nervous James was. Not just nervous but *frightened* – scared for both of them, but especially for Chris. The arrangements for tonight were simple. Chris would be meeting the buyer alone. James would be waiting nearby with the book, close enough to bring it if Chris decided he trusted the man. It was better for them not to be together if things went wrong. After all, it was the book the man wanted. That would give them control over the situation.

A little extra leverage.

James didn't like the idea, and Chris hadn't expected him to. If the situation had been reversed, he would have felt the same. But for him it was non-negotiable. It was he who had taken the book in the first place – he who had got them into this – and so he would get them out. Which wasn't to say he wasn't nervous himself. His chest was growing tighter the whole time they worked. But he was doing his best to ignore it.

James said something.

'What?' Chris said.

'We don't have to do this.'

'We don't really have any choice.'

'Of *course* we have a choice.'

'We'll be fine,' Chris said. 'I promise. And, who knows, after tonight, maybe we'll even be able to afford a coffee each from now on.'

That got him half a smile at least.

'Let's never go that far,' James said.

'All right. Deal.'

Chris continued collapsing the tent. Because they *wouldn't* need it again. Everything was going to be fine.

But even so, James's mention of choice made him think about Alan Hobbes.

All the steps are there at once. Beginning, middle and end – they're all the same.

All the conversations he'd had with the old man came back to him then. Cause and effect. Fate and destiny. And, as he carried on packing, Chris couldn't quite shake the sensation that there were cogs turning below the surface of the world. That events had been set in motion and were now continuing along inevitable paths that had been there all along.

And that however much he tried to reassure them both, he had no real control at all over what would happen next.

26

It's not my story to tell.

Even in the face of Katie's obvious frustration, her mother refused to tell her more about whatever relationship Nathaniel Leland had to their family.

You need to find your brother. And ask him.

As she left the house, Katie wondered bitterly if she was simply being manipulated into continuing the search for Chris – but the emotion on her mother's face had been too genuine for that. Whatever the story behind the newspaper clipping, it clearly upset her in some way. And, regardless, the reality was that she *did* need to find Chris. She needed to understand what had happened to him, and what was happening to her family now.

Back in the car, she rubbed some life into her face and gathered her resolve. Then she set off. She drove to James Alderson's studio first, but it turned out that her luck had run out there. The front door was locked, and when she tried the bell for number six there was no reply. If Chris was inside, he wasn't answering. And if he had returned since she came yesterday and seen her message, he had obviously decided not to call her. Which broke her heart again.

She drove across the city, past the prison on the hill, and parked up on the main road outside Chris's flat. Late afternoon on a Saturday, the street was busier than it had been on her previous visit, and most of the shops were open now, including the estate agent and carpet shop on either side of her brother's front door. She let herself in quietly – locking the door behind her this time – and then searched the flat again. Everything appeared to be the same as she had left it, but there was a sadness to the air now, and the place felt even more abandoned than before, the sense of it being a home like a light growing steadily dimmer. She worked methodically through each of the rooms again but found nothing. Whatever secrets the flat held, it had already given them up.

Where are you, Chris?

She picked up the dice and rolled it across the top of the shelf.

A blank face, the number long since worn away.

She went back downstairs and locked the door, and then sat in her car for a while, trying to think. Trying to work her way through the little she knew as carefully as she'd just searched the flat above her.

Two years ago, her brother had effectively vanished off the face of the earth. At that point he had been an addict and a lost cause. But then he had come back – sober, in what appeared to be a loving relationship, working in some capacity, and building a home and a life for himself here.

It was properly him, she remembered her mother saying. *Like he was* meant *to be.*

Except that a couple of weeks ago something had scared Chris badly enough for him to drop everything and run. He had been being watched and followed, and so it seemed reasonable to assume he had been frightened of *someone*. What she didn't know was who. Was it connected to the work he'd been doing? Someone from his days on the streets? Or did the answer somehow lie even further back in his past?

And, of course, it wasn't just about Chris any more.

Katie looked around the street, remembering being followed back from here two nights ago. There had been the car parked outside Siena's nursery that day. And there had been the intruder in the garden last night, watching her through the kitchen window and then trying the door handle. Any one of those things by itself she might have put down to coincidence – but not all three. Yes, she worried too much. But whatever Sam might think, she wasn't imagining the danger her family was in. The question was whether it was connected to what was happening to Chris.

She kept turning it all around in her head, attempting to make the pieces fit together, if only by accident, the same way her mother had been working on her jigsaw. But it was impossible to make any of them click into place. The harder she thought about everything, the more it all seemed to drift apart.

What the fuck have you got us all mixed up in this time, Chris?

She couldn't think of anywhere else to go to search for her brother and despondency settled on her. Perhaps it was best just to go home. It was late in the day now – in every sense – but if she told Sam *everything* that had happened, then maybe he would believe she wasn't over-reacting. She didn't see what else she could do.

And she was about to do just that when she glanced up at the rear-view mirror and saw the old red car rolling slowly along the high street behind her.

With Michael Hyde at the wheel.

27

Pettifer returned with two coffees but no news.

'I have spent over an hour in the dark room,' she said, 'and I have nothing to show for it beyond a desire to shower.'

The dark room was the department's unofficial nickname for Theo Rowan's office. It was called that in part because of its basement location, but mostly because of the kind of crimes that were dealt with in there. Child abuse; human trafficking; sadistic pornography. Laurence found it hard to imagine delving into that kind of filth day in and day out. While his own work certainly involved its share of horrors, the things Theo and his team investigated seemed to stem from a particularly dark and baffling level of hell.

'Nothing?'

Pettifer started to respond but then stared at the whiteboard and caught herself. In her absence, following his discovery about the provenance of Alan Hobbes's house, Laurence had added a great many more notes about Jack Lock. A photograph of the man had been printed and tacked up.

'What the hell have you done now?' Pettifer said.

'I'll explain in a minute. Theo first – or rather, second.' He reached out his hand. 'Because I appreciate the coffee a great deal.'

'Yeah, you're welcome.'

She handed the cup to him and then sat down and ran through the little that she had learned from Theo. Murderabilia. That was a new one for him – an ugly word for an ugly reality: people buying and selling drawings by serial killers, bricks from crime scenes, items that had once belonged to victims. Everyone involved had their own particular fetish or specialist subject. Theo had told Pettifer he knew a man online who traded exclusively in Third Reich crockery.

'I mean, why would anyone do that?' Pettifer said.

'The same reason people slow down when they're driving past an accident,' Laurence said. 'An interest in death. A desire to touch evil from a safe distance, where it can't touch them back.'

He glanced at the board. 'And with *Jack Lock*,' he said, 'perhaps there is also additional interest because of his supposed ability to see the future.'

'Yeah, maybe. But with Lock it's also the scarcity of it. If you're batshit crazy enough to want to collect cuttings of a serial killer's hair, then there might be a steady supply of that, right? So it's not worth the same. But things associated with Lock like pieces of his writing are one-offs. Theo reckoned they'd be likely to go for a lot more on the black market. Plus, they're just harder to come by.'

Pettifer told him that Theo had trawled through the regular websites and some of the shadier ones without finding a single mention of Jack Lock. It seemed that Hobbes had not been into trading – that he had quietly gathered his collection together over the years and then kept it to himself.

But that situation had changed with his death.

Laurence frowned to himself. If Christopher Shaw had taken the book in order to sell it, then he would need a market in which to do so, and he could hardly advertise in the small ads of the local paper. And if not, why had he taken it at all? It was confounding.

'Theo's going to keep an eye out for us,' Pettifer said.

'But in the meantime we're no further forward.'

'No.' She looked at the board again. 'Unless you've got something?'

'Huh.'

He explained what he'd discovered about the house.

'Huh indeed,' Pettifer said. 'All that tells us is what we already knew. Despite his wholesome appearance, Hobbes was a pretty sick man with an absolutely raging hard-on for all things Jack Lock.'

'Yes. For some reason.'

Laurence considered that. What lay behind Hobbes's fascination with this *particular* serial killer? A straightforward local connection was possible, of course, but he wondered if there was more to it than that. The internet page he'd printed Jack Lock's photograph from was still open in one of the tabs, and he turned to that now, scrolling down and scanning the information there.

And then stopped.

'There were two children there,' he said.

'What?'

'After Lock was arrested and police arrived at the house.' He tapped the screen. 'This account says two children were found alive inside – presumed to be his sons. They were taken into care and adopted, but the details were sealed to protect their identities.'

He did the maths in his head.

'Alan Hobbes would be about the right age to be one of them.'

Pettifer was silent for a moment, considering it.

'So would many people,' she said. 'But even if it's true, how does it help us? All it would tell us is *why* he might have had this lifelong interest in Lock.'

'Everything is connected below the surface.'

'No, it isn't,' she said. 'The house. Jack Lock. The fire. They're all distractions. What we need to focus on right now is finding Christopher Shaw.' She turned to her own computer.

But Laurence continued to stare at his screen. Pettifer was right that Shaw was their priority and that finding him remained key, but the *distractions* she had mentioned continued to occupy him. If Hobbes had been one of the boys found there, who was the other? Why had Hobbes been drawn back to such an awful place as an adult? And, most confusing of all, why had he stayed there after a fire at the property had killed the person he had loved most in his life?

The fire.

Laurence hesitated. Gaunt had told him the fire had been ruled an accident – an electrical fault, if he remembered correctly – but it occurred to him now that he had taken that detail from the lawyer at face value. Perhaps it wouldn't hurt to delve a little deeper. He had been exaggerating before when he said that *everything* was connected below the surface, but it remained true that many things were.

It took him a minute to pull up the file on screen.

The investigation was an old one, which meant the paperwork from the time had been scanned and added to the system at a later date. Laurence swiftly discovered that whoever had done so had been less than thorough. There were several documents missing. In reality, the blame for that probably lay with some bored, underpaid intern doing slapdash work, but he found it difficult not to imagine more nefarious explanations. Hobbes had been a rich man, after all. Money pulled levers.

For some reason that made him uneasy.

Still, there was enough detail in the file to be getting along with. The post-mortem on the boy's charred body concluded that he had died from smoke inhalation without waking. One small mercy, Laurence supposed, in a tale lacking many. Other conclusions appeared far less clear. For example, he found nothing whatsoever to justify the final ruling of the fire being the result of a wiring fault.

Hobbes had been interviewed, and his account was included in the file. Laurence read it through carefully and found it oddly moving. The language was formal and precise, which had the strange effect of making the grief even more apparent, as though he were reading the words of a man struggling hard to hold himself together in the face of impossible heartbreak.

There were several additional documents, including a list of people who had been interviewed at the time. Laurence was about to begin working through those when Pettifer exclaimed behind him.

'Hell's fucking teeth!'

He turned quickly in his chair. 'What?'

'This.' She gestured at her screen. 'Neither hand knows what the other is doing. I've just had a report sent through. Katie Shaw. That would be Christopher Shaw's sister, right?'

'The name is right.'

'She reported a prowler outside her house last night.' Pettifer read the details off the screen. 'Officers attended the scene and found nobody present. Case recorded. No further action at this time. For fuck's sake!'

Laurence was inclined to agree. 'Do we have her number?'

'We do. Somewhere.'

As Pettifer began searching through her notes, Laurence turned back to his screen. Anxious now. He didn't know what this new development meant yet, but it seemed likely that whoever had murdered Alan Hobbes was now searching for Christopher Shaw, and his family would be an obvious place for them to start. And while they might not know who that was yet, they did know the kind of violence that person was capable of.

But for now he looked back at the file on the fire at Alan Hobbes's property. The next document was an interview with a local man.

Laurence clicked it open.

Stared for a moment.

Then spoke quietly.

'Hell's fucking teeth.'

'I copyrighted that,' Pettifer said. 'You owe me money now. What is it?'

Laurence didn't reply. Instead, he quickly scanned the contents of the document. In the early stages of the investigation, a young man had been looked at as a possible suspect who might have started the fire that killed the child. The suspect had been seen close to the property on several occasions prior to the incident, and already had – among other things – arrests on his record for housebreaking and arson. His involvement had been dismissed relatively quickly, and as far as Laurence could tell without any obvious justification at all.

He scrolled back up and read the name again.

Everything is connected below the surface.

'Michael Hyde,' he said.

28

Katie forced herself not to stare at Michael Hyde as he drove towards her.

Instead, she looked down at the steering wheel and rubbed her jaw, trying to give the impression that she was lost in thought and not paying attention to her surroundings. She didn't want him to know she'd seen him.

He was driving slowly, keeping pace with the steady flow of traffic. But as he drew level, she could tell he was staring out of the window, as though daring her to look back at him. It took all her strength to keep looking down. But she caught a glimpse of him turned in her direction, and even out of the corner of her eye she could tell there was something wrong with his face. One of his eyes seemed smaller and blacker than the other.

The skin on the side of her cheek began crawling.

She counted slowly to five before risking looking up.

Hyde had kept driving. Ahead of her, she saw his rusted red car amid the traffic, and watched as it disappeared round a bend in the high street.

She sat there with her heart beating hard and the quiet of the car ringing in her ears. Her skin was still itching. Suddenly, without realizing she was doing it, she found herself rubbing furiously at her cheek, as though attempting to scrub away some kind of filth his gaze had left.

Oh God.

It had been Hyde outside her daughter's nursery. It had to have been.

His face at her kitchen window last night.

He who had followed her – and still was.

As she continued staring at the road ahead, she started to shiver. She had been trying to work out what connection there might be between Chris's disappearance and what was happening to her family, and surely she had just found it. The realization sent a cold spread of fear through her. Sam already thought she was overreacting. If she tried to explain that she thought Michael Hyde was stalking their family, he was only going to be even more certain she was seeing ghosts and jumping at shadows.

You're always scared that something terrible is going to happen.

But she wasn't imagining any of this.

Chris had gone missing. Her family was in danger. And somehow Michael Hyde was involved in it all.

She sat there feeling helpless.

Then:

So . . . what are you going to do, Katie? How are you going to deal with this?

She had no idea. But she just knew she had to do something to keep her family safe – that if she just waited and hoped everything would be all right, then it might not be. Because that was how the world worked. Things came out of nowhere and changed everything, and right now felt like a moment in time she would wish she could come back to and do things differently.

What to do?

Something.

And so, without really thinking about it, Katie started the engine.

She parked up by the corner of Michael Hyde's street.

What exactly are you doing here, Katie?

She had no answer to the question because she hadn't thought that far ahead. What she *had* done was turn round outside her brother's flat and then drive the quickest route here possible, breaking the speed limit along the way whenever it had been safe to do so. So the one thing she *was* certain of was there was no way Hyde could have beaten her back here.

Before she could talk herself out of it, she got out of the car. The slam of the door echoed around the empty street. There was an odd cast to the light, and a chill breeze in the air, and she pulled her jacket round her as she walked towards the end of Hyde's street and turned the corner.

The whole area was run-down, but this street was particularly dilapidated. Many of the properties were boarded up, while the few that appeared still occupied had overgrown gardens strewn with litter and children's toys blanched pale by the sun. Hyde's house was about halfway down. When she reached it, she saw the front door was flimsy and that old graffiti stained the brickwork in places. The mortar had crumbled away beneath the grey windows, creating the illusion of tears.

A narrow driveway led along the side of the house. After one last look around, she headed down it. Round the back, she found an old door, the white paint peeling off the wood in jagged vertical strips.

Are you really going to do this, Katie?

Yes. She had to find out what was happening.

With her heart beating hard she reached out and tried the door handle. It turned easily, and the door opened inwards with a gentle creak. She stepped quickly inside and then stood very still for a moment, listening.

Silence.

She was in a narrow kitchen, dim light filtering in through a single small window beside her. Her gaze moved slowly over the old cabinets on the wall, some of them missing their doors, revealing rows of cans. The counter below was cluttered with dirty plates and empty bottles. The only clear spaces were the hob, crusted with burnt, blackened food, and the sink, where more plates stuck up like pale fins from the grey water. A couple of flies were buzzing mindlessly round.

Her shoes squeaked on the greasy tiles as she moved over to the doorway at the far end of the kitchen. It opened on to a gloomy hallway. Stairs led up to the right, while ahead of her was a living room of sorts, dust hanging in the air. There was a settee and arm-chair that appeared decades old, faded floral curtains, and a portable television resting on a wooden packing crate. Breathing in, she could smell a sweet and sickly odour, like the stink of old wine coming out of a drunk man's skin.

Hurry up, Katie.

Whatever you're looking for, find it quickly.

She moved back into the hallway and headed quietly up the steep, narrow stairs. There were three doors on the landing up here. One was open to a small, grimy bathroom. Another was partially ajar, and through the gap she could see the base of a bed. The sweet smell was stronger there, and bad enough now to make her cover her mouth and take a step back. She turned to the third door instead. It was covered with small colourful stickers, the kind that come free with comics.

A child's bedroom perhaps.

Hyde didn't have children. But looking more closely, she realized the stickers were very old and had probably been on the door for years.

She turned the handle and slowly pushed the door open.

Pitch-black inside. Her hand moved over the wall to her left, searching for a light switch, eventually finding one lower down than felt natural. When she pressed it, the room in front of her burst suddenly into life.

Katie gasped. For a second she didn't understand exactly what she was looking at, only that her mind had immediately registered that whatever she was seeing was profoundly *wrong*. Against the wall to her left, there was a single bed, with a stained pillow at one end and a tangle of covers scrunched up at the other. Tucked in between the base of that and the far wall was a small desk, with a printer on the floor beneath it and a laptop on the surface, closed but humming quietly.

But it was the wall directly opposite that captured her attention.

She stepped across, the floorboards creaking as she approached it, and then tried to make sense of what she was seeing. Hyde had tacked perhaps thirty photographs to the plaster in neat rows and columns. To the right of those he had taped up what appeared to be notes and crude drawings done with felt-tip pens.

And when Katie looked at the photographs more

closely, something tilted inside her. So much so that it felt like the whole house was in danger of toppling over. She had thought that Hyde was stalking her brother, but there was no sign of him on the wall here at all.

But she and Sam were here.

And, most of all, Siena was.

Her gaze moved over the photos, her heart beating harder and a sick feeling rising inside her. They all appeared to have been taken covertly, most of them from a distance. Here were the three of them in a supermarket. Siena was standing between her and Sam, looking back over her shoulder with a curious expression on her face as she made eye contact with the camera.

Their kitchen window. Siena was sitting in her high chair wearing a bib stained with juice, while Katie held a spoon in front of her mouth.

Sam sitting on a bench in the park with his headphones on and his eyes closed, Siena playing in the sandpit in front of him.

Siena's bedroom window at night, her daughter a black shape behind the glass peering down towards the garden. Katie remembered the pale, misshapen face she'd seen in the red car driving past her at her brother's flat.

Moon came to say hello again.

She tried to swallow but her throat failed her. And as she looked at the pictures and notes tacked up beside the photographs, the sick feeling inside her intensified. They were basic and badly drawn, but she could tell what she was seeing. Lists of dates and times – who was where and when. School start and end times. Sam's gigs.

There were maps of the streets around their house and the nursery and the local places they visited, all of them dotted with arrows and circles.

Parking spots, she realized. One-way systems. Cameras.

Escape routes.

She stared helplessly at the whole, awful lot of it.

A soft creak outside the room.

Katie froze. Her gaze moved from the display on the wall to the single bed against the wall – and then something fell away inside her. Because it had clearly been slept in recently. And yet there was another bedroom up here. The one with the door ajar, the air outside it stinking of old, sour wine.

Faltering footsteps now out on the landing.

'Michael?'

A man's voice.

'Is that you?'

Cold panic washed through her. She looked quickly around the room, but there was nowhere obvious to hide. The best she could do was step over behind the open door and press her back to the wall there. A second later, a figure moved into the doorway. The stench coming off him was terrible.

She held herself still. The voice had sounded tentative and wavering. An old man – Hyde's father perhaps. She braced herself for him to come all the way into the room, but he remained on the threshold, just inches away from her. Her heart was beating so hard now that it seemed impossible he couldn't hear it.

And yet he just stood there, breathing shallowly.

The photographs and drawings were right there in

full view, on the wall in front of him. He must have been able to see the family his son was stalking – *her family* – and the plans he had been making. But as Katie listened to the old man breathing beside her, she realized he didn't seem shocked or appalled. He didn't even seem surprised.

A moment later, he turned off the light.

Then he closed the door, and the room was pitch black. Katie heard those same faltering footsteps moving slowly away on the landing. A few seconds later, she was alone again, standing in the darkness, the silence broken only by the quiet hum of the laptop and the thudding of her heart. And then by a sudden blast of music.

She looked around the darkness frantically, not understanding what was happening – and then panic flared as the volume of the music grew even louder, and she felt the vibrations against her chest from her jacket pocket.

Her phone was ringing.

29

Dusk.

When Chris was living out on the street, it had occurred to him that existence was divided into two.

There was the daytime world: the one in which the normal people moved about, living their lives according to schedules. They woke, showered and kissed their partners goodbye; they went to their places of work and then trudged home afterwards.

But then, as the day died, the night-time world took over. The *other* people came out, reclaiming and repurposing the city's streets and spaces. He thought of it like a map being turned over. You might still be able to see an impression of the roads and landmarks through the paper, but the more precise geography of the city disappeared. There was potential there to sketch your own designs and begin to make the map your own.

Those two worlds blurred into each other twice a day. Dawn had its pleasures, of course. There had been times sleeping rough when he had watched the first pink thatches of cloud glowing above the jagged black tops of the buildings, and there was even an odd sort of magic in saluting the first buses as they appeared. But dusk had always suited him best. The bright lights of the shops and offices flicking off. The darkness settling down. The drop in temperature, as though the world was falling asleep without a blanket and had begun shivering slightly.

All of that had appealed to him more. He wasn't sure why.

Maybe it was just that he had always felt more like a night-time person.

But as he sat in the café now, the day dying outside the window, his nerves were singing. It felt like a world was arriving in which he no longer quite belonged. The apprehension he'd felt while packing away the tent earlier was stronger now, and it was taking all his resolve not to walk out of here without looking back.

Because he couldn't do that. For one thing, it didn't feel like there were many other courses of action open to him. This was something he had to do; he and James had no choice. And, for another, the phrasing itself didn't work. *Not looking back* might be a luxury available to some, but it had never felt like an option for Chris. People like him always had to keep looking around them.

He checked his phone. Five minutes until the man was due. No messages from James.

He put the phone away, then looked out past the pale reflection beside him in the glass. The pavement and road outside were illuminated intermittently by the faltering street lights. He wondered if, from across the street, the café window might look a little like that painting, *Nighthawks*, by Hopper – but then again, perhaps not. There was some kind of romance there, whereas there was none to be found here.

The café was one of the few properties still open on this street, and he suspected it wouldn't be for very much longer. It was little more than a harshly lit rectangular room full of folding tables. A rudimentary counter at the side. Back in the day, Chris remembered this place had attracted its fair share of night-time people, and that was why he had suggested it for the meeting. In his memory it was *safe*. But now that he was here, it appeared even the addicts had abandoned this place, and it no longer felt quite so safe.

He was the only customer.

But not the only person. In the reflection Chris could see the owner behind the counter. He was in his sixties, with a shaved head and built like a bull. Right now he was drying a cup with a ragged cloth. But he kept looking at Chris, a conflicted expression on his face.

Chris turned and called over. 'Another black coffee, please.'

The man stared back at him for a moment, then nodded and put down the cup and cloth before turning away. Chris heard the rasp of the machine, like something clearing its throat, and a minute later the man brought the cup over and put it down on the table in front of Chris.

'Thank you.'

'You're welcome.' He paused. 'What are you doing in here, kid?'

'Business.'

'Really?'

'Not *that* kind of business,' Chris said. 'You don't need to worry.'

But the man stood there, looking down at him, and his expression remained conflicted. He was clearly uneasy about Chris being here.

He took a deep breath and seemed to be about to say something.

But then he looked over Chris's shoulder as the bell

rang. Chris turned in his seat to see the door opening. A man walked in, moving slowly and awkwardly. He was very old and his legs seemed stiff. The overhead lights gleamed on a skull from which all traces of hair had long since vanished. He was dressed in an immaculate suit with a bright red rose tucked into the lapel, and he was carrying a briefcase.

Chris held his breath.

Because – just for a moment – it might have been Alan Hobbes he was looking at. There was a *familiarity* there. But then he saw the man's face and the sensation evaporated. Despite his eccentricities, Alan had always been kind. But there was nothing resembling kindness in this man's expression. In fact, there was nothing to see there at all.

'Your business?' the man said quietly.

'I think so.'

The old man used his free hand to brush off the shoulders of his suit as though it had been snowing outside. First one side. Then the other.

The owner called across. 'What can I get you, sir?'

The man didn't look up. 'Coffee.'

His voice was as weathered as his body.

'Black.'

The owner nodded and retreated to the counter.

The man walked slowly over to where Chris was sitting and took the seat across from him, his gaze directed down at the table between them.

'So –' Chris began.

But the man held up a hand. 'No. You already have your drink. You will have the courtesy to wait for mine.'

'OK.'

Chris leaned back and waited, the two of them sitting in silence. He found himself staring at the rose in the man's lapel. The red was one of the deepest colours he could remember seeing. Then the owner came across, breaking the spell. He put the man's cup carefully down on the table. As he did so, Chris noticed his hands were trembling.

The old man picked up his coffee and sipped it. It was surely far too hot to drink right now, but if the temperature bothered the man at all then he did not show it.

'So,' Chris said again.

'So indeed.'

The man still had not looked at him. But now he did – although he seemed to gather himself together a little before doing so. When he finally looked up, Chris could feel his gaze moving over his face, taking in every detail, as though the old man was looking for something there.

And whatever it was, he found it.

The blankness of his expression was interrupted by the briefest flash of anger. *Hatred* even. And whatever the reason for it, Chris suddenly thought that he was in trouble. Faced with the coldness seated across from him, he felt like a child again. And while he had taken precautions by not bringing the book itself to the café, they no longer seemed enough. He was out of his depth here. And he was swimming with sharks.

But what choice did he have?

'You have the money?' Chris said.

'Yes.' The old man tapped the briefcase. 'And you have the book?'

'No, but it's somewhere nearby.'

'With your boyfriend?'

248

Chris stared at the old man for a second.

How did he know about James? But then he remembered how he had felt over the past few weeks. The sensation of being watched and followed. The half-glimpsed figure on the street outside their flat.

There was the slightest of smiles on the old man's face now. As though this was a game in which he was several moves ahead of Chris and knew all the ones ahead were about to play out to his benefit.

'Who are you?' Chris said.

'My name isn't important. All that matters is that I am a man of my word.'

With his gaze not leaving Chris's, the old man placed the briefcase on the table between them and unlocked it.

Click click.

And then he opened it.

30

Leland lifted the lid of the briefcase carefully. It opened towards him, so he rotated it on the table to display the contents to Christopher Shaw, and then watched as the boy stared down at what was inside.

The boy was scared, of course, but Leland could tell the sight before him pulled at him regardless. Money had a way of doing that to people. This was more than most would ever see collected in one place, especially someone like Christopher Shaw. And while Leland was sure Shaw had handled countless old banknotes in his grubby lifetime, he doubted he had ever encountered notes like these ones: packed together tightly, pristine and new. Money was supposed to be crumpled and sullied; like power, it was meant to be used. And like power, it grew dirtier with every transaction. But the notes in the suitcase between them now had the innocence of a newborn baby.

But not for long.

'As you can see,' Leland said, 'I am a man of my word.'

Christopher Shaw looked up at him for a second, then back at the money. Leland could imagine the calculations going through the boy's head. Not about what he could do with such an amount – although nobody was immune from that – but about the situation as a whole. The boy was trying to decide if he had misjudged Leland. Despite his obvious nerves, he was wondering if everything was actually going to play out the way he'd hoped. And for a glorious moment Leland could tell the boy believed it might.

But money never stays innocent for long.

As you can see, I am a man of my word.

And Leland had not been speaking to Christopher Shaw.

He glanced over the boy's shoulder. The owner of the café was a man named Jefferson, whom Leland had arranged for Banyard to speak to yesterday. He watched as Jefferson walked slowly out from behind the counter and over to the door.

The key made only the quietest of sounds in the lock.

Leland could also imagine what was going through this man Jefferson's head. In his experience people had the most astonishing ability to rationalize away their faults and failings, a predictable facet of human nature that had served him well in life. Years from now, Jefferson would believe he had detached his future self from what he was doing right now. If he thought of it at all, it would seem like an action performed by another man entirely, a man who by that point was lost in the past and beyond judgement. But the truth was that God, watching us from outside of time, sees everything at once.

Leland closed the briefcase and slid it to the edge of the table – and from there his hand clamped down on Christopher Shaw's wrist. He could tell from the sudden shock on the boy's face that he hadn't expected Leland to be able to move so fast or to be as strong as he was.

Shaw stood up, fighting against his grip.

And Leland stood up with him. Out of the corner of

his eye he could see their reflections in the window beside them, and the sight of them there pleased him.

Why, it almost looked like they were *dancing*.

'What the fuck are you doing?' Shaw said. 'We had a deal!'

'The deal was for the book.'

Shaw was still trying to fight, panicking properly now, but Leland found it easy to restrain him. The boy was pathetically, contemptibly weak. But then he twisted harder, and the rose in Leland's lapel came loose and fell broken to the floor.

'You'll pay for that,' Leland said.

'Help me!'

'I'm sorry, kid.'

Jefferson. He had already picked up the briefcase and was moving over to the wall. Leland stared down at the remains of the rose for a moment, and then up at the reflection of himself and Shaw in the window.

And then Jefferson flicked off the light, and the two dancers vanished.

31

Katie scrabbled in her jacket pocket for the phone.

When she found it, the screen was bright in the darkness of Hyde's bedroom. She didn't recognize the number, but she cancelled the call as fast as she could, then stood there in the blackness, her heart hammering in her chest.

Please don't have heard.

Please –

But he had, of course. She heard the footsteps on the landing again, faster this time, and with more purpose than before. The bedroom door opened quickly, angrily. The old man's shadow fell across the bare floorboards for a second, and then he flicked the light on.

'Who's there?'

There was no point hiding any more. She moved out from behind the door into the centre of the room, turning to face him. Hyde's father was wrapped in a tattered dressing gown and looked even older than he'd sounded, his thin hair hanging limply around a small, mean face. He had planted himself just over the threshold, one wrinkled hand clutching the end of a stick he was leaning on. He peered at her, saying nothing. He seemed no more surprised to find a stranger in his son's room than he had to see the display on the wall behind her. It was as though part of him had expected this to happen at some point, and he was simply trying to work out who it was that had finally arrived.

Then his eyes narrowed slightly. 'You,' he said.

For a second she didn't understand how he could have recognized her. She'd never seen him before in her life. But then she remembered the photographs.

He would have seen her in those, of course.

Me and my family.

Katie took a step towards him. She was much younger than he was, and probably stronger, but he showed no sign of backing away.

She gestured behind her. 'You knew about all of this, didn't you?'

'*You*,' he repeated.

Either he hadn't registered what she'd said, or it meant nothing to him. He took an awkward step towards her, his eyes blazing, and this time it was her who fought the urge to back off.

The old man raised his cane slightly, gesturing at her. 'It's all your fault,' he said. 'Everything.'

'*My* fault?'

'Everything that happened to Michael. He was a good boy. He's always been a good boy. Until he crossed paths with *your fucking family*.'

Hyde's father almost spat the words at her. She didn't know how to reply. It was like when she'd first seen the display. On one level she understood what he was saying to her, but she also couldn't make sense of it.

'Do you know what they did to him in prison? How badly they beat him?'

He took another step towards her. This time she took one back herself.

'I –'

'Don't lie to me, you bitch.' He raised the cane again. 'He never stood a chance, my boy. My *good* boy. All because of your bastard brother. All because of *you*.'

She shook her head. Whatever logic the old man was working from was so far beyond her that she couldn't even begin to respond. Was he really blaming Chris for being in the wrong place at the wrong time? Was he actually suggesting the attack had somehow been *her brother's* fault?

'It's all your fault,' he said. 'You deserve everything that's coming to you.'

And again, she started to reply. But even though what he was saying was absurd, part of her felt the force of his words anyway.

It's all your fault.

All because of you.

'I –'

But whatever she was about to say was interrupted by a sound from downstairs. The front door opening. Hyde's father heard it too, and an expression of triumph flashed across his face.

'Michael!' he shouted. 'Get up here now, boy. It's her!'

And then Hyde's voice calling up from below. 'What?'

'It's *her*!'

Katie panicked as she heard footsteps on the stairs. All she knew was that she had to get out of this room, away from here, away from *everything*, and without thinking she made a move to get past Hyde's father. But the old man reached out fast, grabbing her wrist. She cried out, twisting her arm over his in an attempt to break the hold.

'No, you don't,' he told her.

The footsteps were coming more quickly now. Fear gave her strength. She turned her arm again – and at the same time shoved Hyde's father with her free hand. The grip disappeared as he stumbled backwards, then lost his balance and clattered to the floor in a tangle of bony limbs.

Get out, get out, get out . . .

She ran to the door and out into the hallway.

Michael Hyde had just reached the top of the stairs, and she collided with him, neither of them really aware of the other until it was too late. The force of the impact seemed to knock the panic out of her for a second, so that she registered everything that happened next in slow motion. The shock on Hyde's face as he fell away from her, arms pinwheeling, hands clawing out for purchase but finding none. His body tumbling backwards down the stairs, the bottom of his dirty shoes flying up and over, the sound of the banister ripping loose, and then the repeated *thuds* as his body collided with the stairs and the walls, each one making the whole house shake to its foundation.

The sharp *crack* as his body hit the floor down below.

The sight of him lying there motionless.

Katie stared down at him. For a few seconds everything in the house was as still and silent as Hyde was now.

And then: 'What have you done?'

She looked back helplessly, momentarily lost to shock. Perhaps spurred by the sounds he'd just heard, Hyde's father had managed to drag himself to his feet. He was emerging from the bedroom now, the cane raised properly, his face contorted with rage.

'*What have you done?*'

Without thinking, Katie set off quickly down the stairs, stepping over Hyde's body when she reached the bottom. He wasn't moving. His arm was bent at a hideous angle beneath him; his head was turned to one side, his face against the dirty wooden floor. The eye she could see – smaller and lower down on his face than it should have been – was closed. A small pool of blood was spreading beside his head.

'You've killed him!'

The old man was at the top of the stairs now, screeching down at her.

'You've gone and done it! You were always going to, weren't you? You've finally gone and murdered my boy!'

She stared up at him, blinking stupidly, then looked back down at Hyde. Part of her brain seemed to have stopped working. What had just happened? And then a primal feeling rose up inside her and took control: she needed to get out of here as soon as possible.

She ran through the kitchen towards the back door. Hyde's father's screams faded away behind her as she went, but his words followed her outside into the evening gloom, and then all the way back along the driveway and up the street, the whole world juddering around her as she ran faster and faster and faster.

You were always going to, weren't you?
You've finally gone and murdered my boy.

The car felt safe.

Katie sat there for a few minutes, taking deep breaths.

Her heart was beating too quickly, and her thoughts whirled in her head. It felt like she was going to be sick. It wasn't just the shock of the accident itself – and it *had* been an accident, she kept telling herself – but everything that had happened before it too. The photographs and notes on the wall and what Hyde's father had said to her.

You shouldn't have run, she told herself.

She realized that now. Because it had been an accident. She hadn't *meant* to hurt anyone, and all the evidence she needed to justify being in the house was taped to Hyde's bedroom wall right now.

But it wasn't too late to put things right.

She took her mobile out to call the police.

It rang again just as she did, and she almost dropped it in surprise. The screen showed another unidentified number, different from the one that had called her back in the house. She stared at it for a couple of seconds, then accepted the call. Her arm was trembling slightly as she held the phone up to her ear.

'Hello?'

'Is this Katie?'

A man's voice. Quiet and nervous.

'Yes,' she said.

'You're Chris's big sister, right?'

She hesitated. 'Yes, I'm Chris's big sister. Who is this?'

Silence again.

As Katie waited for the man to speak, she glanced in the rear-view mirror. A car was approaching, driving a little too quickly. She watched as the vehicle turned into Hyde's street. There were two people inside, although it was impossible to get a proper look at them. A man in the passenger seat. A woman driving. There was something about both of them and the car that made her sure they were police.

Shit, shit, shit.

Surely it wasn't possible for them to have got here so fast?

'It's James,' the voice on the phone said.

Her attention snapped back.

'James Alderson?'

'Yeah. You left a message for Chris at my studio. He didn't want me to call you, but . . . well, I think I have to now. I think we need help.'

Alderson's voice right now was as faltering as Hyde's father's footsteps had been back at the house. He sounded completely lost.

'What do you mean?' Katie said.

'I think Chris is in trouble.'

'What kind of trouble?'

'He's been taken.'

A chill ran through her. Even though she didn't understand what was happening, what he'd just said felt horribly *correct*, like a piece of a jigsaw puzzle clicking into place right where it belonged.

'You need to call the police,' she said.

'He told me not to.'

'He also told you not to call me.'

'Not unless I had to,' Alderson said. 'But if anything happened, I got the feeling it might be OK. Because he trusted you. Because you always looked after him.'

Katie glanced in the mirror again. She knew she should return to the house and explain to the police what had happened. That was the sensible thing to do. But her

brother was in danger. And Hyde's father's words were
still echoing in her head.

It's all your fault.

All because of you.

Katie pressed the phone harder to her ear.

'Where are you, James?'

32

The red car again.

There it was, pulled up at an angle over the tatty grass verge in front of Michael Hyde's house, illuminated by the beam of their headlights. Pettifer was driving, and she parked up behind it without a thought. It meant nothing to her, of course, but there was a moment in which Laurence couldn't take his eyes off the vehicle – at all the stark joins in the metal. The photograph he had looked at yesterday was seventeen years old, but even back then it had felt as though the car somehow existed in both the past and the present simultaneously. Here and now that effect was redoubled. Looking at the car in front of them, he thought that perhaps no single piece of original metalwork remained.

And yet the car persisted.

Everything is connected below the surface.

He took out his phone and tried Katie Shaw's number again. Then gave up.

'A busy signal this time.'

'Perhaps she just doesn't want to speak to us,' Pettifer said.

'It seems so.'

They got out and made their way across to Michael Hyde's front door.

Laurence still wasn't sure exactly what he wanted to speak to Hyde about, only that he had become certain the man was one of those *connections* below the surface. Three decades ago Hyde had been a credible suspect in the fire that killed Joshua Hobbes, and yet his involvement had been dismissed quickly, with what seemed to Laurence a lack of due diligence. Christopher Shaw, who had been working for Hobbes, had been attacked by Hyde as a teenager. And now Alan Hobbes had been murdered.

Coincidences happened, Laurence knew. And sometimes they even arrived in pairs. But this many in a row suggested orchestration of some kind. Even if he didn't quite know what questions to ask Hyde yet, he was hopeful that talking to the man would begin to suggest some.

They knocked on the front door and waited.

No answer. Behind the patchy curtains in the windows, he could tell the light in the front room was on. He looked up. One upstairs too.

Pettifer cocked her head. 'Hear that?'

Laurence listened. 'No.'

'I'm serious. What is that?'

She crouched down and pushed the letterbox open a little, then peered through. She stood up abruptly and grabbed the front-door handle. It turned easily, and Laurence – knowing something was wrong without needing to know what – followed his partner quickly into the room beyond.

'Police!' Pettifer shouted. 'Make yourselves known.'

She'd already cleared the area to the left of the door, and Laurence only briefly took in the shabbiness of the room before his gaze settled on the sight that must have caught her attention through the letterbox. A short distance ahead, a man was lying collapsed at the bottom of the stairs. It looked like one of his arms – at the least – was broken, and there was a pool of blood beneath his head. Laurence could hear the soft gargling noise the man was making as he choked.

Pettifer ran over to him and crouched down again, making an attempt to clear his airways with one hand while she scrabbled for her phone with the other. Laurence joined her quickly, catching a glimpse of the man's face before it was obscured by her attentions. Even with the injuries he had suffered in prison, Laurence recognized him.

Michael Hyde.

What on earth was happening here?

Then he heard a *thumping* noise from somewhere above them and looked up the stairs. There was nobody directly in sight on the landing, but the sound came again anyway.

Someone was up there.

'Police!' he shouted. 'Make yourselves known.'

He started up the stairs – quickly at first, and then more cautiously as he neared the top. To all intents and purposes it appeared that Hyde had fallen, and he had seen no evidence of knife wounds on the man. But he also remembered the terrible violence that had been inflicted on Alan Hobbes and was aware he was unarmed here.

He stepped on to the landing. There was what appeared to be a bedroom to the left – the brightly lit room he had observed from the front of the house – but a light was also on in the room directly to his right, and it was from in there that the sound was coming.

'*Police*,' he repeated – the word the only weapon in his arsenal right now – and then stepped through the doorway.

An old man was standing in the middle of the room. He appeared small and weak, and was by no means an obvious threat, but Laurence kept his distance anyway. Appearances could always be deceptive. The man was wearing a tattered dressing gown and leaning on a cane. He was staring back at Laurence, visibly distraught, although whether that was through grief or rage was harder to tell.

'My boy,' he said. 'My poor boy.'

Downstairs, Laurence could hear Pettifer talking to emergency services.

'An ambulance is on its way,' Laurence told the old man. 'What happened here?'

The man – Hyde's father, Laurence assumed – did not immediately answer. Whatever emotion was driving him was causing his body to tremble slightly, so that the tip of the cane was scratching against the floorboards. Laurence looked around. It was a bedroom – albeit a sparsely furnished one. Just a bed against one wall, with a table at the end. A closed laptop on that. There was no other furniture or decorations. The walls were bare. Except that, looking at the wall directly across from him, Laurence noted numerous patches of paint missing, as though at some point there had been posters up that had been pulled away quickly and carelessly.

'She murdered him,' the old man said.

Laurence looked back at him. 'What happened here, sir?'

'That bitch.'

The old man's body was still trembling.

'She came here. And she killed him.'

33

Night had fallen properly by the time Katie arrived at the address James Alderson had given her.

It was a place on the run-down edge of the centre. After she turned the corner, she found herself driving up a long road lined by dark, derelict buildings that loomed overhead. There were street lights here, but they were long neglected. The plastic bulbs kept flickering and failing, as though the abandoned properties on either side of the road were blinking at each other.

But one further up was still working consistently, and as she drove closer she saw there was a man standing beneath it. He had a coat pulled tightly around him, one hand pushed down in the pocket, the other holding a cigarette. There were a couple of large rucksacks at his feet. She recognized him properly as she pulled in, and without quite knowing why, fear began fluttering in her chest.

What are you doing, James? she thought. *It's not safe to be standing out in the open like this.*

She got out of the car, leaving the door open. 'James?'

He nodded.

'I'm Katie.' She ran her fingers through her hair. 'OK.'

But her voice sounded faint and faraway, as though she were trying to reassure herself rather than Alderson. She glanced around the street. Aside from the two of them it appeared completely deserted. The only sound was the soft buzzing of the street light above.

And yet she had the feeling of being watched.

It's not safe to be standing out in the open like this.

She looked at Alderson. 'What happened?'

'This was where Chris was supposed to meet him.'

She looked at the property behind him. Although it was closed and empty now, it was one of the few buildings on the street that appeared to be still in use. A café of some sort. She stepped to one side of him and peered in through the window, then tried the door handle.

She turned back to Alderson.

'Who was he meeting?'

'I don't know exactly – a man who called us. He knew Chris had the book, and he was willing to pay for it.'

She shook her head. 'What book?'

'Something written by a guy called Jack Lock. This is going to sound crazy, but it's supposed to tell the future.'

Alderson seemed like he wanted to laugh at the idea but couldn't quite bring himself to. Instead, he took a drag on his cigarette and then breathed a plume of smoke out into the amber light. As it spread and unfolded in the air, Katie tried to remember what she'd read about Jack Lock last night. There had been something about a book, hadn't there?

It's supposed to tell the future.

Again, she shook her head. 'What –'

But whatever question she had been going to ask was interrupted by a buzzing in her pocket, and then a trill of accompanying music that felt dangerously loud in this deserted street. She took her mobile out quickly. The screen showed another unidentified number.

She accepted the call and held the phone to her ear. 'Hello?'

'Is this Katie Shaw?'

A man's voice.

She hesitated. 'Yes.'

'Ah, that's great. I'm glad to get hold of you, Katie. I'm Detective Laurence Page. It's good to speak to you again, by the way. Maybe you remember me?'

The name meant nothing.

'No, I don't think so.'

'Well, it's a weird one. Me and your family actually go back a bit. I was involved when your brother was attacked as a teenager. It was me who met you at the cordon that afternoon.'

Now she remembered. Laurence Page. He was very tall with a friendly face. Once she'd stopped trying to see past him that day, he'd made an effort to stoop a little so he was more on her level.

It's my fault, she remembered telling him. Over and over.

He'd frowned and tilted his head. *It's not your fault. Not at all.*

'Yes,' she said quietly now. 'I remember that.'

'And now the two of us are talking again. Maybe that's a coincidence – but honestly? I'm not so sure any more. I can't quite make sense of it all just yet, but I'm hoping you can help me out a little with that. Have you seen your brother recently?'

Be careful, Katie thought. Because he sounded just as friendly as she remembered him. But she wasn't a kid any more, and neither was Chris.

'No,' she said.

'*Heard* from him?'

'Why do you want to know?'

'Ah, we should probably talk about that in person. Whereabouts are you right now?'

She didn't reply. He took her silence for an answer.

'Because the thing is, I'm also calling you about something else. Maybe it's connected, maybe it's not. But I'm sitting outside someone else's house. And you don't need me to tell you who, right? Because my understanding is you were here earlier.'

Dread pooled in her stomach as she remembered the car she'd seen as she was leaving Hyde's.

'Yes,' she said. 'I was there.'

'It's great to get that confirmed. Why were you here?'

That easy-going tone of voice again – as though the two of them were just a couple of old friends chatting. As though her going to Hyde's house had just been an everyday visit during which nothing important had happened at all. Katie glanced around her now. She still had that crawling sensation of being watched, and her gut was telling her she needed to end this call and get away from here. That there was no time for small talk pretending everything was fine.

'How is he?' she said quickly. 'Michael Hyde.'

Laurence hesitated. 'He's on his way to the hospital.' He sounded more straightforward now. Maybe he was as happy as she was to dispense with the pleasantries. 'He's pretty badly hurt, but I think he'll live. Which is another way of saying that things could be a lot, *lot* worse for you than they are. Do you want to give me your side of what happened?'

'Hyde's been stalking my family.'

268

'Really?' She could almost hear his frown. 'How so?'

'You saw his bedroom wall, right?' Katie shifted slightly, swapping her mobile to her opposite hand. 'All the photographs he'd taken of us? My daughter especially. All the notes and maps he'd made. They were all taped up there.'

A pause on the line. 'No sign of any of that, I'm afraid,' he said.

'You went upstairs?'

'I did.'

She tried to think. Assuming he was telling her the truth, it meant Hyde's father had moved quickly to get rid of anything that might implicate his son – his *good boy* – in what he'd been doing.

'It *was* there,' she said. 'He's been following us. Watching us. I even called the police last night about it. He was in our back garden, looking in through the window.'

Another slight pause. It was hard to read silence, but she thought she detected a hint of annoyance in it.

'I did hear that you called,' Laurence said. 'OK. So let's say I believe you about all of this. It makes it all the more important that we meet up. I really think what you need to do is come in so we can talk about all this properly in person. And –'

'Why were *you* there?' she interrupted.

'I'm sorry?'

'It can't have been because Hyde's father called you. You arrived too quickly.'

Silence.

'Was it something to do with Chris?' she said.

'I can't tell you that right now.'

But it was obvious from his tone of voice that it had been. What did that mean? She knew the police had been looking for Chris at her mother's house yesterday, and now something had taken them to Hyde's house today. And yet she'd seen no obvious connection to Chris there at all. It was *her* family that Hyde appeared fixated on now.

'If you tell me,' she said, 'I'll come in.'

'I can't right now. But I think –'

Katie ended the call. For a moment the street was silent aside from the humming of the street light above.

Then Alderson spoke quietly. 'You're in trouble too, I take it?'

'Yes,' she said.

'Is it to do with Chris?'

'I don't know. I think so.'

Alderson nodded to himself, then raised his hand and took a last drag on his cigarette. On the surface he was trying to remain calm. But his hand was trembling and she could tell how scared he was deep down.

He dropped the cigarette and ground it under his heel. 'So what do we do now?'

What indeed?

She wasn't sure how much effort Detective Laurence Page would put into tracking her down, but the first thing she did was turn off her mobile.

She felt a pang of despair as she did so. Not only was she getting herself deeper into trouble, she was cutting herself off from Sam and Siena. The thought of them both created a yearning inside her – an intense desire to go home and for everything to just be OK again. She loved them both so much, and they seemed such a vast distance away from her right now.

After Alderson had put the rucksacks on the back seat of her car, he clambered into the passenger side. They didn't speak as she drove. She took them west out of the city centre, keeping to the minor roads as much as possible, and then pulled in at a high-rise travel hotel on the edge of an industrial park. At the reception she checked them into a twin room, and they took a cramped, stinking lift up to the eighth floor, standing in silence with their heads tilted back to watch the numbers change, two rucksacks resting at their feet. The doors pinged and slid open. She led Alderson down the corridor until she found their room, turning the plastic key card between her fingers as they went.

The room was simple and smelled little better than the lift. But it would do. She walked over to the window and lifted a couple of the slats in the blinds. An intricate carpet of tiny lights was spread out across the dark land, but her attention was drawn upwards instead, towards a sliver of brightness that seemed to be hanging unsupported in the air against the night sky behind. It took her a moment to work out what she was seeing. The prison on the hill. Dark right now aside from a single window, high up in one of its towers.

She lowered the slats and turned round.

Alderson was sitting on one of the beds. He had opened his rucksack and taken out a bottle of vodka, and was now busy pouring a slug into one of the cheap plastic glasses on the table between the beds.

She walked over and sat on the other bed across from

him, then picked up the other glass and held it out to be filled.

'So what happens now?' he said.

She looked at the glass. 'What happens now,' she said, 'is that you tell me everything.'

34

A little over two years earlier, Chris had been at his lowest point.

It had been a couple of weeks since he'd stolen from Katie, and that money had run out quickly. The days since had been a series of worn settees and damp front rooms that blurred into one. He slept fitfully at best, shivering in his thin sleeping bag, frequently unable to remember where he was. He was scared by every creak of the floorboards above, dreading who might be up there and what they might want from him when they came down. There was freezing cold water, assuming the taps ran at all. Chipped porcelain sinks. Broken mirrors in which he could barely see his lank hair as he stubbornly attempted to re-create the centre parting he'd had as a boy, the scar on his face standing out even among the cracks in the glass.

And the constant voice in his head.

This is all that you deserve.

You shouldn't exist.

Now he could only dimly recall the night before that life ended. There were impressions. He was running away from someone's house, an angry voice calling after him, bellowing ugly threats that echoed off the faces of the dark, boarded-up buildings. He was crying and hugging himself, although he remembered thinking he had no right to feel self-pity. Comfort and safety were not things he was entitled to. And he recalled the way the shouts had trailed away in the night air behind him. Because the owner of that angry voice had felt no need to chase him. They both knew he would be back the next morning. That the need he was going to feel by then would compel him.

He spent the rest of that night at the end of a pitch-black broken-down railway arch, huddled on a bed of half-bricks and litter, barely covered by hastily gathered sheets of cardboard and newspaper. To the extent he slept at all, he woke up shivering and feverish, and sat up carefully, easing out the cramp in his limbs. He hadn't moved much during the night, which was a habit he'd acquired over the years. Sleeping on rough, uncomfortable ground didn't allow you the luxury of tossing and turning. The left side of his body felt bruised. The right side of his face, which had been exposed to the air, was damp and numb.

But those sensations were nothing next to the need.

The cold, hard facts of his situation arrived quickly. He had to get back to wherever it was he had run away from. He had to make amends, however hard that would be. And he had to hope – the most terrifying thought of all right then – that he even *could* find his way back there, and that the door wouldn't be closed to him if he did.

He had to do those things because that was all he was.

And he was about to get up when he became aware he wasn't alone.

There was movement at the entrance to the arch, which wasn't far away. It had been dark when he'd sought refuge here last night, and at the time the blackness of the arch had seemed endless and impenetrable. But the entrance was actually only a few metres from him. A man there was now making his way in towards Chris, his gaze focused on the uneven ground and the bricks shifting dangerously beneath his feet.

Chris was more startled than actually afraid. The light in here was dim, but the man was visibly old and frail, and while Chris had always been small, he was sure he could fight him off if he had to. Even so, that drumbeat of *need* was sounding through him. If nothing else, this man was an unwelcome barrier between him and where he knew he had to get to.

Especially because there was a sense of purpose to the man's movements.

Despite himself, Chris drew his knees up as the man reached him.

'Who are you?' he said.

The man didn't answer. Up close, Chris could tell he was older than he'd thought. He was bald, and there was a thumbprint pattern of liver spots crowning his head, as though his skull had been handled and turned by dirty fingers. He was dressed in an expensive three-piece suit that looked like it had fitted once but was a size too large for him now. A pair of ancient spectacles rested on the bridge of his nose.

'What do you want?' Chris said.

The man looked around, taking in the filthy surroundings. There were another few seconds of silence, and then he leaned down slowly on his knee and looked at Chris.

'Your name is Christopher.'

The man's voice sounded as tired and weary as his body appeared, but the use of his name shocked

Chris. He had never seen this man before – didn't know him at all.

And yet somehow the man knew him.

Give nothing away, he told himself.

The man looked around again, and then let out a sigh. It was as though he'd been tasked with doing something he had known in advance would be difficult and unpleasant, but still hadn't been quite prepared for how hard it would be. He leaned carefully off his knee and stood upright again, then looked down at Chris.

The pity he could see on the old man's face now sent a wave of shame through him. There were no mirrors here, cracked or otherwise, but he could imagine how wretched he must look.

'You believe you're at rock bottom, Christopher.' The man spoke quietly. 'You think you're at your lowest ebb. And, in a way, you're right. You're shivering, aren't you? I can see it.'

Chris gritted his teeth and didn't reply.

'Right now,' the man said, 'you are planning on going somewhere you feel you have to. I'm here to tell you that you mustn't. You *absolutely* must not. A terrible thing will happen to you there if you do.'

Chris shook his head in confusion.

The man seemed to take the gesture as a refusal.

'Do you want to die?'

Give nothing away.

'Believe me,' the man said, 'you really don't. It might seem that way right now. And you might not believe me when I tell you this, but there *is a future for you*. You just have a choice to make. You can go back to wherever you were planning to go, and if you do, you will die

276

there. It will be an ugly and squalid death, and not one the newspapers will waste their time reporting.'

There was no way the man could know that. Perhaps it was true, but the voice in Chris's head told him it would be worth it even if it was.

Because that is all you deserve.

Because you shouldn't exist.

Except . . . if that was the case, why had he run last night?

Chris stared at the man for a moment, his heart churning.

'What do you want?' he said finally.

The old man tilted his head and looked off to one side, as though there were a hundred possible answers to that question and he didn't know which one to choose.

'To help you,' he settled on. 'You are suffering right now. But I have access to the best medicines and doctors that money can provide. If you come with me, I will make sure you have everything you need. The life you think is beyond you will be within your grasp again. *That* is what I want. I want to give you the choice to have the future you always should have.'

You don't deserve anything.

Chris stood up slowly. It felt like his body was aching everywhere, and he rubbed his bruised, emaciated arms. But, as weak as he was, he knew he could easily push the old man aside if he wanted to. Step over him. Go back to the life he deserved.

But as he stared at the old man, he recognized the kindness in his face. There was no sense of threat to him. He seemed to be willing Chris to go with him but also resigned to the fact he might choose otherwise. And while none of what was happening here made any sense, Chris found himself believing the man – or at least wanting to.

After a moment, the man nodded in acknowledgement of the unspoken decision that had been made. Then he turned and began clambering awkwardly back the way he'd come, over the rubble towards the entrance. Chris followed him out into the cold, grey morning light. He looked to the right. An expensive car was waiting in the nearby alleyway, its windows tinted black and its engine idling.

Chris hugged himself against the cold. His teeth were chattering.

'Who are you?' he said.

The old man looked at him. Once again, he seemed to be considering the question carefully.

And then he smiled gently.

'Call me Alan,' he said.

35

Katie picked up the bottle of vodka and poured herself a second shot. Then she sipped the liquid, relishing the burn in her throat. There was something grounding about the sensation, and she needed that right now. Her thoughts seemed to be whirling high above her.

'So this man,' she said, 'Alan Hobbes. You're telling me he turned up on the street one day, out of the blue. He rescued Chris, and paid for him to go through rehab? All like some kind of . . .'

She trailed off. The phrase that came most naturally to her felt wrong but what other would do?

'Guardian angel?'

Alderson nodded. 'Yes. Except the way Chris told it, it didn't seem to be out of the blue. He couldn't really explain it, but he said it was like Hobbes had known where he would be that day, and that he was going to need help.'

'Like this Hobbes guy *knew the future*?'

She tried to inflect some sarcasm into her voice, but Alderson didn't seem to notice.

'Yes.'

'And then what happened?'

'After Chris stopped using, Hobbes gave him a job at his estate. Nothing shady. Shopping. Cleaning. Looking after him. The whole thing seemed more like an excuse for Hobbes to have him around than anything else. Most of the time the old man just wanted to talk. He was old and he was dying. I think he just wanted company.'

'What did they talk about?'

Alderson considered that. 'Lots of things. I mean, Chris didn't always tell me. But he liked Hobbes, especially once he got to know him better. Said he was a good guy. And he was generous too. On top of the salary there was the flat. Hobbes owned that and we were living there rent-free.'

That was certainly very generous, which made Katie wonder exactly what had been in it for Hobbes. As a business relationship, it didn't make much sense to her.

'Until the other day, you mean,' she said. 'Until the two of you went on the run.'

'I suppose.'

'Because someone was watching the flat.'

'Yes.'

'Who did Chris think that was?'

'He didn't know. There were just times when he thought he was being followed. Well, times when he was *sure* of it. And it wasn't just his imagination either, because I felt it too. And I saw things. There was a car that kept turning up on the street.'

'A red car?' Katie asked quickly.

Alderson shook his head.

She leaned forward. 'Was it Michael Hyde he was scared of?'

'No, I don't think so. I mean, I know why you asked about a red car. But the one I saw was big and black. Expensive. That's why I noticed it in the first place, because it seemed so out of place in the neighbourhood.'

She leaned back. Once again, she remembered there hadn't been any photographs of Chris pinned to the wall in Hyde's house. It seemed to have been her family Hyde was stalking. But if that was the case, who had been hunting Chris and James Alderson?

Someone who enjoyed doing really bad things to people.

She shivered a little. 'Seems extreme to have gone on the run,' she said.

'It was Hobbes who told him to,' Alderson said. 'Chris mentioned it to him when they were talking, and he said the old man went white. Then Hobbes got angry with himself, as if he'd forgotten something important. He told Chris the two of us had to get out of our flat. We packed up and have been sleeping at my studio for the last few nights.'

Katie sipped the vodka, trying to process what Alderson was telling her. If Hobbes had told Chris to run, perhaps it was something *he* was mixed up in, and nothing to do with her brother at all. But that still left the question of Hobbes's motivation for helping Chris in the first place. And also what had happened to her brother now.

'What about the book?' she said.

Alderson took a deep breath, and then poured himself another drink. Katie waited for him to take a swallow before he continued.

'Right,' he said. 'Jesus. So Hobbes had what you might call a collection.'

'Of what?'

'That's the weird thing. Chris told me Hobbes was a nice guy. Gentle, kind, interesting. He'd been a philosophy lecturer once, and he had a library full of old books.

But there was also something else. Hobbes had collected a lot of stuff connected to this horrible guy. This killer.'

'Jack Lock?'

'Right. I read up on him, and there's too much to get into there. Let's just say that Lock was an absolutely awful human being. He claimed God had shown him the future, and then he killed a bunch of kids because it was His will. A proper nutcase. Hobbes had a lot of Lock's writing, along with other things that had belonged to him. Some of it was worth real money, but apparently the most valuable thing of all was a notebook.'

It's supposed to tell the future.

'And this was what Chris was trying to sell?' Katie said.

'Yeah.'

'He stole it from Hobbes?'

'No.' Alderson shook his head quickly. 'Hobbes *told* him to take it. This was a few days ago. Hobbes said he was dying and wouldn't be able to employ Chris any more. He gave Chris instructions on what he needed to do on his last day. He was to come in at a certain time, take the book, disconnect a camera in the room. Then leave and never look back. And that's exactly what Chris did. He felt like he owed it to him after everything he'd done for him.'

Katie sat in silence for a moment.

'Why did Hobbes want Chris to take the book?'

'I don't know. Chris thought it was maybe because it was worth a lot of money – that it was kind of severance pay. But we had no idea how to sell it or anything. And then this guy phoned us. He said Hobbes had told him to get in touch about it. And so Chris made him an offer.'

'And this is who Chris went to meet at the café?'

'Yeah. He wouldn't give his name, and the money was almost too good to be true, so not taking the book along was meant to be an insurance policy. I was supposed to turn up with it once Chris had had a chance to feel him out and see if he was genuine. But then . . .'

Alderson trailed off helplessly. The guilt he felt over not going with Chris was obvious, and Katie could see him doing the same thing she had done once. Wishing he'd done things differently. Hammering on a door even though he knew it was sealed shut behind him.

'Where's the book now?' she said.

Alderson nodded towards Chris's backpack.

She put her glass on the table, then reached down and opened the cords sealing Chris's bag.

'Hey –' Alderson started.

But she ignored him and began to discard the clothes packed at the top. About halfway down the backpack, her fingers brushed against plastic, and she felt a jolt of electricity. Her hand recoiled as though it had burned her, but then she forced herself to reach in and pull it out.

An old notebook, wrapped in protective plastic.

She turned it around in her hands, her fingertips still tingling slightly wherever they touched it. The covers and spine were made of black leather, and there was a thick wedge of well-preserved pages between them.

The silence in the room began singing slightly.

It's just a book, she told herself.

Which was true. That was all it was — just a horrible relic from the past. No matter what anyone else chose to believe, it contained nothing more than the deluded justifications of a child-killer. And yet the book felt heavier to her than it seemed it should have, as though whatever scrawls of ink had been added to the pages inside had somehow doubled it in weight.

'Have you read it?' she said.

'God, no.'

'What about Chris?'

Alderson shook his head. Then he frowned. 'Are you . . .?'

Katie looked down at the book. Without realizing it her fingers had begun absently toying at the seal.

'No.' She put the book down quickly on the bed beside her. 'I'm not interested in it.'

Then she began rummaging through her brother's rucksack again.

'What are you looking for?'

'Chris's phone.'

'He had that with him.'

Of course he had; she wasn't thinking. She looked up at Alderson and held out her hand.

'Give me yours.'

He hesitated, but the reluctance on his face only held for a couple of seconds. She could tell that part of him wanted to take care of this himself, but the fact remained that he had called her. He was about the same age as Chris, and right then Katie felt very much like the older sister. The one who took charge and sorted things out. The one who looked after people.

When he passed her his phone, she flicked through

until she found the contact number for Chris and then dialled it. The call went to voicemail.

'His phone is turned off,' she said.

'I already tried.'

'So I'll send him a message.'

Alderson sounded alarmed. 'Don't read –'

'I'm really not interested.'

She opened up the SMS conversation between Alderson and Chris. Her brother's phone might have been turned off right now, but if whoever had taken him wanted the book that badly, then perhaps they would switch it back on again at some point.

I have the book, she typed. **We need to talk.**

She hesitated for a moment. And then decided to be forceful.

Hurt him and I'll burn it.

She pressed send and put the phone on the table beside her. Alderson stared at it, as though thinking of asking for it back, then clearly decided it was better to let her handle this.

Katie wished she felt half as confident about that as he did.

'So now what?' he said.

'Now,' she said, 'we wait.'

Which is what they did.

Every now and then she checked the phone, but there was no response to the text she'd sent. At one point Alderson asked if it was safe for him to go outside for a cigarette. She thought about it and decided it probably would be: if anybody was going to find them here, it wouldn't be because they randomly spotted him skulking outside. He was gone a while but she wasn't worried. She figured he was probably chain-smoking – loading up for the night – and being alone gave her a chance to think. Not just about everything he'd told her, although she was still trying to make sense of that, but about her life up until now, and how the events of the past few days had knocked it off course and brought her here.

To this hotel room. To this situation.

And while she didn't properly understand *those* thoughts either, they gave her an odd, incongruous feeling. She was frightened, yes. She was scared for her family. And she also knew she was in real trouble after running from the police. But there was also a strange kind of *relief*. It was like a lever had been pulled that had unexpectedly released her from rails she had been dutifully following without even realizing.

Like she had a chance to put something right *before* it went wrong.

Alderson hooked the chain on the door when he came back, for all the good that was likely to do them. Then he lay down on his bed, with his hands beneath his head and stared up at the ceiling.

'I just want Chris back,' he said quietly.

'I know.'

'I keep kicking myself. If only I'd done this. If only I'd done that.'

I know the feeling, Katie thought. He sounded so despondent that she wanted to console him, but she knew there was nothing she could say that would make him feel better. The past was sealed away. All you could do was your best in the world it had brought you to.

Which reminded her of something.

'I liked your painting by the way,' she said.

'My painting?'

'The one of you and Chris. The one made up of lots of smaller paintings. I know it wasn't quite finished, but I thought it was lovely. And maybe that's something to cling to, you know? That while you might have made some mistakes along the way, you also made lots of *right* decisions too.'

He was silent for a time.

'Thank you,' he said finally. 'But actually, you're wrong about one thing. The painting *was* finished.'

'What about the empty spaces?'

'You got what the picture meant, right?'

'I think so. It was you and Chris in the present, made up of people and places from your pasts. The things that made you both *you*. All the things that brought you together.'

'That's right. And do you know what I was going to call it?'

'Unfinished?'

He laughed despite himself.

'No,' he said. 'Hope.'

She left it a couple of seconds.

'Go on.'

'Hope that actually you're *more* than just that.' He shook his head against his hands. 'The strange thing is I actually started the painting *before* I read about Jack Lock. But when I did, everything there chimed with me. The whole idea of determinism. If every detail of the past is set, then everything in the future must be too. It's the laws of physics. And so life just . . .' He trailed off.

'Continues down its set track?' she said.

He nodded, still staring at the ceiling.

'When I started the painting, I was planning to fill every single one of those spaces. All the things in the past – good and bad – that brought Chris and me to being happy now. But then I thought: how depressing is that? The idea that everything we are, everything we have, has all just been set out for us. That there's no free will or room for chance in what happens. That everything has been preordained from the beginning of the universe.'

She didn't reply.

'And so *that's* why I left the empty spaces,' he said. 'I wanted to cling on to a belief that things could have been different. That we actually have some kind of power or control over what happens in the future. The ability to *change* our paths. Because otherwise . . . I mean, what's the fucking point?'

Again, she remained silent for a moment. She had no answer to his question. But it raised one of her own. Talking about the painting reminded her that the mystery of Nathaniel Leland had been coded into it, and while that might not have been her mother's story to tell, perhaps James Alderson was close enough to her brother for it to be his.

'There was a little boy there,' she said. 'In Chris's part of your painting. Nathaniel Leland. Who is he?'

Alderson stared at her for a moment. And, just as he was about to answer, his phone vibrated on the table. They both started at the noise, and then Katie snatched it up quickly. It was a message sent from Chris's phone, appearing beneath the threat she'd sent earlier.

I will be in touch. Talk to the police and I'll kill him.

She stared at that for a moment, her heart beating a little harder.

Then the phone vibrated again as a second message arrived directly below.

Burn the book and I'll kill you too.

36

Leland stared down at the message.

Burn the book and I'll kill you too.

It wasn't enough.

The knowledge that his father's book was in his brother's hands had tormented him for decades. That it was now in the possession of someone who might destroy it was intolerable. His father's writing was the word of God. If it was destroyed, Leland would do far worse than kill the person responsible. Even the suggestion of damaging it demanded punishment and suffering beyond imagination.

He put the phone away, his hand shaking slightly. Then he turned and walked down the corridor to see Christopher Shaw.

And, as he did so, his thoughts turned to fire.

It is 6 July 1985.

Leland is in church when he understands what he must do. As the last note of the organ music fades away, the congregation is silent for a moment. There is no soft sound of shuffling feet. No throats being discreetly cleared. If Leland were to close his eyes, it would be possible to believe the room is empty. But of course it is crowded. Because many people loved Charlotte Mary Hobbes.

But none more than him.

His gaze fixes on the coffin that rests at the front of the church, which houses the remains of the woman who was meant to be his. In a different world she would have been – *should* have been. In this one he is reduced to sitting at the back of the room. An interloper.

This is not right.

The thought throbs in his head.

This is not what was intended.

Glancing around, even the architecture of the church feels wrong. The corners where the walls met; the angles of the pews; the timber of the wooden beams in the rafters. To Leland everything seems to be *straining*, tilting somehow, as though the entire building – God's own house – is attempting to distance itself from the blasphemy unfolding within it. Candles line the periphery of the room, but while the flames burn brightly there is even an oddness there too. The people here are motionless, the air entirely still. And yet every flame is flickering as though buffeted by an unseen, angry breeze.

And then the silence is broken.

At the front of the church a baby begins crying.

A gentle murmur runs through the crowd at that, more emotion than sound, and a moment later a man stands up. He is cradling a tiny infant in his arms, rocking the child gently. Alan Hobbes wears a mask of absolute grief – a week's worth of tears staining his sallow face – but somehow he is fighting through the pain and loss that appears to have racked him, cooing quietly at the baby in an attempt to soothe it.

Leland stares at his brother. It has been nearly ten years since he first watched Alan and Charlotte laughing together at the dance, and while he is now married to

Eleanor, with a month-old child of his own, he has never been able to forget the fact that Charlotte was *meant to be his*. He has always believed that, over time, the universe would correct its course and bring her to him. Part of him has been waiting patiently for the day. And so the news of her death was impossible for him to accept when he first heard it.

The grief was insurmountable.

Then the anger at what Alan had done. At the future Alan had stolen from him.

And that emotion is *rage* now. It fills him from one burning side of his body to the other, and he has to force himself to watch the revolting pantomime playing out before him. How can Alan bear to show grief – especially *here* of all places? He must have known what was going to happen. He must have known what would come about as a result of his tampering. Or else he had steered the world on to this terrible course with neither care nor concern beyond for his own benefit.

Either way, Charlotte's death is Alan's fault.

But not just Alan's.

Leland's gaze settles on the baby's sobbing face and feels his own expression harden. *Joshua Hobbes* – although it has no business even having a name. No right to comfort or soothing. It *deserves* to cry. Its very existence is an abomination in the eyes of God, the unnatural product of His plan being interfered with.

It should not be in this world.

And that is when the idea arrives.

Sitting there, staring at the baby with his fists clenched hard against the trousers of his suit, Leland realizes that while not everything can be put right, there are some things that still might be. And that rather than waiting for the journey to correct itself, it is within his power to help it on its way. His *duty* even.

He relaxes his hands. And at the front of the church the baby stops crying.

As the ceremony progresses, Leland pays little attention to the words of the priest, and makes no attempt to join in with the hymns that are sung in this black parody of genuine loss. His thoughts have moved elsewhere.

He knows where Alan Hobbes lives now. The home they both grew up in is an old, dilapidated property in which accidents can easily happen – or be made to. It will take time to organize if he is to do it right.

There is no rush.

Even so, he makes a series of calls as he is driven back from the funeral. By the time he arrives home he has already established there is a local man, named Michael Hyde, with a history of burglary and arson, who will be perfect for the task he has in mind.

Inside the house, he finds Eleanor is drunk. She often is. It was as though she too recognized that the life they have found themselves living was not what should have been. Nathaniel is unattended and crying. Leland lifts the baby from its crib and attempts to soothe it, the same way Alan did back in the church.

His actions are sincere. And yet Nathaniel continues to cry.

Leland suppresses the anger he feels. The truth is that he loves his son deeply. Even if Charlotte had been his – as she should have been – surely there would have been room in the world for Nathaniel too. And as he holds his son's small body against his own, Leland imagines all the secret things he will teach him as he grows.

The ways he will shape him.

A few minutes later, Eleanor appears in the doorway, dishevelled and unsteady on her feet. Nathaniel has been soothed into silence now, and Leland is rocking him gently against his chest, staring down at a small face that not only resembles his own but which reminds him of his father as well.

'Was he crying?' Eleanor sounds confused. 'I thought I heard him crying.' She leans against the doorway.

Leland says nothing. There was a time when he thought a marriage might be helpful as a facade – a veneer of normality and acceptability – but he wonders now how long it will be before he is compelled to add her to the burgeoning collection of angels in his secret garden at the back of the house.

But for now he ignores her.

Nathaniel matters, though. And as Leland continues rocking the infant in his arms, he knows the situation can't continue as it is. There are times when he needs to be away for work, and if Eleanor's attention cannot be relied upon, he will have to find another way to make sure his son is properly cared for.

That should be simple enough, he thinks.

They can find a childminder.

Leland stopped outside the door.

There was an endless moment in which he could feel nothing but the blood pounding in his temples. When he could think of nothing but what the babysitter he had hired, Peter Leighton, had ended up doing to Nathaniel.

Thirty years might have been expected to dull some of the hatred and loss, but they had not. Time held little meaning once you understood its true nature. Past, present and future existed as one. The Edward Leland who had once walked down a long corridor to see what had been done to Nathaniel existed just as surely as the one standing here now.

But also as the one who would put things right.

The one who will carry out God's will.

He used the thought to anchor himself. A few short hours from now there existed an Edward Leland who would right the wrongs that had been done, and correct the blasphemous course the world had been set upon.

He unlocked the door before him and opened it.

Christopher Shaw was where Banyard had deposited him upon their arrival: slumped against the bare wall, bound and gagged. His face was scarred down one side, and now badly bruised on the other. As Leland walked slowly across to him, Shaw tried to flinch backwards, but he was already pressed hard against the stone wall behind him and there was nowhere for him to go.

'Look at me,' Leland said.

The boy didn't move.

'I said, look at me.'

The boy did as he was told, raising his face and looking up at Leland. His eyes were wide and scared. There was pleasure to be taken in his fear, but Leland forced himself to remain impassive, leaning down and peering carefully at the boy's features. Searching for another glimpse of what he had seen at the café.

He leaned back. Sure now.

'I spent such a long time looking for you,' he said.

'I always knew I'd find you eventually. I knew Alan wouldn't be able to stay away from you for ever – that he would want to look after you. That he would *need* to. Because you are abhorrent. You should *never have been born*. And, deep down, I think you know that, don't you?'

He reached down and brushed a strand of Shaw's hair away from his face. The boy was so terrified that he didn't even flinch. But there was something in his eyes that suggested Leland's words had resonated with him. That on some level Leland was only confirming a truth he had known his whole life.

He looked at Shaw's scar. At some point the boy had been badly injured. Leland had no idea who had attacked him, but that made sense. Someone else must have laid eyes on Shaw and recognized that he was an abomination that deserved to be removed from existence.

'I can see God has made His own attempts to erase you over the years,' Leland said. 'Now He has brought you to me. And I'm going to enjoy finishing that job for Him.'

Leland crouched down in front of Shaw. And once again he thought that while the boy might not understand exactly what he was being told, he recognized the truth of it.

He knew *what* he was even if he didn't know *who*.

37

It is 13 April 1986.

Alan Hobbes parks his car on Grace Street and then walks slowly up the dark driveway towards St William's Church. It is a warm night, with just a faint whisper of a breeze, and he has no desire to hurry. The world around him is still and silent, and the black sky above so clear it is easy to imagine God looking down at him from beyond the prickle of stars there. A weighty gaze, perhaps, but Joshua – cradled in his arms right now and still half asleep from the journey – is heavier.

Over the years Hobbes has done his best to spend his money decently, distributing it without fanfare to the people and organizations who will use it to do the most good: laundering the gift of his fortune through the lives of others. But two of the more insidious things money can buy are privacy and access, and he has paid handsomely for both tonight. If God is watching, then He is the only observer present right now. And when Hobbes arrives at the door to the church and reaches out for the handle, he finds that the door is unlocked as agreed, and the porch inside empty.

You can't do this, he thinks. *It's not allowed.*

But he does.

He carries his dozing son across and then pushes open the door that leads into the main body of the church. He walks down the narrow aisle between the pews, his footsteps echoing in a space that feels vast. The light from the candles burning in the racks along the walls is unable to reach the vaulted ceiling high above. He glances up into the darkness there. God feels closer in here. It is as though He has leaned forward in His seat and is watching carefully, like a scientist peering into a microscope.

So let Him watch.

Hobbes has come to hate Him a little.

Hobbes still remembers the question he asked his students at the lecture. *If you were a father, which would you prefer? A child who always did as they were told, or a child who disobeyed you and tried to forge their own path, trying to do the best they could?* It had been a rhetorical question, its answer obvious – or at least that was what he'd thought. And yet he has spent much of the time since doubting himself. Because with every bit of good he has attempted – every bit of evil he has worked to prevent – he has felt the world leaning harder against him, like a car ever more determined to drift sideways into a different lane.

You have committed blasphemy.

When Hobbes reaches the front of the church, he looks down at his son. In his arms Joshua is sleeping again now, the side of his face resting against Hobbes's chest.

Can you hear my heart? he wonders. *Do you know how much this hurts?*

He bows his head and breathes in the familiar smell of his son's hair, and then lies Joshua down gently on the stone floor, careful not to wake him. Then he leaves his hands against the soft wool of the blanket, reluctant to take them away now the moment has come. He has kept himself as calm and composed as he can until now, but he knows that his whole world will collapse when he lets go. The realization is stark. He will never hold his son again. For all intents and purposes he will forever be a stranger to the boy.

It will be such a long time until I see you again.

Hobbes tries to tell himself that all moments are present, and so in some way he will always be here, with his hands touching his son to soothe both of them. But it doesn't help. It does nothing to stem the grief that is building inside him. There will be so many stories he will miss as Joshua is growing up. But he also knows that Joshua's story will be cut short if his son remains with him.

Because the world will continue to creak. And Edward will never stop his quest to correct what has been changed.

So he has no choice.

'Are you all right, sir?'

Hobbes looks to his left, startled. A stewardess is standing in the aisle beside his seat, looking down at him with a concerned expression.

For a moment he is confused. Where is he? *When* is he? But then he realizes. It is a little later in the night now, and he is on a plane on his way to Italy for a conference. He will be called home first thing in the morning.

The cabin is trembling.

He swallows. 'I'm fine. It's just . . . the turbulence.'

'Yeah, I get that.' She nods sympathetically. 'Honestly? It's a bit worse than usual, but we'll get through it OK. Promise you.'

'I'm sure we will.'

'Trust me – I've done this *a thousand times* before.'

Hobbes smiles, and she moves away. He turns his head to the small window beside him. The world outside is dark, but after a few seconds the plane tilts slightly and the ground swings up into view. The flight path circles over the north of the city, and Hobbes stares down at the spread of black land far below. It is speckled with tiny lights, one standing out a little brighter than the others.

The fire in his house that Edward arranged in order to kill Joshua.

The one Hobbes knew would come to pass.

The sight of it empties him.

Money can buy many things. Right now, Peter Leighton, the childminder his brother hired to look after his son, Nathaniel, is already settling into life abroad under the new name Hobbes acquired for him. The money Leighton will receive every month until he dies will be sufficient to ensure his silence.

The plane tilts again and the world outside swings up, the sight of the ground replaced by a blue-black sky filled with racing wisps of grey cloud. The cabin continues to tremble for a moment. And then . . . it settles.

The stewardess is making her way back down the aisle and gives him a wink as she passes.

'Told you so.'

Hobbes smiles emptily and closes his eyes.

Right now, Joshua is wrapped in an extra blanket and is being comforted by the cleaning lady who arrived at the church soon after Hobbes left. An ambulance has been called. Joshua's life with Hobbes is over, and his new life with his adopted family will begin a few short weeks from now. It will be a long time before they see each other again. And while all this is necessary, it feels like the valves in Alan Hobbes's heart are crumpling one by one.

I love you so much, my beautiful boy, he thinks. *Do your best for now.*

And then the plane flies higher, and the land below is invisible for a while.

It is 15 April 1986.

Edward Leland is walking down a long, narrow corridor, a nurse on one side of him and a policeman on the other. Despite the warnings they have given him, he is filled with hope. Nathaniel has been missing for over a week now – vanished off the face of the earth, along with his childminder – and Leland had all but accepted his son must be dead. The grief and loss and *rage* have consumed him, soaking him through like torrential rain.

But now a baby boy has been found abandoned in a church. Who else can it possibly be?

Leland walks into the room and looks down at the child. And then freezes. He gradually becomes aware of a terrible noise building in the air, and then realizes it is coming from him. It is something between a scream and a sob, an awful keening that grows ever louder and more desolate as he stares down at *the thing* – he can no longer think of it as a child – that is lying before him.

Charlotte's eyes are staring up at him from Joshua Hobbes's face.

And he understands what has been done to Nathaniel.

Standing there, the horror building inside him, Leland can see it all in his mind's eye. Alan has organized it all so carefully. Using their father's book, he has learned how Leland was intending to correct the course of the world by killing Joshua. And even though part of him must surely have recognized the blasphemy of his actions, he made the choice to save his son. He arranged for Nathaniel to be abducted and delivered to him. And then he swapped the infants, so that instead of Joshua, it was Nathaniel who perished in the fire.

The fire that Leland had arranged.

The fire that killed his own child.

He blinks.

'Not him, right?' the officer says.

Leland will realize later that, had he had better control of himself in this moment, he should have pretended it was. *Yes*, he should have said. *Yes, it's my son*. Even if they didn't believe him, all he would have needed was enough time alone with the infant. And he knew that God would have nodded along in encouragement of his actions. But reason has deserted him right now. He is too consumed by the horror of what Alan has done.

What he *himself* has done.

'No,' Leland says instead.

And then repeats it, over and over, as they lead him from the room. 'No, no, no.'

It is 4 October 2017.

Hobbes clicks the top on to the fountain pen, sensing the ribbon of its history as he does so. Nearly a century ago a little boy called Jack Lock is already scribbling incessantly with it, attempting to translate the strange tongue he is hearing.

And here it is now.

Hobbes places it in the cabinet, alongside all the other surviving remnants of Jack Lock's life that he has spent the last few decades collecting. Then he stands up and leaves the room for ever.

In the bathroom he looks at himself in the mirror. What appears close to a skull stares back at him, its eyes hollow and blank. There is so little of him left in the present, and it is nearly time for the pages of his own life to come to an end.

He has done his best.

With his hands trembling, he pours himself a tumbler of water. And then he begins swallowing pill after pill.

PART FOUR

38

'Is my wife in trouble?' Sam Gardener said.

Laurence pursed his lips and considered the question.

It was the next morning. Gardener was sitting in his front room, with a little girl beside him on the settee wrapped in an odd piece of fabric. The child was young but perhaps old enough to understand the conversation, and so Laurence had suggested he and Gardener talk somewhere more private. The man had said no. He claimed his daughter was feeling clingy due to Katie Shaw's absence. Laurence had actually seen very little evidence that this was the case – the girl seemed almost entirely oblivious, lost in the picture book she was reading – and he suspected Gardener was keeping her close right now more for his own reassurance than hers. Laurence couldn't really blame him.

Is my wife in trouble?

Yes, Laurence thought. No. Maybe. On one level he didn't really know. His gut instinct edged very strongly towards the first response, but he still couldn't put the pieces of what was happening here together well enough to form a satisfactory picture.

On a different level, of course, the answer was obvious.

'Yes,' he said. 'Your wife is wanted for questioning on suspicion of assault.'

Gardener blinked. 'Assault?'

'Yes.' Laurence nodded. 'And breaking and entering too, although that would be of lesser importance right now.'

'But –'

'*Yesterday evening,*' Laurence said, holding up a hand, 'we believe she assaulted a man named Michael Hyde. The attack took place inside his home. It was very serious.'

Gardener just stared back at him for a moment, and from the expression on his face Laurence imagined he was putting together some pieces of his own. The suggestion his wife had assaulted someone might have been unbelievable at first, but the identity of the victim had clearly caused him to reconsider that idea.

'Katie has more or less admitted it,' Laurence said. 'I spoke to her briefly on the phone last night. Unfortunately she ended the conversation and we've been unable to reach her since. It appears she has turned her mobile off. I must ask whether you have heard from her.'

Gardener shook his head and looked away.

But there was guilt there, Laurence thought. Self-recrimination. Gardener blamed himself in some way for what was happening here.

'Mr Gardener?'

'We had an argument,' the man said. 'Yesterday morning. Katie stormed out. I thought she needed a bit of space – and, honestly, I was angry too. Really angry. But I didn't try to call her until later, and by then her phone was turned off. It has been all night. I was trying to think what the best thing to do was when you turned up.'

Laurence looked around the room again. It seemed a very nice house to him. It was a home that had been gathered together over the years with love. But while that love remained, it also felt to him like something that had slipped down behind the cushions and got lost under the chairs. That maybe there wasn't enough talking in this house any more and too much was being left unsaid.

'What was the argument about?'

Gardener slumped slightly. 'It was me being an idiot,' he said. 'Katie had called the police the night before because she saw someone outside. Or thought she did. I didn't take it as seriously as I should have done. I just thought the thing at the nursery had freaked her out, along with all the stuff with her brother.'

The stuff with her brother.

One thing at a time, though.

'What is it that happened at the nursery?'

'Some of the kids thought there was a man in a car who was watching –'

'What colour was this car?'

Gardener shook his head. 'I really don't know.'

'Because when I spoke to your wife on the phone last night, she told me that Michael Hyde has been stalking your family. You, her and – I'm sorry, I don't know your daughter's name.'

'Siena.'

'Right. And Michael Hyde drives a red car, doesn't he?'

'*Red car,*' Siena said.

Laurence and Gardener both looked at her for a few seconds.

'Maybe I *should* have taken it more seriously,' Gardener said. 'But it didn't seem like a big deal. And I *know* how Katie gets sometimes. She takes the weight of the world on her shoulders. She's always so scared that something bad is going to happen. Especially when it comes to her brother.'

'Ah, yes,' Laurence said. 'What exactly has happened with Christopher?'

He listened as Gardener explained, although it very quickly became clear that the man did not know the answer to that question. Katie had received a phone call from her mother three nights earlier that had something to do with Chris. She had gone out, and then returned later that evening. It frustrated Laurence that Gardener was married to the woman and yet did not appear to know anything more than that.

It clearly frustrated Gardener now too.

'I didn't ask,' he said. 'Because I don't want anything to do with her brother – and I think it's best for Katie's sake that *she* doesn't either. All he ever does is hurt people and let them down. But she doesn't think straight when it comes to him. She always blames herself for what happened.'

It's my fault, Laurence remembered.

It's not your fault. Not at all.

'And yet she reported him two years ago,' he said.

'Because I made her.' Gardener looked pained. 'I know it sounds bad when you put it like that. But Chris had screwed up so many times, and it just felt like the final straw to me. She was so hurt. So upset. But I could tell she was going to forgive him again, and so I persuaded her not to. I convinced her that going to the police was the best thing to do – that it was time to cut ties and walk away.'

I know it sounds bad.

Perhaps it did, and yet Laurence found it hard to blame Sam Gardener for pressing her on the issue. The situation was a complicated one – in large part because families were always complicated – but again, he remembered how guilty Katie Shaw had felt seventeen years ago. It occurred to him that she had been with Sam Gardener that afternoon, and that the man before him now might blame *himself* too. Regardless, it was obvious from the distress on Gardener's face that he loved his wife deeply and was worried about her, and Laurence had no doubt his actions two years ago had been driven by those same emotions.

'Has she had any recent contact with her brother?' he said.

'I don't know.' Gardener hesitated. 'That was partly what the argument was about. She lied to me about being at work on Friday, and I was angry about that too. I don't know what she was doing; she wouldn't tell me. But I looked through her jacket the next morning and found something weird.'

An old newspaper clipping regarding a missing boy. *Nathaniel Leland.* The name meant nothing to Laurence, but he felt a chill go through him even so. Why was Katie Shaw interested in a missing child? It was another piece of the puzzle. He didn't know where it fitted yet, but the more pieces he had, the better the chance that some would begin to slot into place.

'There was an address and a phone number too,' Gardener said. 'I think they might have been Chris's.'

Jesus Christ.

'Did you make a note of them?'

Gardener nodded. 'Hang on.'

He stood up and walked through to the kitchen. Laurence waited in the front room, alone with the child. She was still immersed in her book, and for a moment Laurence simply stood there. Then he crouched down and tried to catch her eye, smiling at her when she finally looked up.

'Siena, right? My name's Laurence.'

'Hello.'

'I want you to think hard,' he said quietly, 'and to remember as best you can, because it's important. Did you really see a red car?'

The little girl nodded.

Gardener walked back into the front room. Laurence stood up and accepted the piece of paper the man held out to him. An address and a phone number. He was familiar with the general area of the former; it was close to the location of the cash withdrawals Christopher Shaw had made in recent months. He folded the paper and placed it in his pocket. He needed to call Pettifer.

'Thank you, Mr Gardener. We will be in touch as soon as we have any news. It goes without saying that if you hear from Katie, you should let us know immediately. It's urgent that we find her.'

Gardener slumped on to the settee. 'Because she *is* in trouble.'

'Yes.'

Because while Laurence still had no idea of the cogs turning below the surface here, the face of the clock was easy enough to read. Christopher Shaw was in possession of a book that someone was prepared to kill to get their hands on. And now his sister was involved too.

Laurence turned and headed to the door – but, just as

he reached it, someone outside knocked. Gardener was out of his seat immediately, but Laurence was closer. He opened the door to find a man dressed in black trousers, a white shirt and a red baseball cap.

He was holding a package in one hand and a scanning device in the other.

'Delivery for Katie Shaw?'

39

Katie parked up round the corner from her mother's house, the car tyres squelching in the wet mulch of fallen leaves in the gutter, and then walked the rest of the way on foot. She kept an eye out as she went but there was nobody else in sight. When she let herself into the flat, it felt emptier than before. There was an absence in the air and a heaviness to the silence. The familiar corridor stretching away before her was gloomy and still.

'Hello?' she called.

No reply. But it was early, of course. Her mother was probably still in bed.

'It's just me,' she said quietly.

She headed down the corridor to the spare room. The morning light was streaming thinly through the closed curtains, revealing motes of dust hanging in the air. The box remained where she'd left it yesterday on the floor beside the old desk, and nothing in the room appeared to have been touched. Of course, her mother had no reason to come in here. Even if the story was not hers to tell, she already knew it.

And now – after she had asked Alderson about Nathaniel Leland last night – Katie did too.

She walked across and kneeled down beside the box, and then began to search through everything inside. She found what Alderson had told her was here almost straight away, only a little way under the news clippings her father had collected about Nathaniel Leland's murder.

Her hands trembled slightly as she carefully picked up the envelope. It was very old. But while the writing scrawled on the front had faded with time, the words remained visible, and the weight of them was undiminished by age.

Chris – adoption details.

She felt tightness like a clenched fist in her chest, and opened the flap of the envelope, then pulled out the thin sheaf of folded papers inside and began flicking through them.

There was a certificate of adoption, complete with her brother's name, Christopher William Shaw, and those of her parents.

There was his original birth certificate.

'William Grace' – Date of birth: 13 April 1985.

And then a sheet explaining the reasons for his adoption.

On 13 April 1986, the child was discovered, having apparently been abandoned, in one of the vestibules of St William's Church on Grace Street. The child's age was impossible to determine, and so date of birth has been estimated as the date of discovery minus one year. Staff were extremely moved by the circumstances and the child was provisionally named in reference to them.

Subsequent investigations to establish the child's identity were comprehensive and exhaustive but failed to uncover his parentage. At the time of writing such investigations continue, and the prospective adoptive parents are aware of this. With that in mind we wholeheartedly recommend and endorse the attached application. All our investigations and evaluations suggest Ann and David Shaw, along with their daughter Katie, will provide a loving home for William Grace, and that they are prepared for the eventuality that he may, at some point, be reunited with his birth family, along with whatever complications such a development might entail.

She read the document a second time, and then tried to absorb it. Most obviously of all, it didn't change anything. Her brother was her brother; he always had been and he always would. If anything, this revelation even made sense of some things. The way Chris had always seemed so at odds with the world. Always adrift and out of place. Never quite fitting in. The paperwork in her hand right now didn't really explain that, of course, but in some strange way it felt like it did.

'So now you know.'

She looked round to see her mother in the doorway, leaning on her cane.

'Chris was adopted,' Katie said.

'Yes.'

'What about me?'

'No.' Her mother shook her head. 'Your father and I tried to have children for a long time. It didn't happen for us, and we gave up hope it ever would. So we applied to adopt – which was when I finally got pregnant. You know what they say about men planning and God laughing. But it seemed right for us to remain on the list; it felt like something we should do. And that's how your brother ended up coming to us after you were born.'

Katie swallowed. 'Did Chris know?'

'No. Although I always wondered if part of him suspected. And I assume he knows now. He must have found out when he was looking through the photographs. He was in here for a long time that day. I'm sorry about that. Like I said yesterday, I'd forgotten these things were even here.'

'How did he react?'

Her mother smiled sadly. 'He didn't mention it. Part of me wishes he had done. We could have spoken about it then. But I hope the reason he didn't is because he knows it doesn't matter. And it doesn't, does it?'

'No,' Katie said.

Except that it did. She kept picturing Chris reading these documents and news clippings and trying to imagine how he would have felt. *It doesn't matter*, her mother had just said – and perhaps it didn't to the two of them. But she thought it would have mattered to Chris. All she could see in her head right then was the sensitive little boy he had been, and she wanted to reach backwards in time and hug him. She should have been there for him when he made this discovery. He should have *wanted* her to be.

And then came a different memory. The four of them visiting her father's shop that day, when her brother had started across to join her at the barrier and their mother had called out to him but not to her.

Chris, don't. It's dangerous.

'Is this why?' she said.

Her mother shook her head. 'Why what?'

'Why you always loved him more than me?'

She had barely known those words were coming, and part of her regretted them as soon as she'd spoken them.

But another part of her felt *relieved* – as though she'd been carrying this resentment for such a long time and had finally managed to cast some of it out of her. When her mother understood what she'd said, her face started to crumple. But then she caught herself. She looked down at the cane and began turning it round carefully in her grip. There was something about the movement that suggested all the mistakes of her life – all its disappointments and regrets – were playing out in her mind at once.

'Oh, Katie –' she started. But then she looked up, over Katie's shoulder.

At the same time, Katie was aware of the light in the room shifting, and she turned to see shadows flitting across the closed curtains.

Footsteps in the garden outside.

And then, a moment later, the doorbell rang.

'Wait here,' her mother said.

She turned and disappeared, hobbling awkwardly out of sight down the corridor. With her heart beating faster, Katie crossed the room to the doorway and listened as best she could. Her mother opened the front door.

'Mrs Shaw?'

A woman's voice.

'Yes,' her mother said. 'We met the other day.'

'That's right. Detective Pettifer. This is my colleague, Sergeant Reece. We're trying to locate your daughter, Katie.'

'Why? What's happened?'

Her mother was old and frail, and Katie imagined she was still leaning on her cane for support, but there was the same firmness to her voice she remembered from childhood.

'We'd just very much like to talk to her. And your son as well, of course.'

'I told you I've not heard from him in years.'

'What about your daughter?'

Katie leaned against the door frame. Waiting.

'She came by yesterday,' her mother said. 'I've not seen her since.'

'Why was she here?' the woman asked.

'She brings me my shopping. That's about the only real contact we have any more. Just doing her duty. She'll be at home now, I'd guess. You might want to try there.'

If it wasn't for the cane, Katie could imagine her mother folding her arms at that. There was a moment of silence, and then she heard the distant sound of a radio crackling. It was followed a few seconds later by the noise of feedback, and then quiet and muffled conversation. She listened carefully.

'OK,' she heard someone saying quietly. 'OK.'

Then, more loudly: 'We're sorry to have bothered you, Mrs Shaw. If you do hear from either of your children, we'd very much appreciate you letting us know.'

'Of course.'

A moment later, shadows passed across the curtains again. Katie heard the front door close and then the rattle of the chain. She stepped back into the room and waited until her mother appeared in the doorway.

'The police are looking for you,' she said.

'I know.'

'But I know you won't have done anything wrong.'

'Do you, though?'

Her mother looked down at the cane.

319

'I know full well that – whatever's happened – it will be because you were trying to help your brother. To help *people*. Because that's what you've always done. And I also know I haven't been as supportive as I could have been.'

She began turning the cane thoughtfully.

'But what you said just now,' she told Katie, 'it's not right and it's not fair. I understand you feeling that way. Perhaps your father and I did treat the two of you differently. And maybe that *was* because of the manner in which Chris came to us. Sometimes it felt like he'd been left there for us in that church. Like we'd been trusted with something we needed to keep safe.'

The cane was still turning. 'You just told me we never loved you as much as Chris,' she said. 'But we did. *I do*, Katie. It's just that you were always so confident. So capable. So strong-willed. You knew exactly what you were going to do, and you just went right out and did it. But Chris was never like that. And that's really all there is to it. You never *needed* our help the way he did.'

Her mother looked up at her.

'But you needed my help just now, I think. And so you had it.'

A beat of silence in the room.

'Thank you,' Katie said. 'For that.'

'You're welcome.'

Katie looked at the box. The newspaper clippings about Nathaniel Leland were still on top, and she reached down and picked one out.

One of your father's fancies.

Her mother's phrasing had disturbed her yesterday, but having learned what she had, she thought she understood now.

'Dad thought this might be Chris?'

'He wondered. Your father was always interested in finding out who Chris really was. He knew it didn't matter – that Chris was our son, and that was the end of it – but he also thought that one day it might be important for *Chris* to know where he'd come from. I didn't really appreciate that at the time. But I do a little more now. People need to know who they are.'

'Why did Dad think this boy might be Chris?'

Her mother shrugged. 'Because Chris came from somewhere. Children don't simply appear – however much you wish them to. And that little boy, Nathaniel Leland, was about the right age and had vanished at about the right time. That's all there was to it.'

'But the police must have checked?'

'Yes, of course. We found that out when your father began looking into it. We spoke to the adoption people and they told us the possibility had been investigated and ruled out. The man – that poor missing baby's father – they took him to see Chris in the hospital, just after he'd been found. And he . . .' Her mother trailed off and looked down again.

'What?' Katie said.

Her mother sighed softly. 'Nathaniel Leland's father *screamed* at the sight of Chris,' she said. 'Screamed as though his whole world had just come apart.'

There was another moment of silence in the room.

And then Katie felt a vibration in her pocket.

Alderson's phone was ringing.

40

Chris allowed himself to be led out of the house.

He was too exhausted and scared to resist. The old man guided him. He was holding Chris round the upper arm with a grip so hard he was sure the old man's fingers would be leaving more bruises on his skin. His hands were still bound, and the gag remained in place, but he had been blindfolded now as well, and the claustrophobia from the multiple restraints was as bad as anything he had ever felt. He had never been so afraid.

The old man gave him the slightest of shoves, and he stumbled a little. His legs and back were stiff from lying on the stone floor all night in that pitch-black room. He had not slept and, devoid of sensation, time had begun to lose meaning. Although he had been conditioned by the physical discomfort of sleeping on the streets over the years, last night had been worse than anything he'd experienced before. When you were sleeping rough, you were at least surrounded by *something*. But in that absolute darkness it had started to feel like everything had been taken from him. As though he was nothing more than a small, forgotten memory at the back of someone's skull.

But there was sensation to make up for that now.

When the old man led him outside, he felt a cool breeze on his face. His feet crunched across gravel of some kind. It was raining lightly. He breathed in as best he could, and even through the damp, dirty cloth of the gag the air tasted crisp and fresh. There were so many sudden reminders of being alive that his heart fluttered at the realization he would not be for long.

'Stop.'

Chris did as he was told. Although the blindfold was tied tightly around his head, a little light was making it through the fabric, the world reduced to ghostly grey impressions in front of him. He heard the sound of a car door opening, and one of those ghosts resolved itself into the shape of a vehicle. When the old man put his hand on Chris's head, he understood what was required of him. He ducked down. Manoeuvred himself awkwardly into the back seat.

The door *whumped* shut beside him.

The creak of leather now. The stench of lemon air freshener. He couldn't make out much through the blindfold, but he could sense a presence in the driver's seat ahead, and he reached out tentatively with his bound hands and touched a screen of glass separating the front seats from the back. Then he withdrew them quickly as the other back door opened, and the old man clambered in beside him.

A few moments later, the engine started and the car began to move.

'Where are we going?' he tried to say.

'Be quiet.'

'Are we going to meet James?'

The old man laughed. Chris wasn't sure if the man had understood him or was simply laughing at his attempts at speech. Either way, there was no humour in the sound, and the old man did not answer him. Chris supposed there was no need for him to. The old man wanted the book, which meant he must have convinced James he was prepared to exchange Chris for it.

The idea brought a fresh bloom of terror, one more vivid than any he had ever felt for himself. His whole life, the world had seemed to have been set against him, and part of him had eventually hardened to that and welcomed the moral freedom it offered. There had been occasions when he had not only accepted help when it was offered but taken it when it wasn't. He had been self-ish and thoughtless, putting his own needs above those of others. He had done things that made him more ashamed than he could bear.

And yet now all he felt was a desperate desire for James to be safe.

Don't trust this man, Chris thought. *Run.*

But he knew that James wouldn't do that. No more, had their situations been reversed, than he would have abandoned James.

So you'll have to be ready, won't you?

Yes, he thought. *I will.*

Tensing his muscles slowly, trying not to attract attention, he tested the bindings around his wrists again. It might have been his imagination, but was there a little more give in them now than there had been during the night? Perhaps. Not enough, though. He entertained himself with the fantasy of somehow getting his arms around the old man's neck from behind and pulling with all his might. A knee in his back, and then see which gave first – the bindings or the man's throat.

The old man laughed again, as though reading his mind.

Chris held on to the fantasy anyway.

But another thought was growing too. For as long as he could remember there had been that voice in his head telling him he was worthless – that he deserved all the bad things that happened to him. Ever since Alan had found him, the voice had become quieter, but he could hear it again now, growing in volume. Stronger than before. More confident. And while he didn't understand half of what the old man had said to him last night, he knew this much: he didn't deserve any of this.

You should never have been born.

He had always believed that, and once upon a time the voice would have listened to those words, nodded in agreement and then repeated them back to him with glee.

But not now.

Fuck you, he thought.

Who are you to tell me what I should be?

They drove for some time.

Eventually the car began rolling languidly from side to side, and then Chris heard the sound of its tyres crunching over gravel. They came to a stop and the driver and old man got out. Chris sat in silence for a while, his heart thudding in his chest. Where were they? After what felt like an age, the door beside him was opened and he was pulled roughly out of the car.

He winced. Wherever this was, it was much colder here.

'Where are we?' he tried to say.

And then the blindfold was pulled off.

There was no sign of the driver now, but the old man stood before him in the grey light. He had a knife in one hand. The other was holding something down by his side, slightly behind his leg. But Chris's attention was drawn more to the familiar building looming over the two of them. Back when he had worked here, it had felt like a place of salvation and hope, but the sight of it now delivered only dread. Because part of him understood that this place in which he had come back to life was the place in which he was going to die.

He looked back down and registered the hatred on the old man's face. And he realized what the man was holding by his side.

A can of petrol.

And the old man finally answered him.

Where are we?

'Home,' he said.

41

Katie drove through the winding roads north of the city.

There seemed to be little around her but empty fields and trees. She passed a few abandoned buildings. They were relics of a forgotten era: cottages and farmhouses that were so broken down now they might as well have been cairns of rock by the roadside. Aside from those there were no distinctive features to the land. It was a world of endless fields, dotted with distant clusters of trees that seemed as small as toys. Perhaps it would have been idyllic here in spring or summer but right now the sky above was a vast canopy of grey-black cloud that seemed to be drizzling darkness.

She was about halfway there when she made a decision and pulled over.

She got out of the car and was immediately shocked by the coldness of the wind. The hedgerow beside her was shivering from the force of it. But if she was going to go through with this meeting, there was something else she needed to do first. So she took a deep breath, turned her back to the wind, and then switched her phone on. There were numerous voicemail messages waiting for her. She scrolled down the list. Most of them were from Sam, but there were several from what she assumed must be the police.

She clicked on the list of contacts and found her husband's number.

He answered the call immediately.

'Hello?'

Her name must have come up on his screen, and yet there was such desperation in his voice that it was as though he didn't quite dare to believe it was her. It broke her heart to hear him like that. And to know it was her fault – her responsibility – that he was going through this.

'It's me,' she said quietly.

'Katie. *Oh God*. Where are you?'

She looked around. Having relied on the GPS to take her this far, she couldn't have told him even if she'd wanted to. But, of course, she wouldn't tell him anyway. That wasn't why she'd stopped to make this call. She was phoning him because she was scared. Because she needed to tell him something. And, most of all, because she wanted to hear his voice again, even if it was for the last time.

Where are you?

'I'm not sure,' she said.

'The police are looking for you.'

'I know.'

'They were here this morning.'

She hesitated. 'Are they there now?'

'No. They haven't been back yet. It's just me and Siena here.'

The mention of her daughter's name sent a crack through her heart. For a moment she was desperate to speak to her, but she also knew that if she heard her voice, she wouldn't be able to go through with what she had to do. If Sam asked her to come home, she would still have the strength to refuse him. But not Siena.

'Did the police say why they were there?' she asked him.

'They said you broke into Michael Hyde's house and attacked him.'

She waited.

'They said you claimed he'd been stalking us.'

'I went to his house,' she said. 'There were photographs on the wall there. Sketches. Plans. I think he was after Siena. But his father must have taken them down before the police arrived, to protect him, and I don't think they believe me. And I know you don't either. But I *need* you to, Sam. It's so important.'

He hesitated. 'I'm actually not sure *what* the police believe right now.'

'But what about you?'

Silence on the line again. He still wasn't sure. He didn't want to tell her that and have her hang up on him, but he couldn't bring himself to lie to her either.

'Please just come home,' he said finally.

'I can't.'

'*Why*, Katie? What are you doing?'

And again, she wouldn't have been able to tell him even if she'd wanted to. Where was she? What was she doing? There were basic, everyday answers to those questions, but right now they landed on a deeper existential level. She felt unmoored and adrift on currents she did not understand.

The wind changed direction. She turned her body against it.

'Listen to me,' she said. 'I *need* you to believe me.'

'I do.'

'No – don't just say it. Because Hyde might come back. He might still try to hurt Siena. In fact, I'm sure he will. He's fixated on us for some reason. And when he does, you're going to need to be ready for him.'

Another moment of silence. And then the implication of what she'd just said dawned on him.

'But what about you?'

She swallowed. 'I love you, Sam. I'm sorry.'

'You shouldn't be,' he said quickly. 'No. You should not be sorry at all. *I'm* sorry. I love you so much. I always have. I haven't said that enough recently.'

'I know. Just the same. But there's something I have to do.'

'*Just come home to us.*'

'I'll try,' she said. 'I promise.'

'Wait. Siena's here –'

'Give her a hug from me then,' she said. 'And tell her I love her very much.'

Sam started to say something else, but she moved the phone away from her ear and his words were lost in the wind. She cancelled the call and turned off her phone.

And then she stood beside the car, her palm pressed to her forehead, sobbing.

It wasn't wise. If another car came along the driver might notice and stop to help. But the tears came anyway. She wanted so badly to be back with her family where she belonged. It was easy to imagine how confused and upset Siena must be, and she already knew how frightened Sam was. But it also felt like her course had been set and there was no escaping from it now.

Perhaps that had always been true.

After a minute she calmed herself down and got back in the car. Jack Lock's book, still wrapped in its protective packaging, rested on the passenger seat beside her.

There was a sense of malevolence to it. It was just a book – the fantasies of a mad man – but it was still hurting people after all these years, and through a chain of cause and effect she couldn't fathom it had made its way into her family's life and was continuing to spread its poison.

Just come home to us.

Katie started the engine and set off again.

I'll try, she thought. *I promise.*

42

The law firm that Richard Gaunt worked at was situated on a pleasant leafy street to the north of the city centre, nestled into a row of shops between a bakery and a barber shop, a driveway leading down beside the latter. As Laurence drove along the road towards it, Pettifer hung up the call she had been on.

'Anything?'

He could already tell from her body language that it wasn't.

'No,' she said. 'They've finally tracked down Kieran Davies.'

'Who?'

'Well, exactly. The last member of Hobbes's staff. He's finally turned up, alive and well, and there's an officer talking to him now.'

'Huh.'

It seemed like a long time ago since he'd been concerned with the abruptly dismissed staff members. Then again, it was important to dot the i's and cross the t's. Especially because the developments of the day so far had only confirmed how little they still knew. The whole picture might have been coming slowly into focus, but it remained far too complicated for him to understand what the hell he was looking at.

The address Sam Gardener had given them had indeed been Christopher Shaw's home – a flat that also turned out to be part of Alan Hobbes's portfolio of properties – but it had obviously been abandoned. They had a name for his travelling companion now – a boyfriend, it appeared – and were trying to locate him, but there were several James Aldersons in the city to work their way through, and even if they came up with the right address, Laurence highly doubted they were going to walk in to find the two of them curled up by the fire.

There had been no further sightings of Christopher Shaw.

Laurence had arranged for Katie Shaw's mother to be spoken to again. Assuming Gardener was correct, there *had* been some level of contact between her and her son, which meant she had been lying to them the other day. If so, she was still lying to them now; she remained adamant she had not seen Chris, and had apparently sat there the whole time with her face set like stone. The officer had asked Laurence if he wanted her arrested, but Laurence had decided not. Despite his frustration, he found himself almost admiring the woman. Her stubbornness verged on the elemental.

But there had been two more interesting developments.

Pettifer sighed. 'Remind me what we're doing here again?'

'Following a hunch,' Laurence said. 'Besides, what else can we do?'

He flicked the indicator and turned into the law firm's driveway.

'Ah!' he said. 'And would you look at that?'

Because they encountered Gaunt sooner than he'd been expecting. The lawyer was in his own vehicle, on his way off the premises, and their cars came to a halt nose to nose, blocking each other's way. Gaunt stared at the pair of them through the windscreen for a few seconds, a blank expression on his face.

Laurence smiled patiently. Beside him, Pettifer raised a hand and waved. Gaunt got the message. A few seconds later, he reversed backwards, and Laurence rolled their car slowly down the driveway and parked up alongside.

Another minute and we'd have missed him.

Which felt like a coincidence. Except he was beginning to think there were fewer coincidences in this case than he was comfortable with.

Laurence and Pettifer got out of the car, and he signalled for Gaunt to do the same. Again, the lawyer seemed reluctant, but then he joined them on the tarmac. Laurence thought he seemed even younger now than he had when they'd spoken in the churchyard. He was pale and nervous about something. Not *guilty* exactly – more like he'd got himself involved in something that scared him without him quite understanding why.

'Mr Gaunt,' Laurence said happily, 'we meet again. How are you today?'

'Busy.'

'Managing Mr Hobbes's estate?'

'Yes.' Gaunt looked slightly sick. 'Among others.'

'Excellent. That's actually one of the reasons we're here.'

He had brought the padded envelope with him. He held it up briefly to show Gaunt, and then slid the contents out of the open end.

'I was at the house of a woman named Katie Shaw earlier when this was delivered. The details on the reverse indicate that it was sent by you. Can you tell me what it is?'

Gaunt stared at it. 'A book,' he said flatly.

'Thank you. It is a book, yes – and a valuable one. But not *only* a book.'

The book itself was wrapped in a transparent cover. But there had been something else included in the package. A photograph. Laurence held it up carefully for Gaunt to see.

'This is Professor Hobbes, isn't it? And I assume the woman beside him must have been his wife?'

Gaunt looked at the image. 'Yes,' he said. 'I mean, I never asked, but he used to keep that by his bed.'

'And so what do you make of this?'

Laurence flipped the photograph over, revealing what had been written on the back.

Gaunt read the message there and then looked a little helpless.

'I've honestly no idea,' he said. 'I mean, I didn't even know the photograph was there. Mr Hobbes left very detailed instructions for what to do with his library after he died, and he'd packaged a few of them up already. Some of them had to be delivered to people, and this was one of those. I remember it needed to arrive at a specific time on a Sunday. But I have no idea why, or who the woman is it was sent to – Katie Shaw?'

'Yes.'

'OK. I don't know who she is.'

Laurence waited. But he knew by now that Gaunt was not good at leaving silences unfilled, and it became obvious he was telling the truth. Hobbes had arranged for this book – with a photograph and a message secreted within – to be sent out to Katie Shaw for reasons unknown. Interesting.

He put the items back carefully into the envelope.

'Does the name *Edward Leland* mean anything to you?' he said.

Another hunch. But Sam Gardener had told him Katie Shaw had a newspaper clipping about a missing child named Nathaniel Leland, and there had to be a reason for that. Laurence had looked into the case. The date of Nathaniel's abduction was only a few days earlier than the fire that killed Alan Hobbes's son – and the similarities did not end there. Nathaniel's father was also a very wealthy man, albeit one who had remained curiously absent from the public eye. A man who made his money in the dark and kept it there. He was only two years older than Alan Hobbes.

And then there was the name.

You have committed blasphemy and it will be corrected.
~ Edward

And even though it was only a hunch, he could tell from Gaunt's expression that the name was familiar. That it was perhaps even responsible for some of the sickness the lawyer appeared to be feeling right now.

'Mr Leland is also one of our clients,' he said.

'Your firm seems an odd choice for him.'

'How so?'

'He lives fifty miles away.'

Despite himself, Gaunt gave a nervous laugh.

'Tell me about it,' he said. 'I have to do the round trip all the time.'

'Really? When was the last time you visited?'

'Yesterday.'

'For what purpose?'

'Well, money, of course. It's always money with these people. And they have so much that they don't understand how it works.' Gaunt looked away briefly. 'I can't go into details. Let's just say Mr Leland wanted to withdraw a significant amount of money from one of his accounts, and it was my job to facilitate that.'

Laurence was aware of Pettifer tensing beside him. He himself felt a thrill. All the other details they had were small and meaningless by themselves. They might have pointed towards Edward Leland being connected *in some way*, but they were in no way conclusive. But this felt a little more solid. They had Christopher Shaw in possession of a stolen book he might wish to sell. And now they had a man withdrawing a large sum of money, with which – perhaps – to pay for it.

'What did Mr Leland want the money for?'

'I don't know. It's not my job to ask things like that. All I know is that Mr Leland is a valued client, and has been for many years, and that grants him certain privileges. It's much easier when he sends one of his people here to us, but . . .' He glanced behind him at the office building for a second, then back at Laurence. 'But I just do what I'm told. If he wants me to go there and arrange something, I go there and arrange it. That's how it works.'

Laurence peered at him. Gaunt still seemed nervous, he thought. There was something else going on here that he was reluctant to reveal. Was it there in the glance he'd just given?

'You said Mr Leland sometimes sends one of his people here?'

Gaunt started to look at the office again and didn't quite stop himself in time.

Laurence smiled at him. 'Mr Gaunt,' he said patiently, 'a man is dead. Other lives are at stake. You are very busy. So let me be simple. Signal to me with blinks if you like – two for yes, one for no. Is one of Mr Leland's men here now?'

'No. But one was earlier.'

'Wishing to arrange more money for him?'

Gaunt shook his head. 'Like I told you, we're in the process of managing Mr Hobbes's estate. There is a huge amount to deal with, and some of our existing clients are aware of potential sales. It's only speculative at this point, of course, and it's not strictly above board. But these are valued clients. And it makes our lives easier to begin planning things now.'

'Go on.'

'Mr Leland is interested in buying the house. He wanted to look around.'

Gaunt looked sicker than ever. It was as though he was sure, deep down in his bones, that he had done something wrong – something that went well beyond being *above board* – but couldn't quite understand what.

'He wanted to borrow the key.'

43

Home.

It had been more than sixty years since Edward Leland had been inside his father's house, and he felt a jolt now as he stepped over the threshold.

It was partly one of recognition. Little had changed down here. The entrance hall remained as vast and cavernous as ever, the ceiling lost in darkness high above. The same chessboard tiles on the floor. The same shadowy doorways leading off to either side. Even the air smelled the same. He breathed in deeply and it was like pressing his face into a long-forgotten childhood blanket.

But it was more than memory alone. There was a feeling of electricity here, as though the property had been cut off for a long time and his arrival had reconnected it to the grid, setting the walls and foundations humming. As though the house itself knew that a terrible wrong had been committed and was now going to be corrected.

Leland's footsteps echoed as he led Christopher Shaw across to the twinned staircases, the knife pressed into the base of the boy's spine. The two ascended. Leland knew where to go. He had researched what Hobbes had done to the layout of the house thirty years earlier while planning the fire.

The fire that should have erased the child from existence.

More recognition came as he followed Shaw into the small, enclosed flat at the heart of the building, but here it was tempered by disgust at the sight awaiting them. His father had allowed him in here on occasion. Leland would sit cross-legged on the rug and listen to tales of his future, a fire burning beside him in the iron grate, the flames crackling and popping and casting flickers of golden light across the walls and ornate fittings.

But Alan had stripped it down since taking owner-ship, reducing what had been a grand room into an empty, utilitarian space, fit for existence but not for life. The fireplace had been bricked up and painted over. The rich, soft carpet had been ripped away. The furniture was spartan and the painting was gone. There was barely comfort here now, never mind the opulence he remem-bered. And in that moment Leland hated his brother more than ever.

You can't do this. It's not allowed.

He looked across the room. There was just a dark, empty archway there. The door that led to the deeper chamber was gone.

Along with the rules their father had given them about never entering it.

He led Christopher Shaw across the room. The boy hesitated as they approached the archway. Not because he was frightened of what lay beyond – he would be familiar with that, of course – but because he had seen the bloodstains on the wall around the old bed frame. His father's blood. Perhaps he didn't know who Alan Hobbes had really been, but he knew the man had been good to him, and Leland savoured the expression of dawning horror on the boy's face.

But only for a moment.

He pressed the knife a little harder into the boy's back and the two of them continued on through the archway.

There was no sense of recognition now. Leland had always done what he was told – what he was meant to do – and so he had never entered this chamber, and had nothing with which to compare the empty bookshelves and cases that he saw here now. His gaze moved over them anyway, finally settling on a large wooden cabinet. He felt the pull of its contents – the items within it had once belonged to their father before being scattered to the four winds, and Alan had then spent his life and wealth gathering them together.

And, of course, one which Alan had stolen as a boy. The sacred text he had used to commit the foulest and most unforgivable of blasphemies.

Leland forced Christopher Shaw over to the opposite side of the room, where the roof and part of the wall were open to the elements and a small, burnt bed frame rested against the wall.

'Sit down.'

The boy did as he was told, slumping on to the floor-boards beside the remains of the bed. He was shivering and beaten – but appearances could always be deceptive. Leland had seen him testing the bindings around his wrists in the car, and he thought they looked a little looser now. It didn't matter. He put the canister of pet-rol down and retrieved the handcuffs he'd brought with him from the inner pocket of his suit. Keeping hold of the knife, he cuffed one of the boy's hands to the heavy leg of the bed.

Because it mattered that he died *here*, where he had been meant to.

Then Leland picked up the can, unscrewed the cap and splashed the contents all over Shaw, soaking the boy and the bed and the floorboards around him. He shook out every last, rattling drop as Shaw spluttered and screamed into the gag, his eyes screwed tightly shut and his legs kicking helplessly.

Leland tossed the can aside and stood back.

As he did, he heard a faint sound drifting in from the open wall above them. Tyres crunching over gravel.

Someone was here.

Shaw heard it too. And despite his pain and distress, he tried to say something. It was difficult to make out the words, but, as he had before, Leland could certainly make out the sentiment. *Don't hurt him.*

'No, no,' Leland said. 'It's your *sister* who's coming. And I'm afraid I am going to hurt her very badly indeed.'

Shaw looked back at him for a moment, then blinked rapidly and screwed his eyes shut again, calling out more meaningless noises now.

'I'll be back soon,' Leland told him. 'Don't worry.'

And then he made his way downstairs to finish things.

44

As she was driving up the dirt path that led away from the road, the full weight of what she was doing hit Katie hard. She fought down an urge to stop and reverse out of here. To go home. But if she did that, what would happen to Chris? And so she forced herself to continue. A few minutes later, the trees fell away, revealing a wind-swept field ahead of her, an old mansion house squatting in the centre. There was something dark and hooded about the way the windows seemed to watch her as she drove closer. The building itself appeared even blacker than the dark-grey clouds that filled the sky above.

Not totally black, though.

Most of the property was shrouded in darkness, but as she parked up behind the car that was already there, she noticed a soft glow coming from high above. She stared up through the windscreen and saw a broken-down section of blackened stone around what had once been a window. The light was coming from in there.

What was this place?

She wondered if it belonged to the man she was here to meet. It was a building that felt well suited to some-one both obsessed with the murderabilia of Jack Lock and rich enough to pay for it. But although the property seemed vast, there was also something dilapidated and abandoned about it.

She looked down again. There was nobody visible in

the car in front of her, and the enormous wooden doors of the house were open. Whoever she was meeting was already inside. Perhaps they were even three storeys above where the glow was coming from.

Waiting for her.

But so was Chris.

She looked at the ground by the door and noticed there was a long, thin stretch of tape trampled into the wet ground there. And when she realized what she was seeing, she blinked.

The remains of a police cordon.

She stared at that for a moment, taking a few deep breaths to steady herself, and then picked up the book from the passenger seat. Even through the plastic, her fingertips tingled from the feel of the thing.

'OK,' Katie said quietly. 'You know what you have to do.'

She got out of the car, pulling her jacket around her against the wind. It was much colder here than it had been back on the road. Despite the vast house, it seemed like a wild and untamed place. Isolated and exposed. She left the car door open behind her and walked slowly across the gravel towards the door. And then she stepped over the old police cordon and went inside.

It was dark over the threshold, but enough gloomy light was spreading in from outside to give an impression of the huge open space ahead of her. She registered the black-and-white-tiled floor. The dark doorways leading off to either side.

And then a steady *tapping* noise began echoing around.

She waited. A few seconds later, she saw a figure making its way down one of the two staircases ahead.

A man. He was moving slowly, taking his time. When he reached the bottom, she registered how old he was, and wondered if the care he was taking was due to his age. But as he began to approach her across that chessboard floor, the impression disappeared. *Be careful,* she told herself. Because there was a confidence to him – a sense of strength and power – that set an alarm ringing inside her. However old he was, he was clearly dangerous.

He stopped in the middle of the floor and smiled politely. 'You must be the sister,' he said.

She looked around again. The doorways on either side of the entrance hall remained dark. The old man had come down alone and there was no sign of her brother.

'Where's Chris?'

The old man smiled again. 'He's safe for now. And he will be even safer in a few minutes when we've conducted our business. But after his behaviour last night, neither of you can blame me for taking precautions. He didn't bring the book to that exchange and so, for this one, I have not brought him. But he's safe right now. I am a man of my word.'

He had stopped at the edge of where the light from outside could comfortably reach, and beyond that impression of old age it was hard for her to make out any of his features. But from what she could see of his smile, she didn't trust it. And while his tone of voice was superficially pleasant and friendly, she didn't trust that either.

'I want to see him,' she said.

'And I want to see the book.'

She held it up. And while she couldn't see the old man's

eyes properly, she could tell his attention had locked on to the book. She even felt the force of his gaze and had to fight to stop her hand from shaking slightly.

She lowered the book. 'I told you I'd burn it if you hurt him,' she said.

'You will damn your soul if you do.'

'I don't care – it's just a book. And I want to see Chris. *Right now.*'

Her words echoed around the entrance hall. There were a few seconds of silence then as the old man gathered himself together. Any trace of friendliness had disappeared following her threat, and he had become what he was. A businessman laying out the terms of the deal.

'You are younger and faster than me,' he said. 'I'm sure you could reach your car before I reach you. But I want you to understand this. If you leave here with that book, your brother will die. And he will never be found. You won't even be able to bury what's left of his body.'

She said nothing.

'And this place.' The old man gestured around. 'It has no connection to me. I will never be found. And even if I were, I would never be held to account. So you have to bear in mind which of us here has the most to lose.'

Again, she said nothing.

'All that pain and suffering,' he said. 'For *just a book.*'

And with that it was clear the negotiation was over. The silence stretched out. While she didn't trust him, Katie also understood that everything he had just told her was true. She could still take her chances and run – dart back over that cordon and escape from here – but she would be leaving her brother to his fate.

She racked her brain for options she didn't have.

And then she walked slowly towards the old man.

He extended his hand, but she wasn't prepared to get that close to him. Instead, a little way across the entrance hall, she leaned down and placed the book on the floor – then kicked it across to him. It spiralled across the tiles before coming to a stop at his feet.

The man stared at her.

'It's just a book,' she said.

He crouched down. And then, carefully and reverentially, he picked it up. If her own skin had tingled at the touch of it, it seemed like an actual *jolt* went through the old man; it was as though he had just made contact with a live wire. He squatted there for a few seconds with his head bowed, his fingers the only part of him moving. They were stroking the cover, as though attempting to read Braille through the polythene. And then he stood up.

'I'm sorry,' he said absently.

'What?'

'Like I told you, I'm a man of my word.'

And then he turned and walked back to the staircase.

Katie hesitated, unsure if she was intended to follow. But then a sudden sinking feeling in her chest told her she was not – and she heard movement behind her. She turned round and saw a man had emerged silently from one of the dark rooms off to the side and was now standing between her and the open door.

She heard footsteps *tapping* away up the stairs.

The man she had been left with down here was tall and wide, dressed in a black suit, his face hard and implacable.

Someone who enjoyed doing really bad things to people.

She took a step back. 'Help,' she said.

The man took a step towards her. She realized her voice had been too small and quiet. That, faced with this man, she might even have whispered the word.

And so, for what it was worth, she repeated it more loudly.

'Help!'

And this time it was loud enough.

OK. You know what you have to do.

James Alderson had spent the car journey hunkered down out of sight in the back seat of her car. He came sprinting through the door now, much faster than she'd have given him credit for, and leaped on to the man's back. They both tumbled over and began wrestling on the tiles.

She started over to help, but as the two of them rolled around and started exchanging blows, Alderson shook his head at her, his teeth gritted with effort.

'*Go,*' he managed.

With her heart pounding Katie turned and ran for the stairs.

45

Leland walked back into what had once been his father's opulent quarters and had since become Alan Hobbes's bare flat.

As he stepped over the threshold, he felt another *jolt* inside him. It was a little like when he had touched the book downstairs, but this one was much stronger. For a moment the past was superimposed upon the present. The fire was burning beside him, crackling and flickering, and yet it was somehow also black and dead, the coals cold in the iron grate, and it was also gone entirely, bricked up behind the featureless wall. He stared around, keeping tight hold of the book, and watched as furniture appeared and vanished. A baby laughed. The painting of a flayed saint appeared on the wall and then danced away. A door that was not there any more suddenly was.

And his father's voice swirled like a storm.

You must never go in there.

Do you hear me, Edward? Nothing matters more.

Leland shook his head. The present solidified around him again. Now there was just the squalid chamber with its bad air and bloodstains. The door was gone. And only the faintest trace of his father's voice remained echoing in his head.

You must never go in there.

He headed through.

Christopher Shaw was where he had left him. In the

time Leland had been downstairs, the boy had removed his gag and loosened the bindings around his wrists sufficiently to free his hands. Neither mattered. He was still cuffed to the leg of the bed, which was bolted securely to the floor. The boy was trapped in the place where he had been meant to die all those years ago.

Leland took a lighter from his pocket and flicked the flame alive.

Shaw flinched. 'Don't. Please.'

Leland just smiled. And he was about to toss the burning lighter into the corner of the room when he heard a sound from outside again.

He stopped and listened.

Tyres on gravel.

Another car.

He snapped the lighter closed, and then stepped over to the ruined wall and stood on tiptoes to peer out through the open brickwork. Far below, he could make out the flicker of red and blue lights at the front of the house.

The sound of a car door slamming.

And then quick footsteps behind him.

He turned, knowing it was too soon for the police to have made their way up. It was the woman – the boy's sister. Somehow she had got past Banyard downstairs and followed him up here. But she hadn't known what she would find, and the sight stopped her cold. Even as Leland darted towards her, she was still trying to make sense of what she was seeing.

'Katie!' Shaw cried out behind him.

Thank you, Leland thought. Because her attention snapped over to where her brother was lying, and that gave Leland the chance he needed to close the distance.

With the lighter clenched in his fist, he punched her hard in the face, felt her nose crunch beneath his knuckles, and then watched as she crashed backwards against one of the cabinets and fell to the floor.

Blood began pouring down over her mouth.

'You brought the police,' he said.

She shook her head, half dazed, then spat blood out to one side.

'Not me,' she said, slurring the words.

'Who then?'

'Maybe you're not as untouchable as you thought.'

He took a step towards her, the anger rising. While everything he had told her downstairs was true, the police being here right now meant it would be difficult for him to walk away unscathed. Money could buy many things, but even money had its limits. This was not what was meant to happen. It was not right.

Leland had the sensation of being a puppet. Of his brother still somehow pulling everyone's strings.

You can still burn the boy.

That was true. Not only would the fire send Christopher Shaw down to hell with his father, where the two of them belonged, it would have the benefit of confusing the scene up here. It might give him the chance to work out a story he could sell.

And if not . . . well. His faith was strong.

Deus scripsit.

He turned round. Shaw was staring at him with open hatred now. The fear from earlier was gone, replaced by rage at what Leland had just done to his sister.

'Leave her alone,' the boy said.

Despite everything, Leland actually laughed.

The boy's expression darkened with frustration. He knew Leland could do whatever he liked. And the fear resurfaced as Leland approached him.

Leland clicked the lighter on and –

The police won't let you keep it.

Leland looked down at the book he was holding in his other hand. The realization was stark, and it sent a chill through him. Whatever story he told the police now, he would inevitably be placed into custody at first, and the book would be taken from him – perhaps never to be returned. The thought was intolerable, and it caused the fury inside him to blaze up in him once again.

Even now, Alan had thwarted him.

Except . . .

He had a couple of minutes, didn't he?

Yes. If he was quick enough, he did – and that might at least be something. Keeping hold of the lighter, he began to tear the protective wrapping from the book. It came away easily. If he had been thinking clearly, it might have occurred to him that the book *wanted* to be read, but he was too distracted by the urgency of the task, and then any thoughts at all were knocked off course by the much stronger jolt as his fingers finally touched the leather cover itself.

His father's words . . .

The book's pages fell open easily. He flicked through, scanning a few of the entries. Every sentence was clearly visible to him, but he still couldn't understand what he was seeing.

He turned quickly to the final page in the book.

And then Edward Leland read what had been written.

46

Katie.

Why had she put herself at risk for him?

Cuffed to the bed on the floor, Chris stared across the room at his sister. She was struggling to get to her feet now, but he could tell the old man's punch had badly disorientated her. She kept shaking her head, sending droplets of blood flicking off to either side. His heart clenched at the sight. Her being hurt horrified him, especially because she had come here trying to help him. After everything he'd done, he didn't deserve that.

Even now she was still trying to stand.

He wanted to call out to her to stop – or tell her that if she managed to get to her feet she should run. Leave him. Right now he would have done anything to protect her, even if it was simply giving her permission to stop protecting him. But then she collapsed back down and shook her head again.

The old man hadn't noticed. In fact, he seemed wholly entranced by the book he was holding, staring down intently at a page at the end. Chris could see the man's eyes moving, his gaze tracking back and forth, but aside from that he was motionless.

Chris would have killed him right then if he could.

Not for what he had done to him, or even to save himself, but because of what he'd done to *Katie*. And yet he was no more able to reach the old man than his sister was capable of rising to her feet. All he could do was stare at him, *hating him*, while imagining the hundred things he should have done differently so that he and his sister had not ended up here.

I'm sorry, Katie.

The room was silent for a moment.

And then there was a gentle creak of leather.

The old man closed the book and turned slowly to look at Chris. His face had gone white, and his expression was slacker now. For a moment he didn't seem able to process what he'd just read. But then he shook his head, as though trying to dislodge something, and walked slowly across the room, anger beating off him in waves. Still holding the lighter.

Chris felt his heartbeat accelerate as the old man approached. *Keep calm*, the voice inside his head told him. If he was going to have a chance of surviving this, he needed to do everything right. The man crouched down in front of him, his fingers flicking against the top of the lighter.

Chris could almost feel the soft *whump* of the fire taking sudden hold.

The lick of it everywhere against his skin.

The agony as he burned.

You should never have been born.

'Look at me,' the old man said.

Chris did. The expression on the man's face was the naked hatred of someone who had been tricked. Who had just had everything taken away from him at the very moment he had been supposed to succeed.

'What have you done with it?'

With his free hand Chris reached under his leg. While

the man had been downstairs, he had remembered
something that Alan had told him once, when it had
seemed like his mind had been slipping.

Oh God, it's under the bed. It's under the fucking bed!

Chris took out the knife he had found taped there.
And with all the strength he could muster he plunged
the blade upwards into the old man's throat.

47

It was the sight of the old man crouching over Chris that dragged Katie up.

The stink of petrol filled the air, and part of her understood what was about to happen. Whoever this man was, he had lost his mind and he was going to set them all on fire. That certainty landed inside her harder than his punch had, and the panic got her upright. Without being aware of how it happened she was back on her feet again, the room whirling around her so sickeningly that she wasn't even sure which direction she was facing.

It was the noise that centred her.

A loud clatter – and then a terrible gargling sound. She turned her head towards the source. Her vision moved further than it should, reeling past the sight at the far end of the room before righting itself again. Chris. He was sitting up beside the rusted remains of a bed. The old man was on the other side of it now, collapsed on the floor. He was lying on his back with his hands clenching his neck, an awful cawing sound rattling out of his mouth.

'Katie!'

Her brother's voice.

'Katie, over here!'

She shook her head, then made her way across the room as quickly and carefully as she could. It felt like the floor was tilted at an angle, and her body kept leaning over and threatening to fall away to the side. She grabbed hold of the rusted ends of the bed like a lifeline. And then she registered the sound of metal clinking against metal. Handcuffs. She couldn't see them right then, but she knew that her brother was trapped here.

'There might be a key,' he said. 'Look –'

'Yeah, yeah.'

Her thoughts and words were slurred. Keeping hold of one bedpost for balance, she manoeuvred herself round, like the hand of a clock circling the centre of a dial. The old man was lying in front of her, his fingers still clutching helplessly at his throat. There was blood everywhere: all over his shirt and scrabbling hands, and the floor beneath his head. It came bubbling out of his lips as he rasped and choked on it.

His hands were empty now, and she frowned to herself as she leaned down. Hadn't he been holding something before? A book? A lighter? She couldn't see either of them now, and her vision was beginning to star at the edges.

She reached inside his suit – and his hands immediately shot towards her wrists, trying to grab them. But he was growing weak now, and she just batted them away. She slipped her fingers into the silk pockets in his jacket, under the bright red rose that was pinned to his lapel. Searching.

'Katie,' Chris said.

'Shhhh.'

She found the key – or at least, it felt like a key – then circled back round the bed. Her hands began trembling as she attempted to get the key into the lock.

Chris snatched it off her. 'Let me.'

'*Fine.*'

She heard a few scrapes and clicks of metal, and then her brother was standing up and grabbing hold of her. She was surprised by how strong he seemed. It was her job to help him, and yet it was he who was supporting her as they moved towards the archway. Maybe they were both supporting each other.

They reached the arch. It was going to be OK.

'You shouldn't be here,' her brother told her.

'Yes,' Katie said, 'I should.'

And then she heard a sound behind them.

Scritch.

She looked back over Chris's shoulder and saw the old man had somehow managed to rotate his body around in the pool of blood. She wasn't sure he could even see them any more, but he was staring mindlessly in their direction, a flame now dancing above the lighter gripped in his hand.

There was a sudden *whump* that reminded her of the boiler coming on at home.

A flicker of green and blue light.

Then everything spun – suddenly and violently – and she had the sensation of rough, dank stone slamming against her as her brother threw them both into the corridor ahead, casting them forward just as the whole room burst into flame behind them.

48

An explosion of light at his back.

Michael Hyde saw his shadow cast suddenly against the door of the house in front of him. He spun round so quickly that he almost fell and had to reach out for a nearby lamp post to steady himself. The movement caused the pain in his other arm – his bandaged, broken one – to flare, and the side of his head began pounding violently. And all for nothing. Just the sun emerging briefly through a break in the thick clouds.

Hyde held on to the post and closed his eyes.

Focus.

A few seconds later, he opened his eyes and glanced to either side. There was nobody around – nobody to notice him or to pay any attention. It was such a nice neighbourhood, and the house before him was tucked away in one of its quietest little curls. It felt like he knew every cobblestone by now. He has spent so much time on this street since his release from prison that it might as well have belonged to him.

He reached for the door handle with his good hand.

There was a slight click – the sound of something slotting into place – and then the door opened easily into the front room he had stared at from outside the window so often.

He listened. Music was beating softly somewhere below him.

But the little girl was sitting on the settee, just as she always was, with that scarf of hers wrapped round her. The curtains across the window were drawn, and the light from the television flickered over her. She looked up at him curiously as he stepped inside, as though she'd been expecting someone else, but not with any real concern. That didn't surprise Hyde. She was a brave child – or at least she hadn't learned yet how awful the world could be. Or perhaps it was even simpler. That on some level she understood she had no right to exist and part of her welcomed an end to it.

It had all started after that fire he set thirty years ago.

Ever since then everything had felt *wrong* to Hyde. The cast of the light; the tilt of the world. There was a voice in the back of his mind that spoke in a language he didn't recognize. The whole of existence had seemed to be leaning on him – pushing him to do something, and while he couldn't quite understand it, the voice seemed to be insisting that things were not how they were supposed to be. That a mistake had been made and it was his job to correct it.

It was hard to remember now, but he was sure there had been a moment when the voice had become clear, and he had acted upon it.

Or tried to at least.

But then there had been that time in prison afterwards when the men had come into his cell. His thoughts had been scrambled after that. The voice had been just as insistent as before but now it was even more garbled and indecipherable. All he had really been sure about since was that there was *something* that needed to be put right. He had been doing his best to do what was required of him – to follow the voice as best he could – and even if this little girl here wasn't quite the person he was looking for, it felt like she was close enough.

The music was still beating beneath him.

Hyde walked across to where the little girl was sitting.

'Red car?' she said.

She recognized him. That made everything settle a little for him. Deep down, she really did understand, and that would make this whole thing easier for them both.

'Yes,' he said quietly. 'That's right.'

'Daddy?'

'No,' he said. 'Not Daddy.'

But then he realized she hadn't been talking to him at all – that, in fact, she was looking over his shoulder towards the closed curtains by the front door. And then the side of his head bloomed with white fire, and suddenly he was on his side on the floor. He rolled over on to his back. A man – the father – was standing above him, rubbing his wrist.

The man looked to one side. 'It's OK, sweetie.'

The words seemed to be coming from far too high above, as though Hyde himself was trapped underwater. The voice in the back of his mind grew louder – desperate and angry, and then howling with frustration and rage that drowned out everything in Michael Hyde except the impulse to fight back. To do what needed to be done. He had to get up. He had to –

The man's foot was on his free hand.

He was taking out his mobile phone, still talking to his child.

'It's OK, sweetie. Nobody's going to hurt you while I'm here.'

49

Laurence stared up at the fire burning high above him.

It had taken hold properly now and the entire top floor of the house was ablaze, the flames stretching out into the wings on either side and beginning to lick their way eagerly downwards. Flickers of light and shadow played across the windows of the floor below. He watched as the glass in one of them shattered and billows of black smoke began unfolding out.

Beside him, Pettifer glanced back towards the treeline.

'Where the fuck are they?'

'On their way.'

The first time they had come here Pettifer had remarked about money buying privacy. Which was true, of course – but the flip side of that was isolation. When the fire that killed Joshua Hobbes began here three decades earlier, there had at least been staff on hand to tackle it as best they could. There was nobody now. Fire engines, ambulances and more police were currently on their way from the city, but the house would be left to the whims of the blaze for a while yet.

A section of wall towards the centre crumbled suddenly away. Dust and timber tumbled down and scattered in front of the open door, embers swirling in the air above.

'Shit,' Pettifer said, then called out more loudly: 'Move away, please!'

Laurence watched as James Alderson and Katie and Christopher Shaw moved a little further back from the building. They were gathered close together – survivors supporting each other. He was relieved to see it. The three of them were alive at least, if not entirely unharmed. Christopher Shaw was bruised and shaken, and Katie Shaw's nose had been broken, but both had escaped the flames in time, and both would live. James Alderson had taken slightly more of a beating. When Laurence and Pettifer had arrived, they had found Alderson fighting a man in the entrance hall and immediately intervened. Alderson hadn't resisted them, and they had left him free for the moment. The other man – who had under-estimated what it might be like to take on an angry Pettifer and her baton – was currently handcuffed in the back of their car.

Pettifer's phone rang now.

'Shit.' She stepped away to take the call.

Laurence looked up at the flames again. From what he understood, Edward Leland was up there somewhere – but so far beyond help that he and Pettifer had made only a cursory effort to force their way up the stairs against the wall of heat and smoke that was pushing down from above. The fire had been moving quickly even then.

The whole place was going to burn down today.

Along with everything inside it.

And that was a thought he could not quite get away from. Among the many questions the last few days had brought, two in particular had been preoccupying him. Why had Alan Hobbes – a man with the means to live anywhere – chosen to live in a place with such a terrible

363

history? And while Hobbes had devoted his life to learning and philanthropy, why had he also spent time and money collecting all the items associated with a monster like Jack Lock?

But, as Laurence watched the fire consume the house and its contents, he couldn't shake the feeling that he was looking at the answer to both those questions. Alan Hobbes had gathered everything together in this place so that it would all be destroyed in this moment right now. That it was what he had planned all along.

Which was impossible, of course.

If Laurence was correct, then Hobbes and Leland were the sons of Jack Lock. But their father's book was nothing more than a description of abuse. It was a record of the damage that had been done to him as a child, and the damage he had then perpetuated as an adult. It could no more foretell the future than the past defined the measure of the men who emerged from it.

Pettifer finished her call and stepped back over.

'Anything?' he said.

'Michael Hyde. He just broke into Katie Shaw's house.'

Laurence looked at her.

'Everything's fine,' she said quickly. 'It looks like Hyde really was after their daughter for some reason. But the husband was there. He managed to subdue him. Hyde's in custody right now.'

Laurence looked back up at the flames dancing in the air above. At the play of embers there. They seemed to be forming patterns against the sky behind, and for a moment it was like he was seeing words in a language he couldn't read, which dissolved before he could see them well enough to try.

But the mention of Hyde reminded him of being at Katie Shaw's house earlier – and of something that Alan Hobbes really *had* arranged from beyond the grave. He headed over to their car, ignored the man handcuffed in the back, and retrieved the package that had been delivered to Katie Shaw's house. Then he walked across to the three of them, his feet crunching softly on the gravel, the heat from the fire growing warmer on his face as he approached.

They looked up at him expectantly. Christopher Shaw had a blanket wrapped round his shoulders but was still shivering a little. Even so, he was not quite what Laurence had been expecting. Everything he had read had suggested a man lost and adrift – at odds with the world and unable to find his footing – but Shaw looked stronger and more determined now, as though he had been standing on something precarious that had begun to stabilize for him.

Laurence handed the package to Katie Shaw.

'This arrived for you earlier,' he said. 'And I suppose that it helped to lead me here today. I would be grateful if you could tell me why and how.'

Katie took it and slid the contents out.

The photograph first.

She stared at it for a moment, and then turned it over and read the message on the back. From what Laurence could tell neither the image of Hobbes and his late wife nor the words that had been written on the reverse meant anything to her.

Then she unwrapped the book.

Laurence had been able to read the cover through the transparent packaging it was protected in. It was a rare second-edition copy of *Théorie Analytique des Probabilités* by Pierre-Simon Laplace, and it seemed to mean nothing at all to Katie Shaw. But as she opened it and flicked through its pages, Laurence frowned. It was obvious that the book was far more tattered than it had appeared within its protective casing. The cover was torn and creased, as though it had been carefully unstitched from one book and then stretched and folded round a much larger one.

After a few seconds Katie Shaw looked up.

'It's not for me,' she said.

And then she turned to her brother.

'It's for you.'

50

It is 4 October 2017.

Hobbes is in bed when Christopher arrives. He lies very still and keeps his eyes closed as his son enters the flat and walks quietly across the room towards the archway.

The pills are taking effect. He is already dying.

He is not scared of that. If all moments exist at once, then his life will always be there – every instant of it as vivid and real as the ones that came before him and the ones that will follow.

And he isn't afraid of what might await him either.

The question he once asked in a lecture theatre returns to him now. *If you were a father, which would you prefer? A child who always did as they were told – as you thought they should – or a child who disobeyed you and tried to forge their own path?* Even if you know your child will make mistakes along the way, the answer remains obvious to Hobbes. And so he has watched much of Chris's life unfold with a sense of anguish, and there have been moments when he might have done more. But it is a parent's job to guide their children gently and hope for the best, not to control them.

If God disagrees, then so be it.

Untethered from time now, Hobbes begins to drift.

Four days from now, Edward is standing in the room beyond the archway, with a notebook in one hand and a lighter in the other. He has already flicked through the book and begun to understand what it is. Not their father's notebook at all, but the diary Hobbes has spent much of his life writing. Each word within it is neat and clear, and it gives an accurate account of everything, good and bad, that has happened. It describes the world as it has been – how *he* has made it – irrespective of what was intended for him.

He remembers how he ended his final entry.

And then Edward Leland read what had been written.

Hobbes drifts further.

It is 16 September 2015.

In a different universe – one you might find described in an entry somewhere in Jack Lock's notebook – Chris would be lying dead in the home of a stranger. But in this one, Hobbes finds his son beneath a railway arch a few hours beforehand and makes him an offer.

Call me Alan.

It is 3 May 2000.

Hobbes spends the afternoon drinking alone in his flat. Twenty miles from the house, Christopher begins walking home from school by himself, while a red car patrols the neighbourhood, its driver beset by demons and voices, haunted by a mistake he senses he has made without quite understanding what it was. But as the car swerves across the pavement in front of Chris, a delivery truck is already turning into the other end of the street. The driver of the truck is a good man. He is also a diligent one. After he saves Chris's life, he will attempt to complete his delivery – only to find an empty property with a note taped to the door. *Please open the package you are holding.* Within it he will find a substantial sum of money and a thank-you note. And although he will never understand the nature of the gift Alan Hobbes has arranged for him, he will never reveal it to anyone either.

It is 27 July 1996.

Chris and his family are parking up outside a sunlit mill. Inside, the floors smell of freshly sanded wood. Chris stops briefly by the window of one unit and stares at the dice inside, and then the father unlocks a door and turns on a light, and the family marvels at the sight awaiting them within.

It is a moment worth recording.

'Would you mind?' the mother asks.

Hobbes has arranged to be passing just then.

'Not at all,' he says.

He takes the camera and then waits as the family line up in front of the candle shop. Chris is staring back at him with a curious expression on his face, as though he recognizes him but can't quite remember from when. It causes Hobbes's heart to break; he misses him very much. But the boy is happy right now, and that has to be enough.

He takes the photograph.

It is 4 October 2017 again.

Hobbes can feel that Chris has returned from the other room and is now standing beside the bed. Part of Hobbes aches to say something to his son, but the time for that has passed, and it won't help. He has already said goodbye to Chris, and the sadness of seeing someone for the last time will always be the what and why of it, not the when.

He hears Chris walk away.

And now – finally – it is an hour earlier.

Hobbes wraps Jack Lock's notebook in the cover he has torn from Laplace's book and then slips it into the protective sleeve. Perhaps there is still knowledge within it that his son might use, for good or for ill. If so, he hopes Chris chooses wisely. But, regardless, the choice must be his. His son must find his own path.

Hobbes takes the photograph of himself and Charlotte out of the frame and places it face down on the desk.

Then he picks up the pen.

I love you so much, he writes on the back.

Do your best.

Acknowledgements

Every book is difficult to write, but this one has been especially hard. There are several people to whom I owe an enormous debt of gratitude, not only for their expertise but also for their patience. Joel Richardson, my UK editor, and Ryan Doherty, my US editor. Cecily van Buren-Freedman and Rebecca Hilsdon, for additional editorial input. My wonderful agent, Sandra Sawicka, along with everyone else at Marjacq. Jennie Roman and Erica Ferguson, for catching my mistakes. Lee Motley and Will Staehle for their wonderful cover art. Jaime Noven, Emma Henderson, Ellie Hughes, Rebecca Ritchey, Jennifer Jackson, Grace Long, Anna Belle Hinderlang, Rachel Chou – and everyone else at Michael Joseph and Celadon. I couldn't ask to work with better people.

The crime fiction community is famous for being a friendly, welcoming and supportive place. I am indebted not only to my fellow writers but also to all the critics, bloggers and readers that have given the previous books a chance and been so kind about them. There are too many to name, but I want to thank Colin Scott in particular: all the advice and support aside, the world would be much less fun without you.

Although this novel was started during lockdown in the UK, it was completed in the usual places I go to write. So thank you to, among others, the Pack Horse, the Bower's Tap and the West Riding in Leeds for their hospitality.

Thank you to my friends and family. And most of all, to Lynn and Zack. I couldn't do it without you, and I wouldn't want to try. Thank you for everything.

One final note. Having studied philosophy at university, I would like to apologize to academics in that discipline for oversimplifying and possibly even butchering various philosophical concepts in the name of entertainment. What can I say? Perhaps I had no choice . . .

Read on for an extract from
THE WHISPER MAN

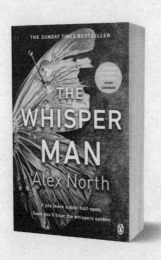

'The best crime novel of the decade'
Steve Cavanagh

Jake.

There is so much I want to tell you, but we've always found it hard to talk to each other, haven't we?

So I'll have to write to you instead.

I remember when Rebecca and I first brought you home from hospital. It was dark and it was snowing, and I'd never driven so carefully in my life. You were two days old and strapped in a carrier in the back seat, Rebecca dozing beside you, and every now and then I'd look in the rear-view mirror to check you were safe.

Because you know what? I was *absolutely fucking terrified*. I grew up as an only child, completely unused to babies, and yet there I was – responsible for one of my own. You were so impossibly small and vulnerable, and me so unprepared, that it seemed ludicrous they'd allowed you out of the hospital with me. From the very beginning, we didn't fit, you and I. Rebecca held you easily and naturally, as though she'd been born to you rather than the other way around, whereas I always felt awkward, scared of this fragile weight in my arms and unable to tell what you wanted when you cried. I didn't understand you at all.

That never changed.

When you were a little older, Rebecca told me it was because you and I were so alike, but I don't know if that's true. I hope it isn't. I'd always have wanted better for you than that.

But regardless, we can't talk to each other, which means

I'll have to try to write all this down instead. The truth about everything that happened in Featherbank.

Mister Night. The boy in the floor. The butterflies. The little girl with the strange dress.

And the Whisper Man of course.

It's not going to be easy, and I need to start with an apology. Over the years, I told you so many times that there was nothing to be afraid of. That there was no such thing as monsters.

I'm sorry that I lied.

PART ONE
July

One

The abduction of a child by a stranger is every parent's worst nightmare. But statistically, it is a highly unusual event. Children are actually most at risk of harm and abuse from a family member behind closed doors, and while the outside world might seem threatening, the truth is that most strangers are decent people, whereas the home is often the most dangerous place of all.

The man stalking six-year-old Neil Spencer across the waste ground understood that only too well.

Moving quietly, parallel to Neil behind a line of bushes, he kept a constant watch on the boy. Neil was walking slowly, unaware of the danger he was in. Occasionally, he kicked at the dusty ground, throwing up chalky white mist around his trainers. The man, treading far more carefully, could hear the *scuff* each time. And he made no sound at all.

It was a warm evening. The sun had been beating down hard and unrestrained for most of the day, but it was six o'clock now and the sky was hazier. The temperature had dropped and the air had a golden hue to it. It was the sort of evening where you might sit out on the patio, perhaps sipping cold white wine and watching the sun set, without thinking about fetching a coat until it was dark and too late to bother.

Even the waste ground was beautiful, bathed in the amber light. It was a patch of shrub land, edging the village of Featherbank on one side, with an old disused quarry on the other. The undulating ground was mostly parched and dead, although bushes grew in tough thickets here and there, lending the area a maze-like quality. The village children played here sometimes, although it was not particularly safe. Over the years, many of them had been tempted to clamber down into the quarry, where the steep sides were prone to crumble away. The council put up fences and signs, but the local consensus was that they should do more. Children found ways over fences, after all.

They had a habit of ignoring warning signs.

The man knew a lot about Neil Spencer. He had studied the boy and his family carefully, like a project. The boy performed poorly at school, both academically and socially, and was well behind his peers in reading, writing and maths. His clothes were mostly hand-me-downs. In his manner, he seemed a little too grown-up for his age – already displaying anger and resentment towards the world. In a few years, he would be perceived as a bully and a troublemaker, but for now he was still young enough for people to forgive his more disruptive behaviour. 'He doesn't mean it,' they would say. 'It's not his fault.' It had not yet reached the point where Neil was considered solely responsible for his actions, and so people were forced instead to look elsewhere.

The man had looked. It wasn't hard to see.

Neil had spent today at his father's house. His mother and father were separated, which the man considered a good thing. Both parents were alcoholics, functioning to wavering degrees. Both found life considerably easier when their son was at the other's house, and both struggled to entertain him when he was with them. In general, Neil was left to occupy and fend for himself, which obviously went some way to explaining the hardness the man had seen developing in the boy. Neil was an afterthought in his parents' lives. Certainly, he was not loved.

Not for the first time, Neil's father had been too drunk that evening to drive him back to his mother's house, and apparently also too lazy to walk with him. The boy was nearly seven, his father probably reasoned, and had been fine alone all day. And so Neil was walking home by himself.

He had no idea yet that he would be going to a very different home. The man thought about the room he had prepared and tried to suppress the excitement he felt.

Halfway across the waste ground, Neil stopped.

The man stopped close by, then peered through the brambles to see what had caught the boy's attention.

An old television had been dumped against one of the bushes, its grey screen bulging but intact. The man watched as Neil gave it an exploratory nudge with his foot, but it was too heavy to move. The thing must have looked like something out of another age to the boy, with grilles and buttons down the side of the screen and a back the size of a drum. There were some rocks on the other side of the path. The man watched, fascinated, as Neil walked over, selected one, and then threw it at the glass with all his strength.

Pock.

A loud noise in this otherwise silent place. The glass didn't shatter, but the stone went through, leaving a hole starred at the edges like a gunshot. Neil picked up a second rock and repeated the action, missing this time, then tried again. Another hole appeared in the screen.

He appeared to like this game.

And the man could understand why. This casual destruction was much like the increasing aggression the boy showed in school. It was an attempt to make an impact on a world that seemed so oblivious to his existence. It stemmed from a desire to be seen. To be noticed. To be loved.

That was all any child wanted, deep down.

The man's heart, beating more quickly now, ached at the thought of that. He stepped silently out from the bushes behind the boy, and then whispered his name.

Two

Neil. Neil. Neil.

DI Pete Willis moved carefully over the waste ground, listening as the officers around him called the missing boy's name at prearranged intervals. In between, there was absolute silence. Pete looked up, imagining the words fluttering into the blackness up there, disappearing into the night sky as completely as Neil Spencer had vanished from the Earth below it.

He swept the beam of his torch over the dusty ground in a conical pattern, checking his footing as well as looking for any sign of the boy. Blue tracksuit bottoms and underpants, Minecraft T-shirt, black trainers, army-style bag, water bottle. The alert had come through just as he'd been sitting down to eat the dinner he'd laboured over, and the thought of the plate there on his table right now, untouched and growing cold, made his stomach grumble.

But a little boy was missing and needed to be found.

The other officers were invisible in the dark, but he could see their torches as they fanned out across the area. Pete checked his watch: 8.53 p.m. The day was almost done, and although it had been hot this afternoon, the temperature had dropped over the last couple of hours, and the cold air was making him shiver. In his rush to leave, he'd forgotten his coat, and the shirt he was wearing offered scant protection against the elements. Old bones too – he was fifty-six, after all – but no night for young ones to be out either. Especially lost and alone. Hurt, most likely.

Neil. Neil. Neil.

He added his own voice: 'Neil!'

Nothing.

The first forty-eight hours following a disappearance are the most crucial. The boy had been reported missing at 7.39 p.m. that evening, roughly an hour and a half after he had left his father's house. He should have been home by 6.20 p.m., but there had been little coordination between the parents as to the exact time of his return, so it wasn't until Neil's mother had finally phoned her ex-husband that their son's absence was discovered. By the time the police arrived on the scene at 7.51 p.m., the shadows were lengthening and approaching two of those forty-eight hours had already been lost. Now it was closer to three.

In the vast majority of cases, Pete knew, a missing child is found quickly and safely and returned to their family. Cases were divided into five distinct categories: throwaway; runaway; accident or misadventure; family abduction; non-family abduction. The law of probability was telling Pete right now that the disappearance of Neil Spencer would turn out to be an accident of some kind, and that the boy was going to be found soon. And yet, the further he walked, the more his gut instinct was telling him differently. There was an uncomfortable feeling curling around his heart. But then, a child going missing always made him feel like this. It didn't mean anything. It was just the bad memories of twenty years ago surfacing, bringing bad feelings along with them.

The beam of his torch passed over something grey.

Pete stopped immediately, then played it back to where it had been. There was an old television set lodged at the base of one of the bushes, its screen broken in several places, as though someone had used it for target practice. He stared at it for a moment.

'Anything?'

An anonymous voice calling from one side.

'No,' he shouted back.

He reached the far side of the waste ground at the same time as the other officers, the search having turned up nothing. After the relative darkness behind him, Pete found the bleached brightness of the street lights here oddly queasy. There was a quiet hum of life in the air that had been absent in the silence of the waste ground.

A few moments later, stuck for anything better to do right now, he turned around and walked back the way he'd come.

He wasn't really sure where he was going, but he found himself heading off to the side, in the direction of the old quarry that ran along one edge. It was dangerous ground in the dark, so he headed towards the cluster of torchlights where the quarry search team were about to start work. While other officers were working their way along the edge, shining their beams down the steep sides and calling Neil's name, the ones here were consulting maps and preparing to descend the rough path that led into the area below. A couple of them looked up as he reached them.

'Sir?' One of them recognized him. 'I didn't know you were on duty tonight.'

'I'm not.' Pete bent the wire of the fence up, and ducked under to join them, even more careful of his footing now. 'I live locally.'

'Yes, sir.' The officer sounded dubious.

It was unusual for a DI to turn up for what was ostensibly grunt work like this. DI Amanda Beck was coordinating the burgeoning investigation from back at the department, and the search team here was comprised mainly of rank and file. Pete figured he had more years on the clock than any of them, but tonight he was just part of the crowd. A child was missing, which meant that a child needed to be found. The officer was maybe too young to remember what had happened with Frank Carter two decades earlier, and to understand why it was no surprise to find Pete Willis out in circumstances like this.

'Watch yourself, sir. The ground's a bit shaky here.'

'I'm fine.'

Young enough to discount him as some old man as well, apparently. Presumably he'd never seen Pete in the department's gym, which he visited every morning before heading up to work. Despite the disparity in their ages, Pete would have bet he could outlift the younger man on every machine. He was watching the ground all right. Watching everything – including himself – was second nature to him.

'Okay, sir, well, we're about to head down. Just coordinating.'

'I'm not in charge here.' Pete pointed his torch down the path, scanning the rough terrain. The beam of light only penetrated a short distance. The bed of the quarry below was nothing but an enormous black hole. 'You report to DI Beck, not to me.'

'Yes, sir.'

Pete continued staring down, thinking about Neil Spencer. The most likely routes the boy would have taken had been identified. The streets had been searched. Most of his friends had already been contacted, all to no avail. And the waste ground was clear. If the boy's disappearance really was the result of an accident or misadventure then the quarry was the only remaining place that made sense for him to be found.

And yet the black world below felt entirely empty.

He couldn't know for sure – not through reason. But his instinct was telling him that Neil Spencer wasn't going to be found here.

That maybe he wasn't going to be found at all.

He just wanted a decent book to read ...

Not too much to ask, is it? It was in 1935 when Allen Lane, Managing Director of Bodley Head Publishers, stood on a platform at Exeter railway station looking for something good to read on his journey back to London. His choice was limited to popular magazines and poor-quality paperbacks – the same choice faced every day by the vast majority of readers, few of whom could afford hardbacks. Lane's disappointment and subsequent anger at the range of books generally available led him to found a company – and change the world.

'We believed in the existence in this country of a vast reading public for intelligent books at a low price, and staked everything on it'
Sir Allen Lane, 1902–1970, founder of Penguin Books

The quality paperback had arrived – and not just in bookshops. Lane was adamant that his Penguins should appear in chain stores and tobacconists, and should cost no more than a packet of cigarettes.

Reading habits (and cigarette prices) have changed since 1935, but Penguin still believes in publishing the best books for everybody to enjoy. We still believe that good design costs no more than bad design, and we still believe that quality books published passionately and responsibly make the world a better place.

So wherever you see the little bird – whether it's on a piece of prize-winning literary fiction or a celebrity autobiography, political tour de force or historical masterpiece, a serial-killer thriller, reference book, world classic or a piece of pure escapism – you can bet that it represents the very best that the genre has to offer.

Whatever you like to read – trust Penguin.